TURN OF MIND

This Large Print Book carries the
Seal of Approval of N.A.V.H.

TURN OF MIND

ALICE LAPLANTE

THORNDIKE PRESS
A part of Gale, Cengage Learning

GALE
CENGAGE Learning™

Detroit • New York • San Francisco • New Haven, Conn • Waterville, Maine • London

GALE
CENGAGE Learning

Thorndike Press® Large Print Basic.
The text of this Large Print edition is unabridged.
Other aspects of the book may vary from the original edition.
Set in 16 pt. Plantin.

LIBRARY OF CONGRESS CATALOGING-IN-PUBLICATION DATA

LaPlante, Alice, 1958–
    Turn of mind / by Alice LaPlante. — Large print ed.
      p. cm. — (Thorndike Press large print basic)
    ISBN-13: 978-1-4104-4097-6
    ISBN-10: 1-4104-4097-4
    1. Women surgeons—Fiction. 2. Memory—Fiction. 3. Murder—
Investigation—Fiction. 4. Large type books. I. Title.
PS3612.A6438T87 2011
813'.6—dc22   2011020847

Published in 2011 by arrangement with Grove/Atlantic, Inc.

Printed in the United States of America
1 2 3 4 5 6 7 15 14 13 12 11

For Alice Gervase O'Neill LaPlante

ONE

Something has happened. You can always tell. You come to and find wreckage: a smashed lamp, a devastated human face that shivers on the verge of being recognizable. Occasionally someone in uniform: a paramedic, a nurse. A hand extended with a pill. Or poised to insert a needle.

This time, I am in a room, sitting on a cold metal folding chair. The room is not familiar, but I am used to that. I look for clues. An office-like setting, long and crowded with desks and computers, messy with papers. No windows.

I can barely make out the pale green of the walls, so many posters, clippings, and bulletins tacked up. Fluorescent lighting casting a pall. Men and women talking; to one another, not to me. Some wearing baggy suits, some in jeans. And more uniforms. My guess is that a smile would be inappropriate. Fear might not be.

I can still read, I'm not that far gone, not yet. No books anymore, but newspaper articles. Magazine pieces, if they're short enough. I have a system. I take a sheet of lined paper. I write down notes, just like in medical school.

When I get confused, I read my notes. I refer back to them. I can take two hours to get through a single *Tribune* article, half a day to get through *The New York Times*. Now, as I sit at the table, I pick up a paper someone discarded, a pencil. I write in the margins as I read. These are Band-Aid solutions. The violent flare-ups continue. They have reaped what they sowed and should repent.

Afterward, I look at these notes but am left with nothing but a sense of unease, of uncontrol. A heavy man in blue is hovering, his hand inches away from my upper arm. Ready to grab. Restrain.

Do you understand the rights I have just read

to you? With these rights in mind, do you wish to speak to me?

I want to go home. I want to go home. Am I in Philadelphia. There was the house on Walnut Lane. We played kickball in the streets.

No, this is Chicago. Ward Forty-three, Precinct Twenty-one. We have called your son and daughter. You can decide at any time from this moment on to terminate the interview and exercise these rights.

I wish to terminate. Yes.

A large sign is taped to the kitchen wall. The words, written in thick black marker in a tremulous hand, slope off the poster board: My name is Dr. Jennifer White. I am sixty-four years old. I have dementia. My son, Mark, is twenty-nine. My daughter, Fiona, twenty-four. A caregiver, Magdalena, lives with me.

It is all clear. So who are all these other people in my house? People, strangers, everywhere. A blond woman I don't recognize in my kitchen drinking tea. A glimpse of movement from the den. Then I turn the corner into the living room and find yet another face. I ask, So who are you? Who are all the others? Do you know *her?* I point to the kitchen, and they laugh.

I *am* her, they say. I was there, now I'm here. I am the only one in the house other than you. They ask if I want tea. They ask if I want to go for a walk. Am I a baby? I say. I am tired of the questions. You know me, don't you? Don't you remember? Magdalena. Your friend.

The notebook is a way of communicating with myself, and with others. Of filling in the blank periods. When all is in a fog, when someone refers to an event or conversation that I can't recall, I leaf through the pages. Sometimes it comforts me to read what's there. Sometimes not. It is my Bible of consciousness. It lives on the kitchen table: large and square, with an embossed leather cover and heavy creamy paper. Each entry has a date on it. A nice lady sits me down in front of it.

She writes, January 20, 2009. Jennifer's notes. She hands the pen to me. She says,

Write what happened today. Write about your childhood. Write whatever you remember.

I remember my first wrist arthrodesis. The pressure of scalpel against skin, the slight give when it finally sliced through. The resilience of muscle. My surgical scissors scraping bone. And afterward, peeling off bloody gloves finger by finger.

Black. Everyone is wearing black. They're walking in twos and threes down the street toward St. Vincent's, bundled in coats and scarves that cover their heads and lower faces against what is apparently bitter wind.

I am inside my warm house, my face to the frosted window, Magdalena hovering. I can just see the twelve-foot carved wooden doors. They are wide open, and people are entering. A hearse is standing in front, other cars lined up behind it, their lights on.

It's Amanda, Magdalena tells me. Amanda's funeral. Who is Amanda? I ask. Magdalena hesitates, then says, Your best friend. Your daughter's godmother.

I try. I fail. I shake my head. Magdalena

gets my notebook. She turns back the pages. She points to a newspaper clipping:

Elderly Chicago Woman Found Dead, Mutilated
CHICAGO TRIBUNE — February 23, 2009
CHICAGO, IL — The mutilated body of a seventy-five-year-old Chicago woman was discovered yesterday in a house in the 2100 block of Sheffield Avenue.

Amanda O'Toole was found dead in her home after a neighbor noticed she had failed to take in her newspapers for almost a week, according to sources close to the investigation. Four fingers on her right hand had been severed. The exact time of death is unknown, but cause of death is attributed to head trauma, sources say.

Nothing was reported missing from her house.

No one has been charged, but police briefly took into custody and then released a person of interest in the case.

I try. But I cannot conjure up anything. Magdalena leaves. She comes back with a photograph.

Two women, one taller by at least two

inches, with long straight white hair pulled back in a tight chignon. The other one, younger, has shorter wavy gray locks that cluster around chiseled, more feminine features. That one a beauty perhaps, once upon a time.

This is you, Magdalena says, pointing to the younger woman. And this here, this is Amanda. I study the photograph.

The taller woman has a compelling face. Not what you'd call pretty. Nor what you would call nice. Too sharp around the nostrils, lines of perhaps contempt etched into the jowls. The two women stand close together, not touching, but there is an affinity there.

Try to remember, Magdalena urges me. It could be important. Her hand lies heavily on my shoulder. She wants something from me. What? But I am suddenly tired. My hands shake. Perspiration trickles down between my breasts.

I want to go to my room, I say. I swat at Magdalena's hand. Leave me be.

Amanda? Dead? I cannot believe it. My dear, dear friend. Second mother to my children. My ally in the neighborhood. My sister.

If not for Amanda, I would have been alone. I was different. Always apart. The cheese stands alone.

Not that anyone knew. They were fooled by surfaces, so easy to dupe. No one understood weaknesses like Amanda. She saw me, saved me from my secret solitude. And where was I when she needed me? Here. Three doors down. Wallowing in my woes. While she suffered. While some monster brandished a knife, pushed in for the kill.

O the pain! So much pain. I will stop swallowing my pills. I will take my scalpel to my brain and eviscerate her image. And I will beg for exactly that thing I've been battling all these long months: sweet oblivion.

The nice lady writes in my notebook. She signs her name: Magdalena. Today, Friday, March 11, was another bad day. You kicked the step and broke your toe. At the emergency room you escaped into the parking lot. An orderly brought you back. You spat on him.

The shame.

This half state. Life in the shadows. As the neurofibrillary tangles proliferate, as the neuritic plaques harden, as synapses cease to fire and my mind rots out, I remain aware. An unanesthetized patient.

Every death of every cell pricks me where I am most tender. And people I don't know patronize me. They hug me. They attempt to hold my hand. They call me prepubescent nicknames: *Jen. Jenny.* I bitterly accept the fact that I am famous, beloved even, among strangers. A celebrity!

A legend in my own mind.

My notebook lately has been full of warnings. Mark very angry today. He hung up on me. Magdalena says do not speak to anyone who calls. Do not answer the door when she's doing laundry or in the bathroom.

Then, in a different handwriting, Mom, you

are not safe with Mark. Give the medical power of attorney to me, Fiona. It is best to have medical and financial powers of attorney in the same hands anyway. Some things are crossed out, no, obliterated, with a thick black pen. By whom?

My notebook again:

Mark called, says my money will not save me. I must listen to him. That there are other actions we must take to protect me.

Then: Mom, I sold $50,000 worth of IBM stock for the lawyer's retainer. She comes highly recommended for cases where mental competency is an issue. They have no evidence, only theories. Dr. Tsien has put you on 150 mg of Seroquel to curb the episodes. I will come again tomorrow, Saturday. Your daughter, Fiona.

I belong to an Alzheimer's support group. People come and they go.

This morning Magdalena says it is an okay day, we can try to attend. The group meets in a Methodist church on Clark, squat and gray with clapboard walls and garish primary-colored stained-glass windows.

We gather in the Fellowship Lounge, a large room with windows that don't open and speckled linoleum floors bearing the scuff marks of the metal folding chairs. A motley crew, perhaps half a dozen of us, our minds in varying states of undress. Magdalena waits outside the door of the room with the other caregivers. They line up on benches in the dark hallway, knitting and speaking softly among themselves, but attentive, prepared to leap up and take their charges away at the first hint of trouble.

Our leader is a young man with a social-worker degree. He has a kind and inef-fectual face, and likes to start with introduc-tions and a joke. My-name-is-I-forgot-and-I-am-an-I-don't-know-what. He refers to what we do as the Two Circular Steps. Step One is admitting you have a problem. Step Two is forgetting you have the problem.

It gets a laugh every time, from some because they remember the joke from the last meeting, but from most because it's new to them, no matter how many times they've heard it.

Today is a good day for me. I remember it. I would even add a third step: Step Three is remembering that you forget. Step Three is the hardest of all.

Today we discuss *attitude.* This is what the leader calls it. You've all received this extraordinarily distressing diagnosis, he says. You are all intelligent, educated people. You know you are running out of time. What you do with it is up to you. Be positive! Having Alzheimer's can be like going to a party where you don't happen to know anyone. Think of it! Every meal can be the best meal of your life! Every movie the most enthralling you've ever seen! Have a sense of humor, he says. You are a visitor from another planet, and you are observing the local customs.

But what about the rest of us, for whom the walls are closing in? Whom change has always terrified? At thirteen I stopped eating for a week because my mother bought new sheets for my bed. For us, life is now terribly dangerous. Hazards lie around every corner. So you nod to all the strangers who force themselves upon you. You laugh when others laugh, look serious when they do. When people ask do you remember you nod some more. Or frown at first, then let your face light up in recognition.

All this is necessary for survival. I am a visitor from another planet, and the natives are not friendly.

I open my mail myself. Then it disappears. Whisked away. Today, pleas for help to save the whales, save the pandas, free Tibet.

My bank statement shows that I have $3,567.89 in a Bank of America checking account. There is another statement from a stockbroker, Michael Brownstein. My name is on the top. My assets have declined 19 percent in the last six months. They apparently now total $2.56 million. He includes a note: It is not as bad as it could have been due to your conservative investment choices and a broad portfolio diversification strategy.

Is $2.56 million a lot of money? Is it enough? I stare at the letters on the page until they blur. AAPL, IBM, CVR, ASF, SFR. The secret language of money.

James is sly. James has secrets. Some I am

privy to, more I am not. Where is he today? The children are at school. The house is empty except for a woman who seems to be a sort of housekeeper. She is straightening the books in the den, humming a tune I don't recognize. Did James hire her? Likely. Someone must be keeping things in order, for the house looks well tended, and I have always been hostile to housework, and James, although a compulsive tidier, is too busy. Always out and about. On undercover missions. Like now. Amanda doesn't approve. Marriages should be transparent, she says. They must withstand the glare of full sunlight. But James is a shadowy man. He needs cover, flourishes in the dark. James himself explained it long ago, concocted the perfect metaphor. Or rather, he plucked it from nature. And although I am suspicious of too-neat categorizations, this one rang true. It was a hot humid day in summer, at James's boyhood home in North Carolina. Before we were married. We'd gone for an after-dinner walk in the waning light and just two hundred yards away from his parents' back porch found ourselves deep in a primeval forest, dark with trees that dripped white moss, our footsteps muffled by the dead leaves that blanketed the ground. Pockets of ferns unfurled through the debris and the occasional mushroom gleamed. James gestured. Poisonous, he said. As he spoke, a bird called. Otherwise, silence. If there was a path, I couldn't see it, but James steadily moved ahead and magically a way forward appeared in front of us. We'd gone perhaps a quarter of a mile, the light diminishing minute by minute, when James stopped. He pointed. At the foot of a tree, amid a mass of yellow green moss, something glowed a ghostly white. A flower, a single flower on a long white stalk. James let out a breath. We're lucky, he said. Sometimes you can search for days and not find one.

And what is it? I asked. The flower emitted its own light, so strong that several small insects were circling around it, as if attracted by the glare.

A ghost plant, James said. Monotropa uniflora. He stooped down and cupped the flower in his hand, being careful not to disengage it from its stalk. It's one of the few plants that doesn't need light. It actually grows in the dark.

How is that possible? I asked.

It's a parasite — it doesn't photosynthesize

but feeds off the fungus and the trees around it, lets others do the hard work. I've always felt a kinship to it. Admiration, even. Because it's not easy — that's why they don't propagate widely. The plant has to find the right host, and conditions must be exactly right for it to flourish. But when it does flourish, it is truly spectacular. He let go of the flower and stood up.

Yes, I can see that, I said.

Can you? James asked. Can you really?

Yes, I repeated, and the word hung in the heavy moist air between us, like a promise. A vow.

Shortly after this trip, we quietly got married at the Evanston courthouse. We didn't invite anyone, it would have felt like an intrusion. The clerk was a witness, and it was over in five minutes. On the whole, a good decision. But on days like today, when I feel James's absence like a wound, I long to be back in those woods, which somehow remain as fresh and strong in my mind as the day we were there. I could reach out and pluck that flower, present it to James when he comes back. A dark trophy.

I am in the office of a Carl Tsien. A doctor. *My* doctor, it seems. A slight, balding man. Pale, in the way that only someone who spends his time indoors under artificial light can be. A benevolent face. We apparently know each other well.

He speaks about former students. He uses the word *our. Our students.* He says I should be proud. That I have left the university and the hospital an invaluable legacy. I shake my head. I am too tired to pretend, having had a bad night. A pacing night. Back and forth, back and forth, from bathroom to bedroom to bathroom and back again. Counting footsteps, beating a steady rhythm against the tile, the hardwood flooring. Pacing until the soles of my feet ached.

But this office tickles my memory. Although I don't know this doctor, somehow I am intimate with his possessions. A model of a human skull on his desk. Someone has painted lipstick on its bony maxilla to approximate lips, and a crude label underneath it reads simply, MAD CARLOTTA. I know that skull. I know that handwriting. He sees me looking. Your jokes were always a little obscure, he says.

On the wall above the desk, a vintage skiing poster proclaims *Chamonix* in bright red letters. *Des conditions de neige excellentes, des terrasses ensoleillées, des hors-pistes mythiques.* A man and a woman, dressed in the voluminous clothing of the early 1900s, poised on skis in midair above a steep white hill dotted with pine trees. A fanciful drawing, not a photograph, although there are photographs, too, hanging to the right and left of the poster. Black-and-white. To the right, one of a young girl, not clean, squatting in front of a dilapidated shack. To the left, one of a barren field with the sun just visible above the flat horizon and a woman, naked, lying on her belly with her hands propping up her chin. She looks directly into the camera. I feel distaste and turn away.

The doctor laughs and pats me on the arm. You never did approve of my artistic vision, he says. You called it precious. Ansel Adams meets the Discovery Channel. I shrug. I let his hand linger on my arm as he guides me to a chair.

I am going to ask you some questions, he

says. Just answer to the best of your ability.

I don't even bother to respond.

What day is it?

Going-to-the-doctor day.

Clever reply. What month is it?

Winter.

Can you be more specific?

March?

Close. Late February.

What is this?

A pencil.

What is this?

A watch.

What is your name?

Don't insult me.

What are your children's names?

Fiona and Mark.

What was your husband's name?

James.

Where is your husband?

He is dead. Heart attack.

What do you remember about that?

He was driving and lost control of his car.

Did he die of the heart attack or the car accident?

Clinically it was impossible to tell. He may have died of cardiomyopathy caused by a leaky mitral valve or from head trauma. It was a close call. The coroner went with cardiac arrest. I would have gone the other way, myself.

You must have been devastated.

No, my thought was, that's James: a perpetual battle between his head and his heart to the end.

You're making light of it. But I remember that

28

time. What you went through.

Don't patronize me. I had to laugh. His heart succumbed first. His heart! I did laugh, actually. I laughed as I identified the remains. Such a cold, bright place. The morgue. I hadn't been in one since medical school, I always hated them. The harsh light. The bitter cold. The light and the cold and also the sounds — rubber-soled shoes squeaking like hungry rats against tile floors. That's what I remember: James bathed in unforgiving light while vermin scuttled.

Now you're the one patronizing me. As if I couldn't see past that.

The doctor writes something in a chart. He allows himself to smile at me.

You scored a nineteen, he says. You're doing well today. I don't see any agitation and Magdalena says the aggression has subsided. We'll continue the same drug therapy.

He gives me a look. Do you have a problem with that?

I shake my head. Okay, then. We'll do everything we can to keep you in your home. I know that's what you want.

He pauses. I must tell you, Mark has been urging me to make a statement that he can use to declare you mentally incompetent to make medical decisions, he says. I have refused. The doctor leans forward. I would recommend that you not let yourself be examined by another doctor. Not without a court order.

He takes a piece of paper out of his file. See — I have written it all down for you. Everything I just said. I will give it to Magdalena and tell her to keep it safe. I have made two copies. Magdalena will give one to your lawyer. You can trust Magdalena, I believe. I believe she is trustworthy.

He waits for my answer, but I am fixated on the photo of the naked woman. There is doubt and suspicion in her eyes. She is looking at the camera. Behind it. She is looking straight at me.

I can't find the car keys, so I decide to walk to the drugstore. I will buy toothpaste, some dental floss, shampoo for dry hair. Perhaps some toilet paper, the premium kind.

Normal things. I'm inclined to pretend to

am suddenly very tired. I sit down in front of the tea, push it away, but not before getting a waft of chamomile. So many old wives' tales about chamomile have proven true. A cure for digestive problems, fever, menstrual cramps, stomachaches, skin infections, and anxiety. And, of course, insomnia.

A fix for whatever ails you! Magdalena had exclaimed when I told her that. Not really, I said. Not everything.

We are listening to St. Matthew's Passion. It is 1988. Solti is at the podium in Orchestra Hall, and the audience is held captive until the cadences resolve. The diminished seventh chords and the disturbing modulations. The suspense barely tolerable. I can feel the warmth of James's fingers intertwined with mine, his breath warm against my cheek.

Then suddenly it is a cold winter day. I am alone in my kitchen. I fold my arms on the table and lean my forehead against them. Did I take my pills this morning? How many did I take? How many would it take?

be normal today. Then I will go to the supermarket and pick out the plumpest roast chicken for dinner. A loaf of fresh bread. James will like that. Small comforts — we share our love of these.

But I must go quickly. Quietly. They will try to stop me. They always do.

But no purse. Where is it. I always keep it beside the door. No matter, there will be someone nice there. I will say, I am Dr. Jennifer White and I forgot my purse and they will say oh of course here is some money and I will nod my head just so and thank them.

I stride down the street, past ivy-covered brownstones with their waist-high wrought-iron fences enclosing small neat geometrically laid-out front gardens.

Dr. White? Is that you?

A dark-skinned man in a blue uniform, driving a white truck with an eagle on it. He rolls down his window, slows to a crawl to keep pace.

Yes? I keep walking.

Not the nicest day to be out and about. Nasty.

Just a walk, I say. I make a point of not looking at him. If you don't look, they may leave you alone. If you don't look, sometimes they let it go.

How about a ride? Look at you, completely soaked. No coat. And my goodness. No shoes. Come on. Get in.

No. I like the weather. I like the feel of my bare feet against concrete. Cold. Waking me out of my somnolent state.

You know, that nice lady you live with won't like this.

So what.

Come quietly now. He speaks soothingly while pulling the truck over to the curb. He holds out both hands, palms up, and beckons with them. Gently.

I'm not a rabid dog.

No, you're not. Indeed you aren't. But I can't stand by and do nothing. You know I can't, Dr. White.

I brush my icy hair out of my face and keep

32

going, but he idles his truck along takes out his phone. If he punche numbers, it's okay. If he punches numbers, it's bad. I know that. I sto wait. Onetwothree. He stops. He bring phone to his ear.

Wait, I say. No. I run around the front the truck. I yank the door open and clambe in beside him. Anything to stop the phone. Stop what will happen. Bad things will happen. Put the phone down, I say. Put the phone down. He hesitates. I hear a voice on the other end. He looks at the phone and flips it shut. He gives me what is supposed to be a reassuring smile. I am not fooled.

Okay! Let's get you home before you catch your death.

He waits at the curb until I reach the front door. It is wide open, and wind and sleet are gusting through into the hallway. The thick damask curtains on the front window are drenched. I step on a sodden carpet a dark Tabriz runner we bought in Bagh thirty years ago, now considered muse quality. James had it appraised last year be furious. Magdalena's shoes are go lukewarm cup of tea sits on the tabl drunk.

33

I am almost to the point. I have almost reached that point. And hear an echo of Bach: Ich bin's, ich sollte büßen. It is I who should suffer and be bound for hell.

But not yet. No. Not quite yet. I sit and wait.

A man has walked into my house without knocking. He says he is my son. Magdalena backs him up, so I acquiesce. But I don't like this man's face. I am not ruling out the possibility that they are telling me the truth — but I will play it safe. Not commit.

What I do see: a stranger, a very beautiful stranger. Dark. Dark hair, dark eyes, a dark aura, if I may be so fanciful. He tells me he is unmarried, twenty-nine years old, a lawyer. Like your father! I say, cunningly. His darkness comes alive, he glowers — there is no other word for it.

Not at all, he says. Not in the slightest. I cannot hope to fill those mighty McLennan shoes. Give counsel to the mighty and count the golden coin of the realm. And he gives a mock half bow to the portrait of the lean, dark man that hangs in the living room. Why didn't you give me your name, Mom? The shoes would have been just as large but of a different shape altogether.

Enough! I say sharply — for I remember my son now. He is seven years old. He has just run into the room, his hands clutching at his thighs, a glorious look on his face. Water spattering everywhere. I discover his front pockets are full of his sister's goldfish. They are still wiggling. He is astonished at my anger.

We save some of them, but most are limp cold bodies to be flushed down the toilet. His rapture is not dimmed, he stares fascinated as the last of the red gold tails gets sucked out of sight. Even when his sister discovers her loss he is unrepentant. No. More than that. Proud. Perpetrator of a dozen tiny slaughters on an otherwise quiet Tuesday afternoon.

This-man-who-they-say-is-my-son settles himself in the blue armchair near the window in the living room. He loosens his tie, stretches out his legs, makes himself at home.

Magdalena tells me you've been well, he says.

Very, I say, stiffly. As well as a person in my

condition can be.

Tell me about that, he says.

About what? I ask.

About how aware you are of what's happening to you.

Everyone asks that, I say. They are astonished that I can be so aware, so very . . .

Clinical, he says.

Yes.

You always were, he says. He has a wry smile, not unappealing. When I broke my arm, you were more interested in my bone density than in getting me to the hospital.

I remember someone breaking his arm, I say. Mark. It was Mark. Mark fell out of the maple tree in front of the Janeckis'.

I'm Mark.

You? Mark?

Yes. Your son.

I have a son?

Yes. Mark. Me.

I have a son! I am struck dumb. I have a son! I am filled with ecstasy. Joy!

Mom, please, don't . . .

But I am overwhelmed. All these years! I had a son and never knew it!

The man is now kneeling at my feet, holding me.

It's okay, Mom. I'm here.

I hold on to him tightly. A fine young man and, wondrous of all, conceived by me. There is something not quite right about his face, a flaw in his beauty. But to my eyes, this makes him even more beloved.

Mom, he says after a moment. His arms around me loosen, he pulls back. I miss the warmth immediately but reluctantly let go and sit back in my chair.

Mom, I had something really important to say. It's about Fiona. He is standing now, and his face is back to the dark, watchful look he wore when he entered. I know that look.

What about her? I ask. My tone is not

welcoming.

Mom, I know you don't want to hear this, but she's gone off again. You know how she gets.

I do know, but I don't answer. I have never encouraged this telling of tales.

This time it's bad. Really bad. She won't talk to me. You used to be able to talk her down. Dad, sometimes. But she listened to you. Do you think you could speak to her? He pauses. Do you understand what I'm saying?

Where have you been, you bastard? I ask.

What?

After all these years, you come here and say these things?

Shhh, Mom. It's okay. I'm right here. I never left.

What do you mean? I've been alone. All alone in this house. Eating dinner alone, going to bed alone. So alone.

That's just not true, Mom. Until just last year there was Dad. And what about Magdalena?

Who?

39

Magdalena. Your friend. The woman who lives with you.

Oh. Her. She's not my friend. She gets paid. I pay her.

That doesn't mean she's not your friend.

Yes, it certainly does. Suddenly I'm angry. Furious! You bastard! I say. You abandoned me!

The man slowly gets to his feet and sighs heavily. Magdalena! he calls.

Did you hear me? Bastard!

I heard you, Mom. He looks around, searching for something. My coat, he says. Have you seen my coat?

A woman hurries into the room. Blond. A woman of heft. Better go, she says. Quickly. Here's your coat. Yes. Thanks for coming.

Well, I won't pretend it's been fun, the man says to me, and turns to go.

Get out!

The blond woman puts up her hand. She

moves slowly toward me. No, Jennifer. Put that down. Please put that down. Now, really, did you have to do that?

What has happened. There has been an accident. The phone lies in the hallway amid shattered glass. Cold air sweeps past me, the curtains blow wildly. Outside, a car door slams, an engine starts. I feel alive, vindicated, ready for anything. There's so much more where this came from. O yes, much much more.

From my notebook:

A good day. Excellent day, my brain mostly clear. I performed a Mini-Cog test on myself. Uncertain of the year, month, and day, but confident of the season. Not sure of my age, but I recognized the woman I saw in the mirror. Still a touch of auburn in the hair, deep brown eyes unfaded, the lines around the eyes and forehead, if not exactly laugh lines, at least indicating a sense of humor.

I know my name: Jennifer White. I know my address: 2153 Sheffield. And spring has arrived. The smell of warm, wet earth, the promise of renewal, of things emerging from a dormant state. I opened the windows and waved at the neighbor across the street, already turning over his raised beds, preparing for the glorious array of angel's trumpets, blood flowers, blue butterfly bushes.

Went into the kitchen and remembered how to make the strong, bitter coffee I love: how to shake the beans into the grinder, how to sniff the rich scent as the blades slash through the hard shells, how to count the scoops of fragrant deep brown coarse particles into the coffeemaker, how to pour the fresh cold water into the receptacle.

Then Fiona stopped by. Ah, my girl delights me! With her short pixie haircut and upper right arm entwined by a red and blue rattlesnake tattoo. Usually she keeps it hidden, and only a chosen few in her current life know about it, about her wilder days.

She came to collect my financial statements, go over some numbers that I will not understand. No matter. I have my financial genius. My monetary rock. Graduated from high school at sixteen, from college at twenty, and at twenty-four, the youngest female tenure-track professor at the U of C business school. Her area of specialization is international monetary economics — she routinely gets calls from Washington, London, Frankfurt.

After James died, once I was certain of my prognosis, I signed over financial power of attorney. Her I trust. My Fiona. She places paper after paper in front of me, and I sign without reading. I ask her if there is anything I should pay special attention to, and she says no. Today was different, however. She had no papers but just sat at the table with me and held my hand in hers. My remarkable girl.

At our Alzheimer's support group today, we talk about what we hate. Hate is a powerful emotion, our young leader says. Ask a dementia patient who she loves, and she draws a blank. Ask her who she hates, and the memories come flooding in.

Hatred. *Hate.* The word resonates. My stomach contracts, and bile rises in my throat. *I hate.* I find my hands clenched into fists. Faces turn to look at me. Some men, mostly women. A variety of races, of creeds. A United Nations of the despised, of the despicable. I cannot make out their features

43

exactly. An anonymous mob.

It is becoming hard to breathe. What is that noise. Is it me. Who are you staring at.

Our leader is coming over. Our leader is leaving the room, he returns with a young-ish woman, bleached blond hair, too much makeup. She comes straight over to me.

Dr. White, the woman says. Jennifer. We're going home now. Shhh. No yelling. No. Please stop. Stop. You're hurting me. No, don't call, I can handle this. Jennifer. Come now. That's right. We're going home. Shhh. It's okay. It's okay. It's me, look at me. At me, Magdalena. That's right. We're going home.

On some days, blessed clarity. Today is one of those days. I walk through the house taking joy in claiming things. *My* books. *My* piano, which James played endearingly clumsily. *My* Calder lithograph, purchased by James for me in London, 1976, its lines as fresh as ever. *My* artifacts, the seventeenth-century santos and the ex-votos, doubtless stolen from churches, which we bought from roadside peddlers in Jalisco and Monterrey: all the trappings of the devout without the burden of faith. I touch everything, rejoicing in the feel of leather, mahogany, canvas, porcelain, tin.

Magdalena is what I can only describe as sullen. She breaks a plate, curses, sweeps up the pieces, and drops them again while struggling with the lid of the trash can. Her job cannot be fun. I suspect, however, that she needs the money badly. Her car is at least a dozen years old, with dented rear fenders and a cracked windshield.

She dresses simply, in faded blue jeans and a white man's button-down shirt that hangs over her substantial hips. She bleaches her dark hair, not very competently — you can see the roots. Thick eyeliner and mascara that make her eyes appear small.

Her age: perhaps forty, forty-five. I catch her writing in my notebook. A very good day for Jennifer. A not-so-good day for me. I ask her why, and she shrugs. Her face is haggard, and she has circles under her eyes.

Why should I explain again? she says. You'll just forget anyhow.

I wonder if she is always this rude. I wonder many things. How long has it been raining?

How did my hair get so long? Why does the phone keep ringing, yet never seems to be for me? Magdalena picks it up, and her face closes in secrecy. She whispers into the receiver as if to a secret lover.

I am in the middle of a street. Dirty snow has been pushed to either side, but still treacherous going, I have to tread carefully. There is shouting. Cars everywhere. Horns blaring. Someone grabs my arm, not gently, pulls me faster than my legs want to move, practically hoists me up a curb onto a cement island. I am suddenly surrounded by people. Strangers. From afar a voice calls, a familiar one, and the strangers part like the waters of the Red Sea. Here she comes: bright auburn hair, shivering in a short-sleeved T-shirt that exposes her rattlesnake tattoo.

Wait! I'm her daughter! Please don't call the police!

She arrives, breathless.

Thank you, thank you. Whoever got her out of the street, thank you. She takes a deep breath. I apologize for the trouble. My mother has dementia. She is forcing out the words, and her thin frame is starting to shiver. It is bitterly cold.

As the crowd begins to disperse, she turns to me.

Mom, please don't do that! You scared us all.

Where am I?

About two blocks from home. In the middle of one of the busiest intersections in the city.

She pauses. It was my fault, I was putting my bag up in my old bedroom. You know, I'm spending the night again, Magdalena thought it would be nice for you. We got to talking, didn't notice that you'd wandered off. Where were you going?

To Amanda's. It's Friday, isn't it?

No, actually it's Wednesday. But I understand. You were trying to find Amanda's house?

It's our day.

Yes. I understand. She thinks for a moment, seems to make up her mind. I think we should go to Amanda's, see if she's in.

What's your name?

Fiona. Your daughter.

Yes. Yes, that's right. I remember now.

Let's go. Let's see if we can find Amanda.
Look. The light is green now. She is holding
my arm and urging me forward with purpose. Although I am at least three inches
taller than she is, I have trouble keeping up
with her stride. We move past the thrift
store, past the El station, around the corner
of the church, and suddenly the world tilts
into place again. I pause at one house, a
brownstone, with a short black iron fence
around its yard. A tree stripped of leaves
leans over the path to the front steps.

Yes, this is our house. But we're going to visit
Amanda.

I remember, I say. Three houses down. One,
two, three.

That's right. Here we are. Let's just knock on
the door and see if Amanda's here. If she's
not, we'll go home and have a cup of tea and
do the crossword puzzle. I brought a new
book.

Fiona knocks loudly three times. I press on the doorbell. We wait on the porch, but no one comes. No face appears behind the curtains of the living room window. Not that Amanda would ever peer like that. Despite Peter's admonitions, she always flings open the door without looking. Always ready to face whatever life brings her.

Fiona has her back to the door. Her eyes are closed. Her body is shaking. Whether it's from the cold or something else I can't tell. Let's go, Mom, she says. No one is home.

Strange, I say. Amanda has never missed one of our Fridays.

Mom, please. Her voice is urgent. She pulls me down the steps, so fast I stumble and nearly fall, and pushes me back down the sidewalk. One. Two Three. We are back in front of the brownstone.

Her hand on the gate, she pauses, looks up. Her face is full of pain, but as she gazes at the house, the pain dissipates into something else. Longing.

How I love this house, she says. I'll be so sad to see it go.

Why should it go? I ask. Your father and I

don't intend to move. The wind whistles past and both of us are white with cold, but we stand there on the sidewalk in front of the house, not moving. The frigid temperature suits me. It suits the conversation, which strikes me as important.

Fiona's face is pinched and there are large goosebumps on her arms, but she still doesn't move. The house before us is solid, it is a fact. The warm red stones, the large protruding rectangular windows, the three stories capped with a flat roof emblematic of other Chicago houses of the era. I find myself yearning for it as desperately as when James and I first saw it, as if it were out of our reach. Yet it is truly ours. Mine. I bullied James into buying it, even though it was beyond our means at the time. It is my home.

Home, she says as if she could read my mind, then shakes her head as if to clear it. She takes me by the elbow, propels me up the steps, into the house, helps me off with my coat, my shoes.

I have something to show you, she says, and takes a small white square out of her pocket, unfolds it. Look at this, she says. Just look.

A photograph. Of my house. No, wait. Not precisely. This house is slightly smaller, fewer and smaller windows, only two stories high. But the same Chicago brownstone, the same small square of yard in front, and, like my house, crowded in from brownstones on either side, one in pristine condition, the other, like this one, slightly shabby. No curtains at the windows. A SOLD sign in front.

What is this? I ask.

My house. My new house. Can you believe it? I try to take the photograph from her to see more closely, but she has trouble relinquishing it. I have to pull to get it into my own hands. Even so, she leans toward me, as though she can't bear to let it out of her sight.

It's in Hyde Park. On Fifty-sixth Street. Right off campus. I can bike to my office.

It's eerie, I say. The similarity.

Yes, I thought so too. I paid too much for it, of course. It needs tons of work. But these things don't come on the market very often. I had to act fast.

51

I keep gazing at the house. It could almost be my own, that could almost be my bedroom window, that could almost be the iron gate to my backyard.

When do you move in?

Well, it's a little complicated. Closing was delayed. Because of Amanda. She had co-signed the loan for me.

And why would that be a problem? Did she change her mind?

No. No, of course not.

Well?

Fiona is silent for a moment. Then, I just decided I didn't want to bother her with it after all.

Why didn't you ask me? Or your father?

Fiona twists a purple lock around her index finger. I don't know. Just didn't want to make you feel obliged. It turned out okay. I was able to come up with enough money.

Well, you know if you ever need help . . .

Yes, I know. You've always been very generous.

Mark is a different matter altogether, of course. Your father and I don't trust his judgment in money matters.

You're a little hard on him, you know.

Perhaps. Perhaps.

I have forgotten I am still holding the photograph until she reaches out and plucks it from my hand, folds it carefully, and puts it back in her pocket. Then pulls it out and looks at it again, as if checking that it is real, the way I used to pat her little arms and legs when she slept, amazed I had produced this perfect being.

It is my home, she says, so softly I can barely make out the words. And she smiles.

From my notebook:

I watched David Letterman last night. So, in homage:

TOP 10 SIGNS YOU HAVE ALZHEIMER'S

10. Your husband starts introducing

himself as your "caregiver."

9. You find an hourly activity schedule taped up on your refrigerator that includes "walks," "crocheting," and "yoga."

8. Everyone starts giving you crossword puzzle books.

7. Strangers are suddenly very affectionate.

6. The doors are all locked from the outside.

5. You ask your grandson to take you to the junior prom.

4. Your right hand doesn't know what your left hand has done.

3. Girl Scouts come over and force you to decorate flower pots with them.

2. You keep discovering new rooms in your house.

And the No. 1 sign you have Alzheimer's is . . . It's somehow slipped your mind.

If I could see through this fog. Break through this heaviness of limbs and extremities. Every inhalation stabs. My hands limp in my lap. Pale and impotent, they used to wield shiny sharp things, lovely things with heft and weight that bestowed power.

People would lie down and bare their naked flesh. Invite me to dismember them. *And if thy hand offend thee, cut it off: it is better for thee to enter into life maimed, than having two hands to go into hell, into the fire that never shall be quenched.*

Write about yourself, Magdalena urges. If it helps, write in the third person. Tell me a story about a woman who happens to be named Jennifer White.

She is a reserved person. Some would say cold. Yet others welcomed that quality, saw it as a form of integrity. She thought either was a fair assessment. Both could be attributed to her training. Surgery requires precision, objectivity.

You don't get emotional over a hand. A hand is a collection of facts. The eight bones of the carpus, the five bones of the metacarpus, and the fourteen phalanges. The flexor and extensor tendons that maneuver the digits. The muscles of the forearm. The opposable thumb. All intertwined. Multiple interconnections. All necessary to the balance of motion that separates humans from other species.

But Amanda. She thinks of Amanda's metacarpus, minus four sets of phalanges. A mutilated starfish. Does she cry? No. She writes it in her notebook. Amanda died. Fingerless. But the details won't stick.

I stop, put my pen down. I ask Magdalena, Which neighbor was suspected in Amanda's death? but she will not answer. Perhaps because I have asked and she has answered the question many times. Perhaps because she knows I will forget my question if she ignores it.

But I rarely forget that a question has been asked. When Magdalena ignores me, unfinished business lies heavy between us, disrupts our routine, hangs over us as we drink our tea. In this case, it pollutes the very air. For something is terribly wrong.

My notebook again. Fiona's handwriting:

Came over today to find you uncharacteristically subdued. Anger we see a lot of. Bewilderment. And a surprising degree of intelligent acceptance. But rarely this resigned passivity.

You were slumped at the table, your face flat down, your hands hanging at your sides. I crouched down and put my arm around your shoulders, but you didn't move or say anything. Wouldn't answer any questions or give any sign you knew I was there.

Eventually you sat up, pushed back the chair, and slowly went up the stairs to bed. I didn't dare follow you. Didn't dare ask any more questions for fear of what you would reveal about the dark place you were residing in.

I had never been afraid like that. I wasn't always sure what you were thinking, but I could always ask, and sometimes you would even tell me. If the truth had the power to hurt, you made it palatable by your calm acceptance of it.

You don't really like me very much, do you? I asked you when I was fifteen. No, you said, and you don't like me very much either right now. But we'll find each other again. And we did. If I'd known that within a decade I would lose both you and Dad, would I have acted differently back then? Probably not. I probably would have gone out and gotten another tattoo.

That tattoo. You keep asking about it, Mom, so I'll write it down here. It's a pretty good story. I already had two tattoos. There was the one I got with Eric when I was fourteen. You didn't know about that one. It's very discreet — on my left buttock. A tiny Tinker Bell. Well, I was fourteen.

Then when I was sixteen, the youngest freshman in my class at Stanford, I got another one, this time on my ankle. A cannabis sativa plant. Yes, you can guess why a kid really too young to be away from home would think that was cool.

But the rattlesnake. That was my junior year. I'd done okay the first two years, better than I'd done in high school socially, actually made some friends, did the things you'd expect. Drank too much. Slept around.

But in my junior year, things fell apart. My best friend had a sort of breakdown and went home to West Virginia. He wrote a couple times, made jokes about the skinny dogs and the ugly women, and that was that. Two of my other friends started dating each other, retreated into their own private world, put up a barrier against others. It felt oddly personal.

At that point, I was living off campus in a room

rented from this Silicon Valley marketing type. She wasn't there half the time, either traveling or staying up in the city with her boyfriend. The house was up in the redwoods, high above the university.

When people came up to visit they'd sit in the hot tub and ooh and aah, but I never got used to the place. The quiet disturbed me, as did the fact that the sun went behind the hills at two in the afternoon and suddenly the day was over.

Coyotes trotted boldly through the yard, rats scratched under the floors and in the wood-work, and even the deer spooked me. They'd come right up to the house to forage, and since there were no curtains on the windows — the house was on three acres of redwoods, so there was no need — I'd woken up several times to deer faces pressed against the glass, solemnly observing me as they chewed.

So I took to spending a lot of my time down on the flats, in Palo Alto. There was one cof-feehouse I liked, and I'd sit there for hours, drinking cup after cup of black coffee and studying. By then I was taking grad classes, and my professors were telling me I had a career in academia if I wanted one. Because I wanted one, badly, you could find me at that coffeehouse working pretty much every night.

I was there one Friday night as usual, hyped up on coffee and lonely as hell, and not wanting to go back up the hill to that house without curtains. I had resigned myself to doing just that, however, when a nice-looking young woman — just a little older than myself, I'd guess — came up to me. She had a question about what I was studying — was it math? Sort of, I said, and we fell into a conversation about what economics was and why it mattered.

After a while she motioned to a young man sitting at another table and said, We're going to a party in Santa Cruz, you want to come? I thought, Well, this is strange. And, I'm not sure I like these people. There was something too eager about them. The woman's teeth were too large for her mouth when she smiled. And then, recklessly, Why the hell not?

They told me not to bother with my car, that they'd bring me back when the party was over. That should have alerted me. But I got in the car, and the first thing that happened was they started going up the hill toward where I lived.

I said, Wait a minute, this isn't the way to Santa Cruz, and they told me it was a back

60

way, a really pretty one. Since I'd had enough of that kind of pretty and was beginning to think I'd done a very foolish thing, I asked them to just drop me off at my house — we were passing right by my street — and said that I'd pick up my car in the morning.

But they refused. Said, No, you're coming with us. And I was both very angry and very frightened. I had a kind of a crazy idea that I would wait until the car slowed to go around a corner and then jump out, but when I tried to open the door I found they'd put the child-safety locks on. So I just folded into myself and waited to see what happened.

We got to this old ranch house up in the Santa Cruz mountains — where, I'm still not sure — and there was another poor soul like me who they'd picked up in Santa Clara. We were all in this room and this man came out and welcomed me and this other girl to what he called "the family." Said we shouldn't be alarmed. Said we could go home whenever we wanted, we just had to give them a chance. Keep an open mind.

At that point, I got up and left the room. Didn't run, didn't hurry, just walked right out of that house and down the long driveway and into the road. Astonishingly, no one followed me.

Later, maybe a half mile down the road, I found my hands clenched into fists. I kept walking, it was pitch-black, and I had no idea where I was, but had a vague idea of getting to the nearest house and calling the police. And then I saw headlights. I stuck out my thumb, and a truck with two sixteen-year-old kids from Ben Lomond stopped.

One of them had only that day gotten his driving license and they were both pumped up like hell on excitement. They were on their way into Santa Cruz to get drunk and tattooed to celebrate.

I said, I'm game, and I was. I figured I couldn't get a bus back to Palo Alto until the next morning anyway.

After downing a bunch of tequila shots in a campus bar, we somehow got to a twenty-four-hour tattoo parlor on Ocean. I stumbled into a chair and said Do your worst. Give me the biggest meanest thing you have.

So he started in. It took him all night. He kept popping pills to stay awake, which should have worried me, but it didn't. The pain was almost unbearable, but the booze helped and when I got home and saw my lovely snake it was worth every acid-laced sting.

I aced my finals that week and, my arm throbbing, took a red-eye back to Chicago. You took one look at my arm and prescribed a course of antibiotics, but you never said anything about my snake. Whether you liked it or not. Until after you got sick.

Then you began complimenting me on it. Telling me not to cover it up. Encouraging me to wear sleeveless tops. I think at this point you're as proud of it as I am. Our joint emblem: Don't Tread on Me.

From my notebook. My handwriting:

Two men and a woman were here today. Detectives. I must write it down, Magdalena says, I must keep my head clear. Know what I've said. Think straight.

The men were clumsy and heavy, perched awkwardly on my kitchen chairs. The woman was one of them: coarse, almost, but with a more alert, intelligent face. The two men deferred to her. She mostly listened, putting in a word now and then. The men took turns asking questions.

Tell us about your relationship with the deceased.

What deceased? Who died?

Amanda O'Toole. Everyone says you were very close.

Amanda? Dead? Nonsense. She was here, just this morning, full of schemes for a new neighborhood petition. Something against excessive dog barking, about imposing sanctions and fines.

Let me rephrase the question. What is your relationship with Mrs. O'Toole?

She is my friend.

But one of your neighbors — the man who was talking consulted his notebook — said you had a loud argument on February fifteen. The day after Valentine's Day, around two PM, in her house.

Magdalena broke in. They were always fighting. They were that close. Like sisters. You know how family is.

Please, ma'am. Let Dr. White answer. What was that particular argument about?

What argument? I asked. It is a bad day, I can't concentrate. This morning Magdalena put a red and white stick in my hand at the bathroom sink. Toothbrush, she said, but the word meant nothing. I came to later at the kitchen table with a half-eaten stick of butter in front of me. Then I had another fade-out and a fade-in. I found myself sitting in the same place, but now with a glass half full of an orange liquid on the table in front of me, a pile of multicolored pills. What is this? I asked Magdalena, pointing. The colors were wrong. The bright liquid and the small hard round bursts of blue, magenta, buttercup. Poison. I would not be fooled. Was not fooled. Flushed it all down the toilet when Magdalena was not looking.

But back to the main point:

The argument you had with Mrs. O'Toole in mid-February, the man repeated, somewhat impatiently.

Can't you see that she doesn't remember? asked Magdalena.

Convenient, said the other man. He looked at the first man and raised his eyebrow. Coconspirators.

She's not a well woman, said Magdalena.

You know this. You have her doctor's statement. You are aware of the nature of this disease.

The first man started in again. What was the state of your relationship with Amanda O'Toole in February?

I imagine it was what it always was, I said. Close, but combative. Amanda was in many ways a difficult woman.

The woman spoke for the first time. So we've heard, she said. She allowed herself a small smile. She nodded to the first man to continue.

You had a fight with her in her house seven days before the body was discovered. About the time of the murder.

What murder?

Just answer the question. Why did you go to Amanda O'Toole's house on February fifteen?

We were in and out of each other's houses all the time. We had keys.

But that particular day? What were you doing? According to our witness, you didn't knock but let yourself in the front door. This was at approximately one thirty PM. At two PM this neighbor heard loud voices. An argument.

I shook my head.

Look, clearly she doesn't know, Magdalena said. She won't even remember you were here ten minutes after you're gone. Can't you leave her alone? How many times are you going to ask these questions?

The first man started to talk, but the woman silenced him. That evening was the last time anyone saw Amanda O'Toole, she said. She visited the drugstore, bought some toothpaste, and picked up some food items from Dominick's around six thirty PM. But she didn't take in her paper after that day. The timeline fits. If nothing else, Dr. White was one of the last persons to see Mrs. O'Toole before she was killed.

The world shifted sideways. Darkness descended. My body turned to stone.

Killed? Amanda? I asked. But it was true. Somehow I knew that. This was not shock. This was not surprise. This was grief, continued.

After a short silence, the woman spoke. Her

voice was gentler. That must be difficult. Reliving that moment over and over again.

I willed myself to breathe, to unclench my hands, to swallow. Magdalena put a hand on my shoulder.

And why are you here today? asked Magdalena. We've gone over this several times. Why again. Why now? You have no evidence.

There was only silence to that.

So why are you here? Magdalena asked again. No one was looking at me.

Just routine. Trying to find out if Dr. White can help us in any way.

How could she help you?

Perhaps she saw something. Heard something. Knew something about what was going on in Amanda's life that no one else knew about. The woman turned to me suddenly.

So, was there? she asked. Anything out of the ordinary in Amanda's life? Anyone who had a grudge? Had reason to be . . . disgruntled?

Everyone looked at me. But I was not there.

I was in Amanda's house, at her kitchen table, we were laughing wickedly over her imitation of the head of our block's Neighborhood Watch program, her rendition of the 911 tape in which the woman reported a dangerous intruder trying to break into the church, which turned out to be a stray Labrador urinating under a bush.

It was a humble kitchen, never renovated to the standards of the neighborhood. Peter and Amanda, schoolteacher and PhD student in religious studies, bought the house prior to the area's gentrification.

Plain pine cupboards painted a flat white. Checkered linoleum tiled floors. A twenty-year old avocado green Frigidaire. Amanda brought out a stale Bundt cake, a leftover from a PTA function, and cut us each a dry slice. I took a bite and spitted it out at the exact moment she did the same. We started laughing again. And suddenly I ached with loss.

The female detective had been watching me intently. Enough, she said. That's all for today.

Thank you, I said, and our eyes met for a second. Then the three of them took their leave.

March 1, according to the calendar. Our anniversary. James's and mine. I usually forget, but James, never. He doesn't buy me extravagant gifts on schedule — those he saves for when I least expect them — but the ones he brings on these occasions are nevertheless deliciously unusual. What will it be today? I feel doglike, capable of wearing out the carpet with my pacing. Not that I'm often in this mood. No. And not that I would let him catch me. But nevertheless, there *is* this excitement, this anticipation, that has not dissipated. My parasite, thriving in darkness, his essence remaining mysterious throughout the mundanity of marriage. The shared bathroom, the clothes abandoned on the floor, the crumbs under the breakfast table. Still an enigma despite all this. A gift from the gods, James was. And today, as I wait for his return from parts unknown, I give thanks to them.

◇ ◇ ◇

I pick up the first photo album, labeled *1998–2000.* The woman who helps me insists. She doesn't understand how utterly stupefying it is to be guided through the sea of unfamiliar faces and locales. All labeled in large black capital letters as though for an idiot child. For me.

To be asked, over and over, And who is this? Do you remember her? Do you recognize this place? It's like being forced to see someone's holiday snapshots of places you never wanted to go.

But today I will do what the leader at our support group suggests. I will examine each photo for clues. I will think of the book as a historical document, myself as an anthropologist. Uncovering facts and formulating theories. But facts first. Always.

I have my notebook beside me as I look. To record my discoveries.

The first photo that has Amanda written in the caption is dated September 1998. Amanda and Peter. A vibrant older couple. They could be in an ad for healthy aging.

The woman with longish thick white hair caught up in a ponytail. You can tell how strong and capable she is. Her wrinkles augment this authority. You wouldn't want to be in a subservient position to her. You'd have to hold your own or be vanquished. An executive? A politician? Someone used to controlling crowds, multitudes even.

The man next to her is a different sort altogether. Although his beard is gray, his hair still has traces of black. He stands a little behind the woman and is only very slightly taller. More humor in his smile, more kindness.

You would turn to him for help, advice. To her, for decisive action. I cannot see his left hand. Hers has a wedding band on it. If they were husband and wife, there would be no doubt who would be in charge.

The photo has few other points of interest. They are standing on a porch — a rare feature for the brownstones on this street. It is summer: They are wearing T-shirts, and the honeysuckle vine climbing up the railing is in full bloom.

Behind them are folding lawn chairs, the kind woven from cheap multi-colored plastic strips. A small oval plastic table immediately in front. On it, three empty tall glasses and one full one that contains a flat watery amber liquid. There is a slight blur in the bottom right-hand corner of the photo — perhaps the photographer's hand, gesturing the couple to move together.

The sun must be behind the photographer, because his (her?) shadow shades the woman's neck and breasts.

And suddenly I remember. No, I *feel.* The heat. The insistent buzz of cicadas that were everywhere that year — the seventeen-year plague, every one said, only half kidding. They crunched underfoot, spattered across our windshields, forced us inside during the hottest months of summer.

Peter and Amanda's house had a screened-in porch, which is what made it possible to sit outdoors that day, to relieve the claustrophobia, the sense of incarceration. We were waiting for James, who was late, as usual.

We'd drunk our beers and were debating whether to open some more when Peter suggested capturing the moment. *What moment?* Amanda and I had exclaimed, in such perfectly matched tones that we both laughed.

Peter, characteristically, was unruffled. This moment that will never come again, he said. This moment after which nothing will ever be the same. Amanda made a face but went inside for the camera agreeably enough.

And what is likely to be different after this moment? I teased Peter. Do you have an announcement to make? Some revelation? That made him uncomfortable.

No, of course not, he said. Nothing of the sort. He shifted in his chair, picked up his glass, and raised it to his lips again, even though it was empty.

I guess I'm grateful, he said, finally.

That's an odd emotion to feel when it's more than one hundred degrees at six o'clock in the evening, I said.

He refused to smile. No, grateful is the right word, he said. Grateful for every moment that the bottom doesn't fall out. He paused, then laughed. It's those damn cicadas, he said. They make one think about Old Testament–style wrath-of-God-type things.

You know, he continued, there are remark-able parallels between events documented in an ancient Egyptian manuscript, Admonitions of Ipuwer, and the book of Exodus. Pestilence and floods, rivers turning red, and no one able to see the face of his fellow man for days on end because of locusts. Many a doctoral candidate has been grateful for these points. Although if I never read another thesis with the word locust in it, I myself will be eternally grateful. He stopped, leaned forward, suddenly intent.

And you, Jennifer, he said. What would you be grateful for?

Taken unaware, I gave him a breezy reply: Oh, the usual. Health and happiness. That the kids keep doing as well as they're doing. That James's and my late fifties are as productive as our early fifties and our sixties not too dull as we start to slow down.

He took it more seriously than I had intended.

Perhaps. Yes. Those are not unreasonable hopes.

Well, I'm a reasonable woman, I said. But frankly, you're alarming me.

I don't mean to. But I do have a decade or so on you. Enough to know that the words reasonable and hope don't always fit well in the same sentence.

Then, a bustle and a little noise, and

Amanda was back with the camera. She gestured for Peter and me to stand together. No no, I said. I'm a little spooked by what Peter has been saying. I'd rather not have this particular moment recorded with me in it. Here, let me.

And so I took the picture — my sense memory is so clear I can hear the double click-click of the predigital camera — and at that moment James arrived, bearing flowers and wine and keeping his own counsel on things of import. But I didn't realize that at the time.

It is a day for the rending of garments. For the gnashing of teeth and the covering of mirrors. Amanda.

I rage at Magdalena. How could you withhold this information from me? I may be impaired, but I am not fragile! I accepted my diagnosis. I buried a husband. I am nothing if not resilient.

We did tell you. Many times.

No. I would have remembered this. It would have been as though my own fingers had been severed. As if my own heart sliced open.

Check your notebook. Here. Look at this entry. And this. Here is the news article of her death. Here is the obituary. Here is what you wrote when you first found out. And we've been to the police station twice. Visited by investigators three times. We've gone over this and over this. You have mourned. And mourned again. We went to church. We said the Rosary.

I? Said the Rosary?

Well, I said the Rosary. You sat there. You were calm. Not aware, but not distressed. You get like that sometimes. Calm and accepting. Almost catatonic. I like to take you to church when that happens. Magdalena isn't looking at me when she says this.

I have a theory, that it is a good thing when you're in that state, she says. That those are the times your soul is most open, the possibilities for healing greatest. The echoing silence, the sweet smell, the soothing filtered light. The Presence. This time was different, however. You roused yourself. You saw the people waiting their turn for confession. You got in line. You went behind the curtain. You stayed a very long time. When you came back

77

you had tears on your face. Tears! Imagine that!

I can't, actually. But go on.

But it's true. I swear. You reached out, and took my Rosary. You closed your eyes. Your fingers touched the beads. Your lips moved. I asked you, What are you doing? And you answered, as clear as could be, Amanda. My penance.

That sounds implausible. I wouldn't know how to say a Rosary. Not after all these decades.

Well, you gave a pretty good impression of knowing what you were doing!

I consider this. I am calmer now. I consider the written evidence. I accept that there was no betrayal on Magdalena's part. Just my damaged mind. But this doesn't lessen the agony. Amanda my friend, my ally, my most worthy adversary. What will I do without you?

I think of the time around Mark's graduation from high school. He and James had fallen out. He had, disconcertingly, attached himself to me. Just as I was getting ready to let him go. He was then coming into his dark, dangerous looks. Always good-looking — the girls started calling when he was twelve — he had in the last year been transformed into a dangerous man, a walking risk to those around him.

That summer was memorable for that, and because Amanda was for once not teaching. We spent the long evenings together while the sun lingered on her porch. Fiona, a very mature twelve, preferred to stay at home reading, that summer it was Jane Austen and Hermann Hesse. But Mark would inevitably join Amanda and me, sometimes for a few minutes on his way to a friend's house, sometimes for hours, and sit quietly, listening while we talked. Although he was a year from being of legal age, Amanda would pour him a beer and he'd drink it thirstily and fast, as if we might change our minds and take it away.

What did we talk about night after night in that waning light? Politics of course, the latest petitions and rallies and marches Amanda had participated in, which she was constantly pressuring me to join.

Take Back the Night. Walk for Breast Cancer. Run for Muscular Dystrophy. Books —

we were both Anglophiles, both knew the works of Dickens and Trollope by heart — and travel. The many places James and I had traveled, and Amanda's curiosity, despite her own inclination to stay at home, which I never understood. And Mark there, listening.

Something significant occurred on one of those evenings. James and I had just returned from St. Petersburg, where we had purchased an exquisite fifteenth-century icon of Theotokos of the Three Hands. It had been outrageously expensive.

I had seen it at a gallery in Galernaya Place and had fallen in love. James resisted and resisted and then, on our last morning, disappeared for half an hour and came back with a package wrapped in brown paper, which he held out to me with a mixture of amusement and anger.

I held it on my lap on the flight home, unwilling to trust it to my suitcase or the overhead bin. Now I carefully unwrapped it to show Amanda. Perhaps eight inches high, the icon showed the Blessed Mother supporting the Christ Child with her right hand. Her left hand was pressed to her breast as if trying to contain her joy.

At the bottom of the icon appeared a third hand. The severed hand of Saint John Damascene. As the legend went, it had been miraculously reattached to his arm by the Virgin. Now at her feet, a testament to her healing powers.

Amanda held the icon in silence for perhaps five minutes, intent as when she was deeply engaged in giving a lesson to a difficult student or preparing for an important school board speech. She finally spoke. I like this, she said. I never really understood your passion for religious iconography, but this is different. This one moves me in a way I can't explain.

Then she spoke. I want this, she said. Her voice was soft but firm. Will you give it to me?

Mark, who had been lolling on the steps, sat up straight. I could only look. There was a long silence before a car horn sounded on Fullerton, causing both Mark and me to jump. Amanda didn't move.

Well? she said. I won't ask if I can buy it, because I know I can't afford it. So I think you will give it to me. Yes. I think so.

I stood up, walked over to where she was sitting on the porch swing, and took the icon from her hands. It took some effort, she was holding on so tightly.

Why now? Why this? I asked. You've never asked for anything before. Never.

And you've always been so generous to me, she said. Bringing me gifts from your travels. Lovely things. The most beautiful things I own in the world come from you. But I hope you won't mind me saying that they meant nothing. Mean nothing. Such things never touched me. But this. This is something else.

Mark surprised both of us by clearing his throat and speaking. But Mom loves this. It's not just a souvenir to her. He opened his mouth as if to say more, then blushed and closed it.

I understand that, Amanda said. Which is one of the reasons I want it so much. Not the only reason. But a main one.

No, I said. My voice came out stronger and louder than I had meant it to. This is mine. Anything else, you know I'd be happy to give you whatever you wanted. Money has never been an object.

No, it wouldn't be, she said, and there was a warning in her voice. Mark was watching everything intently.

No, I said again. I rewrapped my icon and placed it back in its box. No and no and no. This time, you've gone too far.

I left her porch, and it was many weeks before I felt calm enough to speak to her again. Many lonely weeks. Then, she knocked on my door one Friday noon. Our standing appointment. And I got my coat and joined her. It was done. She had made a request — something I imagined was a humbling experience — and had been refused. There was nothing more to say.

Yet there was an odd coda to all this. Mark went off to Northwestern in the fall, as planned. Since his dorm was less than twenty minutes away, it was not as momentous a leave-taking as Fiona's was to California four years later.

But it was traumatic for him. During the days before he left he was extraordinarily demanding. I need a study pillow. My roommate doesn't have a TV, we need to buy one. And even, Bake me some cookies.

It was also a particularly busy time at work,

and I gave most of these demands short shrift. Still, it was more draining than I had anticipated. It wasn't until the morning after we'd dropped him off in Evanston, leaving him standing in front of his dorm, that I realized my icon was gone. A blank spot in its position of honor in the front hallway.

I immediately called Mark, but there was no answer. I left an urgent message on his machine, and paced from room to room, to the phone to call James, back to the front window, to the phone to try Mark again. I didn't for a minute think it could be anyone else. I had found Mark standing in front of it on more than one occasion, a bemused look on his face, his hand outstretched as if to caress the Madonna's face. When the doorbell rang, I jumped. Amanda stood there, cradling the icon.

Look at what was on my doorstep yesterday morning, she said, and held it out.

I took it. My hands were shaking. I found I was unable to speak.

Yesterday morning? I managed to ask, finally. What took you so long to come around?

Amanda didn't say anything. She merely

84

smiled. I eventually answered myself.

Because you weren't sure you were going to return it, I said.

Amanda seemed to be considering what to say.

I was touched by Mark's gesture, she said.

And you coveted it. Badly. As badly as I had.

Yes, I did. And I asked you to give it to me. And you said no.

I said no. And I meant no, I said. I held out my hand. She handed over the icon.

I suppose I will pay in some way for that refusal, I said.

Yes, you will pay. Perhaps not in any way you can guess. But eventually, such things have repercussions, Amanda said.

Then she turned and left. My best friend. My adversary. An enigma at the best of times. Now gone, leaving me utterly bereft.

Jennifer you are having a bad day. Jennifer

you have had a bad week. Jennifer this is the worst yet, ten days and counting. Dr. Tsien increased your galantamine. He increased the Seroquel. He increased the Zoloft.

When Mark calls, I lie, I say you are well, you are napping. Or I don't answer the phone at all when I recognize his number on caller ID. Fiona knows, she is here every day. What a good daughter. How lucky you are. I will pray for you, I will say the Rosary. I will pray to Saint Daphne, patron saint of the mentally ill. Or to Saint Anthony, my favorite, the patron of lost things.

What has been lost? Your poor, poor mind. Your life.

Fiona and I go out to lunch. Chinese. My fortune: *It doesn't take a good memory to make good memories.* You couldn't make this shit up, says Fiona.

Amanda has always called me shameless. She means it as a compliment. Shame-less. Without shame. I used to lie to the priests when saying confession because I could

86

never think of things I should be asking forgiveness for. People who take this to an extreme are called sociopaths, Amanda tells me. You have certain tendencies. You should watch them.

Bless me Father for I have sinned.

It has been forty-six years since my last confession.

My how time flies.

This always happens. I wake early, hoping to get some work done before the children start clamoring for their breakfast, but someone is up even earlier. That blond woman. Damn. Only this time she's not alone. Another woman is with her, drinking coffee out of my favorite cup. Large bones. Short light brown hair, tucked behind her ears. Wearing a denim jacket on top of faded jeans, cowboy boots.

Jennifer! What have you done . . . ?

I beg your pardon? I ask, but the blond woman has already left the room. She returns immediately with a blue towel and places it around my shoulders. She puts her arm around mine, turns me around, takes me away from the kitchen.

I notice that I am oddly cold, that rivulets of water are dripping from my nightgown onto the wood floors, that I can see my wet footprints on the polished oak. The blond woman talks at me as she leads me upstairs.

What a morning to pull this stunt. What timing. Didn't I tell you? Didn't I write it down in your notebook? Didn't we talk about it last night? I swear, sometimes I feel like I'm the one going nuts in this house.

She takes off my wet things, towels me down, dresses me in a blue skirt and a blue-and-red striped sweater, talking the whole time.

Now, behave. Just answer the questions. Keep calm. No acting up. This is just an informal visit. Very friendly. There's no need to worry. No need to bother Fiona or that lawyer she's got. It's not that kind of thing, not at all. Just a few questions and off she'll go.

The world is subdued today. Like I am behind a veil, looking out. The colors pastel

88

and faded, my senses dulled. My vision slightly obscured by the veil. It's not unpleasant. But it can be dangerous. You think that you are hidden from them, behind your veil, and suddenly you realize that you've been visible the whole time. Exposed.

It's not that you did anything you are ashamed of. Or that you would change what you did. It's just the thought of what you *might* have said or done. The breathtaking risk you've just taken. Now I am sitting at the kitchen table, facing the strange woman. My jaw feels wired shut. I have no energy to open it. I can barely keep my eyes open. Sleep. Sleep.

I remember turning on the shower. I remember soaping up my arms and my legs. I remember thinking that my nightdress was getting in the way. But I didn't put it all together. Too slow. Too uncaring.

The woman is asking me questions. I'm finding it hard to pay attention.

Where were you again the week of February sixteen?

Here. I'm always here.

On February fifteen and February sixteen in

particular? You were here? You didn't leave the house?

I exert myself, reach out, and pick up my notebook. I leaf through the pages. February 13. February 14. February 18.

The blond woman interrupts.

We try to document as many of her days as possible. She likes to read over them when she's feeling a bit down, when she's having a bad time of it. But I guess we missed that day. Still, if anything out of the ordinary had happened, I would have made a point of writing it down. Her daughter insists upon it.

The brown-haired woman reaches out and takes the book from me. She carefully turns the pages.

I see she wandered from home several times in January.

Yes, she does that occasionally. I watch her, but sometimes she does get away.

Did that happen in mid-February?

No, not in February. Honestly, it's a very rare occurrence.

She was seen by Helen Tighe, from Twenty-one Fifty-six, letting herself into Amanda O'Toole's home on February fifteen. Was that one of those rare times?

We've been over and over that. If it happened, I didn't know about it. She wasn't missing for any extended length of time. Sometimes I do laundry in the basement. Make some soup. If she went over to Amanda's, she was back before I noticed.

Doesn't that worry you?

It does, it does. Honestly, I do my best. We've had locks installed on all the outside doors, but that upsets her and does more harm than good. It's best to leave them unlocked and watch her carefully. Usually a neighbor notices. It's that kind of street. Everyone looks out for everyone else. We always get her back. We had a bracelet made, but she won't wear it.

What about at night?

Oh, nights are no problem. I've been told there are cases where you have to strap them in at night or you wouldn't know what they'd get up to. Not her. She goes down quietly at nine and doesn't make a peep until six in the morning. You could set a clock by her.

The brown-haired woman isn't listening. She is frowning. She holds the book closer, places her index finger in between two of the pages, draws it back, and looks at me.

A page has been removed, she says. And not torn out. Sliced out. With a razor or something like that. She looks at me, moves her chair closer to the blond woman, and speaks more softly. She was a doctor, right? A surgeon?

That's right.

Does she still have any of her equipment? Her scalpels?

I wouldn't think so. Don't those belong to the hospital? I've never seen anything like that around here. I would have, too. There isn't anything about this house I don't know. I have to keep an eye on things. Otherwise, you don't know what she'll do.

The blond woman pauses for a breath.

Last week, she threw all her jewelry in the trash. We only caught it by accident — her daughter found a diamond pendant lying outside in the snow next to the garbage. We dug down and found her wedding ring. Then some family keepsakes — some quite valuable, others just sentimental. We retrieved it all, and at that point we went through everything and I mean everything. Definitely no knives. Her daughter took a couple of trinkets that she wanted home with her — a special necklace that belonged to her mother and her father's college ring — then locked everything away in the safe-deposit box.

I make a noise. It's not until both women look at me that I understand it is laughter.

I stand up. I go into the living room. I go to the piano. To the bench. I open it up. It's full of what looks like junk. It is James's and my don't-but-can't place. As in I don't-know-what-to-do-with-it-but-can't-throw-it-away-yet. Receipts for purchases we might want to return someday. Knobs that fell off things. Unmatched socks.

I dig down. Past old prescription reading glasses, batteries that may or may not have charges, New Yorker magazines. Until I hit bottom. And pull it out, loosely wrapped in a linen napkin.

My special scalpel handle. Shiny. Alluring. Begging to be used. My name engraved on it, along with the date I finished my surgical residency. What do they say about me at the hospital? Get a second opinion. She's the best there is, but she's a hammer looking for a nail. She'll operate on a torn cuticle if you let her.

Some plastic packages fall out of the napkin. Each one holding a glinting sharp blade, ready to be inserted into my scalpel handle. Ready to slice. Both women are standing nearby, watching me closely. The blond one closes her eyes. The brown-haired one reaches out her hand. I'll have to take those, ma'am, she says. And I'm afraid you'll have to come with me.

We are in a car. I am sitting in the back, behind a driver with short brown hair. I cannot tell if it is a man or a woman. The hands on the wheel are strong, coarse even. Androgynous.

Magdalena is next to me. She is on her phone. Speaking urgently to one person, then hanging up, dialing another. It is cold. Snow is in the air. Yet the trees are budding. I roll down the window to feel the wind in my face. A typical Chicago spring.

94

I like being able to use that word, *typical.*
Usually is another good one. And *most of*
the time. Anything that's relative. Any way
of comparing future events to past occur-
rences.

We are in a room. Empty except for a table
and one chair — the chair I am sitting in.
There is no one in the room I know. Four
men. No Magdalena. I am read something
from a piece of paper. I am asked if I
understand. With these rights in mind, do you
wish to speak to me?

I am firm. No. I want my lawyer. There is a
large mirror taking up an entire wall. Otherwise, a barren, forsaken place. A place to
keep one's counsel.

Your lawyer is coming.

Then I will wait.

My scalpel handle and the blades on the
table in a plastic baggie. The men talk
quietly among themselves, but no one can
keep their eyes off the items and me.

I amuse myself by thinking how, in the movies, this room would be filled with cigarette smoke. Unshaved haggard men drinking cold weak coffee out of Styrofoam cups. Yet these men are close shaven, well dressed, dapper even. Two are drinking foamy drinks out of paper cups. One is holding an energy drink, the other a plastic water bottle. No one offers me anything.

A bustle at the door, and in sweep three women. Three tall striking women. Amazons! My daughter or perhaps my niece; the nice woman who helps me; and another one I may have seen before.

This last one, the one I am most uncertain about, holds out her hand, grips mine hard, and smiles. Nice to see you again, she says. Although I wish it were under better circumstances. She searches my face, smiles again, and says, Joan Connor. Your lawyer. To whom you are paying very big bucks indeed.

My daughter/niece comes straight over and puts her arm around my shoulders. It's okay, Mom, she says. They can't do anything to you. This is America. They still have to have some kind of proof.

The third woman, the blond one, just stands in the back, near the door. She is sweating profusely. Her color is curiously high. I reach into my jacket pocket for my stethoscope. Then I remember.

I am retired. I have Alzheimer's. I am in a police station because of my blades. My mind won't take me beyond these facts. My diseased mind. Yet I have never felt more alert. I am ready for anything. I smile at my daughter/niece, who does not smile back.

The lawyer turns to the men. Whereas before they had been standing casually apart from one another, now they are in a line, their shoulders nearly touching, their beverages on the table, forgotten. Men on guard. Against the enemy.

Are you charging Dr. White?

We just have a few questions. She refused to talk without you.

As is her right.

As we explained to her. Can we proceed now?

My lawyer nods. Please, a few more chairs.

The men break rank, two leave the room and come back with four more folding metal chairs, another one returns with two cups of water. He silently offers one to me, one to the young woman.

The lawyer sits down to my right, my daughter/niece to my left. She keeps her arm around my shoulders. The blond woman remains standing near the door, waves off a man when he gestures to an empty chair.

Where were you on February sixteen and seventeen?

I don't remember.

My lawyer interrupts.

She has been asked this time and time again. She has answered to the best of her ability. As you are aware, Dr. White has dementia. She will not be able to answer many of your questions.

Understood. When was the last time you used your scalpel?

I don't know. Some time ago.

You were an orthopedic surgeon, right?

That is correct. One of the best.

The man allows himself a smile.

And you specialized in hands?

Hand surgery, yes.

What do you make of these? He handed me some photographs. I study them.

An adult hand. Female. Medium-sized. The thumb is the only remaining digit. The others disarticulated at the joints between the metacarpal and proximal phalanges.

How would you characterize the cuts?

Clean. But not cauterized. Judging from the amount of coagulated blood, not performed according to protocol. But by all appearances, expertly executed.

What kind of knife would you say has been used?

Impossible to tell from these photos. I, personally, would use a size ten blade for an amputation, but it does not appear that these cuts were made for therapeutic reasons.

Is there a size ten blade in here? He indicates

the baggie.

Of course.

Why 'of course'?

Because it's the most appropriate blade for many of the most common surgical procedures. You would always have one handy.

You know who these photos are of, don't you? Whose hand this is?

I look at my lawyer. I shake my head.

Amanda O'Toole.

Amanda?

That's right.

My Amanda?

That's right.

I am left without words. I look at the young woman who has her arm around my shoulders. She nods.

Who would have done such a thing?

100

That's what we're trying to find out.

Where is she? I must see her. Do you have the digits? Replantation might be possible with cuts this clean.

I'm afraid that isn't likely.

The room contracts. Somehow I know what he is going to say. Those photos. This station. A lawyer. My scalpel handle. The blades. Amanda. I close my eyes.

My daughter/niece breaks in. How many times are you going to do this to her? How cruel can you be?

We have no choice. When Detective Luton found the scalpel we had no choice.

You mean, when my mother handed over the scalpel. Would she have done that if guilty?

Perhaps. If she didn't remember what she'd done. He turns to me.

Did you kill Amanda O'Toole?

I don't answer. I am focused on my own hands. Whole and unbloodied.

Dr. White, pay attention: Did you kill Amanda O'Toole and then afterward cut off four of her fingers?

I don't remember, I tell him. But there are images that nag.

The man is watching me closely. I meet his eyes and shake my head.

No. No. Of course not.

Are you certain? For a moment there . . .

My client has answered. Do not badger her. She is not a well woman.

One of the other men, smallish and blond, the one who had been sipping the energy drink, interrupts.

Strange how she knows some things and not others.

That is the nature of the disease, says the woman sitting next to me. She fades in and out.

I'm just saying. I could have sworn just then she remembered something.

He turns to me.

Anything. Anything at all pop into your head?

I shake my head. I look straight ahead, not at him. I place my perspiring hands on my lap, under the table.

My lawyer rises. Will you be charging my client?

The first man hesitates, then shakes his head. We need to run some tests.

I don't like the way that the woman next to me and the lawyer look at each other. We get up to leave, one of the men hands me my coat. I look for the other woman, the blond one, but she is already gone.

From my notebook. In an odd, backward-slanting handwriting, it is dated January 8 with the name Amanda O'Toole.

I stopped by today to say hello. Jennifer, you seemed to be doing well. You knew me. You remembered my knee surgery from last fall and the fact that this coming spring I plan to plant heirloom tomatoes in pots on the back patio where it catches the sun. You don't look particularly well. You've lost weight and your eyes are ringed with red. I hate losing you like this, old friend.

But today was a day for being content. We sat in the front room and talked, mostly about our men. Peter and James and Mark. You didn't remember that both Peter and James are gone, one to California, the other to a place that is either much better or much worse than here.

Peter loves California. He e-mails me frequently, you know. He asks about you. After forty years of marriage you don't just sever all ties. Peter and his vision quest. To live in a trailer in the Mojave Desert with a new age graduate student. People ask how I can bear that — the abandonment, as they see it.

Isn't the house empty? they ask. Well, it always was, I say, the two of us in that great big cavern. Maybe when you sell this place and move, I'll move too. There's not much else keeping me on this street.

You spoke of your worries about Mark. About how he takes too much after James in all the bad ways, with none of his — James's — strengths.

I can't agree with you there. Mark has a

vulnerable side that may save him. He's aware of it, too. James would never have acknowledged any weakness. Utterly confident of himself until the end. It can be reassuring to be around someone like that, to have a partner who has such an absolute belief in his own place in the world.

But such confidence has its risks. If you make the mistake of following them when they take that inevitable misstep, then you're at hazard, too. Then you're both sunk. A little healthy skepticism is good, even essential, for a marriage. A certain amount of pushing back. You never did enough of that.

Listen to me, my marriage evaporated after four decades without leaving a trace. Should the death of a marriage be odorless, tasteless? No. There should be some residue, there was something wrong with Peter and me that ours didn't have any. That it was so easy, that it ended so quietly.

At least when James died you felt something. It manifested itself in some strange ways, but you felt it very deeply. I know you don't remember that time, but you threw yourself into gardening, oddly enough. You of the black thumbs. Or rather, you started digging holes in your backyard.

And after you'd dug a couple dozen holes, you inserted rose saplings into them that you got from that nursery on Halsted. The first time you'd ever set foot in such a place. Then you abandoned them. They died, of course. Your yard was filled with little mounds of fresh earth with dead plant sprigs lying limply on top of them. The work of a demented gopher.

Do you remember anything at all about those days? You were starting to exhibit some of the signs. You had told me about your fears, of course. You hadn't told James. Did you ever tell the kids? Somehow I doubt it. You just hired a caregiver and let them figure it out for themselves.

Magdalena tells me the episodes of aggression are getting worse. I haven't seen one yet. Magdalena says I seem to have a calming influence on you. I know better than to think I've got some secret power. I've read enough about this disease to know that you can't predict the future by the past. It's like they say about parenting: Just when you think you've mastered it, everything changes.

That's why teachers hate switching from one grade to another, why I taught seventh grade for forty-three years. Try to apply all your best ideas and curricula even one year later in a child's life and it simply won't work.

You talked cogently about Fiona today. No fog there. And about her we are in complete agreement. She is doing well. We're both so proud of her. I was as worried during her adolescence as any parent would be. Her late teens and early twenties were so difficult, so painful to watch.

As you know, I took my godmother duties seriously! I wasn't worried about drugs or sex, although I'm sure she dabbled in both. Perfectly normal. No, I was more worried about her rescue fantasies. Always bailing Mark out. Then that unspeakable boy. Thank God she got rid of him before she reached her twenties. Otherwise she might well have married him.

It wouldn't have lasted, of course. But it would have left a stain, knowing Fiona. Damaged her. She would have felt it deeply. More deeply than I did after forty years.

Enough of this! I've gone on. Be well, my dear friend. I'll stop by again soon.

I spend a lot of time thinking about the

children. They used to be so close. Mark being so much older than Fiona, you'd think he would have gotten bored, would have pushed her away. He never did, not then. But they've fallen out. Mark does that with people. Sours on them, picks fights, renounces them. Then, after six months or a year, comes humbly back, begging pardon.

Early on, she was too young to be of interest to his friends, and I'd see her mooning after one or the other of them without worrying too much. Too thin, gawky, too damn smart to interest the football stars and basketball heroes that were Mark's cronies back then. But there was one — Fiona would have been, what, fourteen? Not cute anymore, and her features hadn't rearranged themselves into the pleasing openness of her adult years. She was a closed, secretive creature in adolescence.

Yet this boy — this young man — Mark's freshman-year roommate from Northwestern, saw possibilities. I had always been alert for predators, but Eric slipped below my radar. Too sallow, too diffident, without any of the charm or resentment I associated back then with successful seducers.

What happened between them I don't know.

Fiona wouldn't tell me. Was her heart broken? Did she catch a venereal disease? Did she have an abortion? Any of those were likely, but I think it was probably something less melodramatic. I thought at the time she was merely helping him through a statistics course. Amanda thought something similar. She thought Fiona had taken pity on him for his social clumsiness. It didn't occur to either of us that Fiona needed anything from Eric. It just wasn't what one thought about Fiona.

I ended it one night, after I caught them together sitting on the front steps. I wasn't spying, hadn't even thought about them, just opened the door and there they were. He had a petulant look on his face, the kind of don't-you-love-me face that young men like to pull. Not one I would have thought Fiona would be susceptible to. Then I saw her expression. Not love. No. Something worse. A kind of despairing responsibility. A tortured acceptance of a heavy burden.

It took every ounce of my strength not to kick that young man in his bony buttocks. I can still picture his aggrieved shoulders as he leaned toward Fiona, willing her to give him some of her strength. And she looked back at me, saw that I saw, and the weight seemed to evaporate from her body as I shook my head. No.

Later that night she accused me, in tears, of ruining her life. And so we played out that particular mother-daughter scene with a gusto that fooled both James and Mark. But we knew what was going on. A timely rescue, met with gratitude.

I find a letter next to my morning pills and juice. My name on it, no address. No stamp. Two pages of unlined notepaper, tiny cramped writing. I read it through once, then again.

Mom:

I'm sorry my last visit didn't end so well. I never even got to the real reason I came over. But, in fact, the episode just proves the point I wanted to make. It's really time to sell the house and move into assisted living.

What's more, it's time for me to exercise the medical power of attorney. I know you don't want this. You value your independence. With Magdalena's help,

65 percent of the time you do well. But the other 35 percent of the time!

The ongoing investigation into Amanda's death is a real worry. The fact that it's even a question that you might have been involved — not that I believe that, of course — is reason enough to make this move.

Do I believe that you are a danger to others? No. Do I believe you are a danger to yourself? Yes, I do. I suspect I don't hear everything. I suspect that Magdalena and Fiona keep things from me.

You gave me this power. I didn't ask for it. But, having been given it, I intend to fulfill my duties. You could take it away, of course. You could do what Fiona is trying to convince you to do (yes, I read through your notebook last time I was there) and strip me of this power. But I think you know it would be a mistake.

About Fiona. I worry about her. Almost as much as I worry about you. As I said when I saw you, you know how she gets. How she does really well for long periods of time, but then things can go south — very very quickly. Remember that time at Stanford? When Dad had to go get her so she could decompress in a safe place?

Anyway, I know Fiona tells you otherwise, but I truly have your best interests at heart. The police have had you in for questioning multiple times. I know that if they had anything at all on you they wouldn't hesitate to try you as a competent adult.

I worry about you a lot. I know I don't always express it in the most diplomatic way. As we've discussed many times, I'm not Dad. I'm not the silver-tongued corporate finance lawyer, just a grunt. But I do care.

Legally, as you once knew (and maybe still do when your mind is clear), incapacity has to be established for each separate task. You may no longer be competent to dress yourself, but you may be competent to make a decision about where you want to live. I accept that.

The fact that you decided to give Fiona financial control was on one hand a wise one. You recognized that you could no longer act in your own best interest financially. You have substantial assets, and you should not risk them. That was the right thing to do — almost.

This is a long-winded way of saying that I would like to declare you mentally incompetent to get some legal protection for you. Just in case.

And an equally long-winded way of saying that I'm not sure that Fiona is the best person to control your money. She's certainly capable. But is she trustworthy? I would feel more comfortable if I were also getting copies of your account statements. Can we perhaps arrange this?

Try to read this letter knowing of my concern for your well-being. Mental competency is a label. It doesn't have anything to do with your actual abilities. You won't suddenly deteriorate because some court of law has ruled. You'll still be the same person. But you may possibly avoid a lot of trouble and expense by making this move now rather than waiting until you are pulled in again by the police or even charged.

I'll come by tomorrow and try again. Believe me, I truly wish to be of service.

Your loving son,

Mark

Today my mother died. I am not crying, it was her time. So it goes. So it always goes.

Oh Mary! My father would say when my mother did something outrageous — danced the cancan on top of a chair at a formal dinner party, stoned a pigeon to death in front of horrified passersby. *Oh Mary!* Their love duet.

Such a lovely man, my father. He had a quiet mind, as Thoreau would say. How did he end up with my mother? She flirted with homosexual priests, told audacious lies, uncorked the whiskey at four o'clock every day. And now, finally, gone.

My flight to Philadelphia is delayed, and so

when I arrive at the hospice the bed is already empty — someone failed to pass on the news that I was coming. I sit on the stripped bed. Does it matter? No. I don't know if she would have known me in any case.

She wandered at the end. A devout Catholic always, in the last months of her life she forsook Christ and the Blessed Mother for the virgin martyrs. Theresa of Avila, Catherine of Siena, and Lucy were her constant companions. She would giggle, swat at the air with a Kleenex, offer them bits of food. A hungry, witty lot, to judge from the constant feeding they required and my mother's constant laughing at their repartee.

She retained her mischievousness. She never lost that. Once, she secreted a ketchup package from her lunch tray and dotted it on her wrists at the lunocapitate joints, on her ankles at the talonaviculars. Bitter, vinegary stigmata. The nurse's assistant screamed, to my mother's obvious delight. She gave a high five to an invisible coconspirator.

Ultimately what did her in was a fall. An innocuous one. Her knees buckled as she hobbled from her bed to the toilet. She collapsed onto the floor, was helped up, and that was the end of her.

That evening, she was running a high fever. Throughout the night she remained deep in conversation with her saints. It was a different kind of delirium than usual: She was saying her good-byes. She kissed the virgins good-bye, gave them long, loving embraces. She waved goodbye to the doctors, the nurses, the orderlies. She waved to the hospice visitors passing by in the hall. She asked for, and received, a large glass of Scotch whiskey. She was given her last rites. Good-bye, good-bye.

My father wasn't mentioned. I wasn't either.

She was a lover of practical jokes until the end. When the orderlies came to remove her body, one noticed an oddly shaped lump between her breasts. Gingerly fishing his hand down the front of her hospital gown, he gave a shriek, jumped back, and shook his hand. *Something bite you?* his coworker said, grinning. Yes, indeed: my mother's false teeth. A beautiful woman when younger, she had never stopped believing in her allure. So one of her last acts was to spring a trap where she apparently still believed someone would want to go.

The nurse told me all this, and I smiled. I wonder what will remain in my mind, at the end. What basic truths will I return to? What tricks will I play and on whom?

Jennifer.

Someone is shaking me. The nurse.

Jennifer, it's time for your pills.

No. I must call the funeral home. Make arrangements for the cremation. Because I cannot bear the thought of a funeral. Ashes to ashes, that is all that is required. The plot is paid for. My father is already there. Beloved husband and father. All that is necessary is to finish carving the double headstone. I can arrange for that tomorrow and be on an evening plane. Back to my surgery, to James and the children.

Jennifer, you are in Chicago. You are home.

No. I am in Philadelphia. At Mercy Hospice. With the body of my mother.

No, Jennifer, your mother died a long time ago. Years and years.

No, not possible.

Yes. Now take your pills. Here's your water. Good. Now. How about a walk? She holds out her hand. I take it. I study it. When I cannot sleep, when I am confused, I label things. I try to remember what matters. And I use their right names. Names are precious things.

I run my fingers across the hand I am holding. This is the *hamate.* This is the *pisiform.* The *triquetrum,* the *lunate,* the *scaphoid,* the *capitate, trapezoid, trapezium.* The *metacarpal* bones, the *proximal phalanges,* the *distal phalanges.* The *sesamoids.*

You have a gentle touch. You were a good doctor, I suspect.

Perhaps. But not necessarily a good daughter. When did you say it happened?

More than twenty years ago. You've told me the stories.

Did I mourn?

I don't know. I wasn't around then. Perhaps. You're not one to display much.

I continue holding her hand, stroking the

118

fingers with my own. The things that matter. The truths we hold on to until the end. *These are things that make life as we know it possible,* I used to say in my lectures, pointing to each phalange in turn. *Treat them with the utmost reverence. Without them, we are nothing. Without them, we are hardly human.*

The beautiful one would leave by the back door as James came in the front. Duplicity. Making rounds with him and needing to be stern. He was so young. Reprimanding him for poorly executed sutures. But we saw the patient's symptoms and functions improve after I reconstructed the traumatized joint, he argued once, almost whining. Not attractive in that context. No.

The sullenness of the inexperienced, sulk of the injured. Why do you treat me this way? he would ask.

Because I cannot show favoritism.

Because people would notice?

Because it compromises my reputation and the reputation of this hospital.

119

If I'm so substandard, why put up with me?

Because you are not substandard. Because you are beautiful.

It did not last long. How could it? And people talked. But I would not have given up a millisecond of it. Still, the loss. To lose and to grieve and to be unable to confide that grief. It is a lonely place to reside.

I stretch out my arm and feel nothing but bedclothes. The clock tells me it is 1:13 AM, and James is still not home. The fact that I know where he is does not alleviate worry. It's a dangerous world, and the hours between 1 AM and 3 AM are the most dangerous ones.

Not just outside, in the city streets, but here, inside. Sometimes I get out of bed to go to the bathroom and relieve myself or to check the windows and doors, and I hear breathing. Rough and rasping. When there shouldn't be anyone else in the house. Not the children, they are long gone. Not James, he has not come in from his wanderings.

I seek the source of the noise, and it comes

from one of the spare bedrooms. The door is open. I see a shape in the bed, large and bulky. Man or woman? Human or homunculus? At this hour, in these confused half-awake times, anything is possible.

I breathe deeply to control the terror, close the door, and back away. I make it to the steps, run downstairs, nearly falling in my haste. I look for a safe place. The only room with a door is the bathroom. I lock myself in, sit down on the toilet, and try to calm myself. To have someone to clutch, to have my hand patted and be told, *It's just a dream. Or just a movie.* For I cannot tell the difference anymore. But no one is here.

Magdalena is out and about, leaving me alone in this house with an unknown thing. I wish suddenly for a dog, a bird, a fish, anything with a heartbeat. I adore cats, but we never got one, because I hated the thought of keeping one trapped indoors when its instinct would be to roam. The risks of letting one out in Chicago were too great.

Did it bother me that first time James didn't come home? The night of his original sin? Briefly. And then I found out the facts, and all the pain disappeared, replaced by anger.

Not anger toward him, or at least nothing more than a slight flare-up that quickly burned itself out. No, anger directed inward. I never took myself for a dupe. I valued myself so highly that I assumed others did, too, especially those closest to me. James. The children, even during the horrors of the teenage years. Amanda, of course. I told no one but Amanda about James, and she disappointed me with the banality of her response.

There's nothing worse than betrayal, she had said. And, When trust is gone, so is respect.

Actually, I told her, there are a lot of things worse than betrayal. And respect always precedes trust to the door.

What's worse than betrayal?

Losing your sight. Losing the use of your arms. Just about any physical affliction or deformity.

Illness.

Yes.

If you've got your health, you've got everything. She made a face as she recited the platitude.

Pretty much.

Well, if that isn't a self-serving attitude for a physician to have, I don't know what is. No wonder they call you the hammer.

There are a lot of bona fide nails out there.

How far would you take this theory?

What theory?

That physical suffering trumps psychological, emotional, or spiritual pain?

Well, clearly they are all interrelated! I'd take it to the point that I always have, as a physician: When patients come to me, I do everything in my power to heal them or, if that isn't possible, to minimize the impact on their ability to live their lives. Clearly, a physical trauma can have severe emotional and psychological effects that must be considered when making a prognosis.

And spiritual effects?

That one puzzles me. How can losing the

123

use of a hand lead to a spiritual crisis? Medieval doctors, of course, believed that things worked the other way around: Spiritual flaws lead to physical illnesses. Lechery led to leprosy, for example. But other than that . . . ?

It can cause someone to doubt their God. Their sense of how the universe works. Their sense of right and wrong. But let me reverse the question. What would cause a spiritual crisis for you? What would shake your belief in your universe?

Well, clearly James having a fling is not going to do it! I know most people wouldn't understand it, but our bond goes deeper than that. It will end. We will survive.

Clearly. Then what?

I thought about it. Some moments passed during which Amanda had time to pour herself another cup of coffee.

I guess, I said, the thing that scares me most is corruption.

And you define corruption as . . . ?

The act or process of tainting or contaminating something. To cause something that has integrity to become rotten.

So when James cheats on you, that's not corrupting your marriage?

You can't corrupt something like what James and I have. Although I am quite aware you question the integrity of our relationship.

I was speaking slowly because I was in the process of working something out.

Yes, indeed I do.

It is a tragedy when something decent and good becomes tainted, I continued. That's what is so horrifying about the Catholic Church protecting their priests. And corruption of the young is truly evil.

And that's why it's not horrifying about James. Because neither of you is an innocent.

Most definitely not.

And what should be the punishment for corruption?

She was playing with me, and I knew it. A

dangerous game.

As I said, pure corruption is pure evil. Something to be eradicated.

Do you mean it deserves death?

Yes, when it manifests itself in its purest form.

Yet you're against the death penalty. You've marched with me. Held candlelight vigils.

Our courts aren't the way to adjudicate good and evil.

What is?

Aren't we getting pretty far from the point? We started out talking about betrayal and trust. And now you're laughing at me.

Never.

Always.

You're right. Always.

The memory fades out, like the end of a movie. I can no longer hear Amanda's voice, but I can see certain words as though they had been written in the air. *Respect. Innocence. Death.* Clearer than my current reality. I sit in the dark and try not to listen to the house breathe.

James was very angry last night. Someone had been in his sock drawer, taking all his clean pairs, he said. Someone had stolen his favorite comb. Someone had been using his razor. He sounded like Papa Bear. Who's been eating my porridge? We both knew who, of course. Fiona is thirteen and in a danger zone.

Need. I hate the word. I hate the very idea. Certain needs are unavoidable. I need oxygen. I need nutrients. I need to exercise this vessel, my body. I can accept all these things. But my hunger for companionship, that's something else altogether. The camaraderie of the OR, of the locker room, of sharing coffee with Amanda at her or my kitchen table.

Since I cannot go out to get this companionship, it is brought to me. I don't see money exchange hands anymore. That's done behind my back, a sleight of hands, since I signed my financial power of attorney over to Fiona. We pretend now. We pretend that Magdalena is my friend. That she is here voluntarily, that I invited her into my home.

So here we live, such an odd couple. The woman without a past. And the woman desperately trying to hold on to hers. Magdalena would like a clean slate, while I am mourning the involuntary wiping of mine. Each with needs the other can't fulfill.

How mortifying to be pregnant at forty. How mortifying not to suspect until a naive co-worker congratulates you on your changing shape. But you haven't had a regular period in your life. It took six years to conceive Mark. You'd given up. Almost agreed to get the dog for James. Never used birth control again. And now this.

How will James react? Will he guess? How will you react when the shock has worn off? You're still staring at the white stick with the pink plus sign on the end of it. You've just peed onto a stick and changed your life forever.

We are sitting in the living room, Mark, Fiona, and I. I vaguely recall some recent trouble between Mark and Fiona, some estrangement that had distressed Fiona considerably. Mark, as far as I could tell, had been unaffected. But there appears to have been some kind of reconciliation. Mark is lolling on the long leather-cushioned Stickley couch, and Fiona is sitting on the rocker smiling at him, remnants of little-sister adoration shining from her face.

They really thought they had you this time, Mark says. But all the tests they ran were inconclusive. He is fiddling with his watch strap. He does not seem overly concerned. I catch a quick worried frown flash across Fiona's face.

What are you talking about? I ask. I am irritable. It is not a day when I feel especially maternal. I have paperwork to complete, and I am more tired than I like to admit. A cup of coffee and a retreat to my office is what I really want, not making small talk with these young people, however closely we are related.

Never mind, Fiona says quickly, and so I

don't. Instead I look at my watch. I notice that Fiona notices, and the frown briefly re-appears, but that Mark is now staring at my Calder, hanging in its usual place above the piano.

Where is your father? I ask. He'll be sorry he missed you. I begin to rise, it is my way of ending the session, which feels strangely like they are deliberately wasting my time, as if it's a ruse to keep me in the room and away from my real work.

I doubt he'll be back before we have to go, says Mark, who doesn't budge from the couch. I don't miss the look Fiona gives him. Something is up, they are withholding information, but I am too annoyed to pursue it.

Where's Magdalena? Fiona asks abruptly. There's something we have to discuss with both of you. She begins to get out of her chair, but just then Magdalena bustles. Her eyes are slightly red.

I'm sorry, I was on the phone, she says, adding, Family stuff.

Fiona has settled herself back in her chair and gives the ground a little push with her right foot to set it in motion. Small and slight as she is, she resembles a child as she rocks back and forth.

We wanted to get on the same page about something, she begins, and looks over at Mark. He has turned his attention back to the Calder, so she continues.

The press has been bugging both Mark and me. There was a leak. They know Mom was taken in for questioning and released. That's about as much as they seem to know, but I'm — and here she gives Mark another quick glance — we're eager to avoid any undue publicity.

Magdalena jumps in. I would never say anything. You know that. I just hang up on them. Or if someone appears at the door I don't recognize, I don't even open it.

Mark speaks up. Yes, but they somehow got hold of Mom last week — she'd wandered out into the front yard.

What exactly do you mean — *got hold of me?* I ask, icily. And under what circumstances would I *wander* out into my own front yard? You make me sound like a two-year-old.

I see Mark smile at this, but it isn't a smile for me. Just some private joke.

Magdalena is looking uncertain and slightly frightened. No one told me, she says.

I got a call from the reporter. Fiona did, too. Apparently Mom was in fine form that day — got it in her head that the reporter was trying to dig up dirt on Amanda and her teaching methods — remember how Amanda was always battling the PTA? Confused the hell out of the guy. It seems they talked at cross-purposes for a moment or two, then Mom dismissed him. He doesn't quite understand what is going on.

If he's any good he can find out about Mom's condition from the hospital or clinic, Fiona says. And of course there's the leak on the police end. But let's not make it easy for him or anyone else.

My condition? I ask. I am standing now. I'll tell you what my condition is — I'm furious.

I'm astonished that no one bothers to look at me. Excuse me, I say, clipping the words short, and deliberately lowering my voice. This invariably gets the attention of the OR. But it doesn't work this time.

No more negligence, Mark is saying, looking at Magdalena. Do you understand? Three strikes and you're out. We've started counting.

Magdalena's breath is uneven. Yes, she says. Understood.

Even Fiona, usually so attentive toward me and gentle toward others, has hardened her features. This is now your number one priority, she tells Magdalena. Protecting the family. Nothing else matters.

We're looking at apples. Piles and piles of apples, all different varieties, colors, sizes. Next to them, mounds of green pears, purple pears. Then oranges. Who stacks them so neatly? Who keeps them in order?

I take one of the apples, a red one, and bite it. A bitter aftertaste. I spit it out and pick up another. Try that one. A little girl is watching me. Mom, that lady is wasting food. Shhh, her mother says, but the girl persists.

And why is she taking off her dress?

Jennifer! I turn around. A large blond woman is running at me. Startled, I bump against the apples, and they start tumbling down off the stand, rolling by the dozens onto my feet, onto the floor, scattering in all directions.

Put your clothes back on! But why should I? Jennifer, no, not anymore. Please leave on your underpants. Oh God, they'll call the police again. A large man hurries over. Ma'am? he asks. The blond woman cuts him off. She has dementia. She doesn't know what she's doing. Here. Here's a letter from her doctor.

The blond woman is pulling a crumpled envelope from her purse. She opens it hurriedly, thrusts a piece of paper at the man. He reads it, frowning. Okay, but get her dressed and get her out of here. What were you thinking, anyway, bringing her here when this might happen?

Usually she's very good. It's just on occasion . . .

Often enough that you have to carry a letter around with you!

Yes, but . . .

Just get her out.

The blond woman is pushing something over my head and down over my hips and then picking up something smaller and balling it up and putting it in her pocket. We leave the store with the cries of children rising over us. But Mommy! Mommy? Mommy, look.

My notebook: Fiona's handwriting.

Mom, we had a discussion today. It's one I've been wanting to have for years, but the time was never right. I was always afraid. But now things are so different. Even if you get mad, it doesn't last. Revelations these days are worth shit. We quickly go back to our safe, comfortable roles. It wasn't always this safe, of course. So it's still a little scary to initiate a talk.

We started out talking about me at fourteen. Remember? Cantankerous, rebellious, rude. Acting everything that was age-appropriate, in fact. I ran away twice, if you recall. The first time was a fit of pure rage. One minute I was screaming at our nanny at the time — what was her name? Sophia? Daphne? — and I don't remember anything else until I was at Union Station, trying to buy a ticket for New York. That's when the cops picked me up. I barely look my age now. I can only imagine what I looked like at fourteen: skinny and knock-kneed with my hair cut like a boy's and greased to stand up straight. The first of my many piercings in my ears and cheeks. Dressed in all black, of course.

What I would have done in New York is anyone's guess. I must have had some of my wits about me, because I'd gone through Sophia's or Daphne or Helga's wallet and stolen what I thought was a credit card but was really a AAA membership card you'd given her in case her car broke down. Very naive I was. The cops brought me back right after you got home from work. You hadn't even taken off your coat. And you just coolly accepted the facts the cops told you, didn't punish me, didn't bring up the subject ever again, just told me to wash my hands for dinner. I was furious, as you can imagine.

The second time was different. I'd just broken up with Colin. Because of you. I was in a panic. I'd been shown the abyss and wasn't sure if I had leaped in or been pulled back

136

from the precipice. It was an almost purely physical sensation, because I certainly wasn't thinking: my heart was racing, I had trouble breathing, and I was even breaking out in odd rashes all over my body. To all of this you seemed oblivious. Just leaving in the morning and coming back at night. Mark was away at college already. Dad was . . . well, who knows where. And I thought I was dying. Everything was getting out of control and I was afraid. So I left again. But I was smarter this time. I packed a bag and went over to Amanda's, requesting asylum. She was delighted. She had always taken her role of godmother very seriously and had always encouraged me to come to her — especially if I was having trouble with you. You probably wouldn't be surprised to hear that she reveled in such complaints. I always adored her. I saw her hardness, the way she treated others, the face she showed the world. But I could always overcome those defenses. I took advantage of her, of course. Shamelessly. And that time was no different. I laid my grievances about you at her feet and watched her mind begin to work.

As I told you today, I think now that she'd planned this for years. She'd just been waiting for the right time. She had been watching me and calculating and hoping. Observing me change from an intense but loving child into a total freak with mother issues. Waiting for her chance. She thought she had it that time. We were sitting at her dining room table, and she had this funny look on her face. Funny for Amanda, who is usually so resolute. But I could see her trepidation when she asked me. To move in with her and Peter. To spend the rest of my teen years with them. To leave you, Mark, and Dad behind, although I'd see you, of course. She would be my foster mother. It shocked me out of my teenage angst. And attracted me. Revenge, ready-made. I asked for some time to think it over. She agreed, naturally, and told me to go home until I made up my mind. I came home that evening in a daze. You noticed something was up — I found you studying me during dinner — but didn't say anything directly. Still, you came to my room that evening, something you rarely did. You sat on the edge of my bed and said something odd. It was as if you knew. You said, three more years. Just three more years. And you patted my arm. That's all it took. Just one touch. Even though at that age I shrank from any physical contact, I welcomed that touch and in one instant abandoned Amanda and her well-laid plans. We never spoke about it, Amanda and I. No questions ever asked. And she never changed her attitude toward me. We continued as before, the iconoclast and the devoted godmother. Until the day she died.

And what did you say, this afternoon, when I told you all this? You smiled, and reached out and patted my arm again. Then withdrew it, sooner than I liked. For I'm no longer at a point where I don't want to be touched. The opposite, in fact. Yet I don't seem to be attracting much these days. I've spent some years in the wilderness and can't seem to find my way out. God help me, I'd thought and didn't realize I'd said it out loud until you said, Yes, please do.

I'm having a bad day, the kind of day when I know that believers would pray, but I just can't allow myself to sink that low. So a single word echoes repeatedly inside my head, little pleadings to little gods. Godlets. Please. Just that one word, over and over again.

Fiona is sobbing. Her head in her hands at my kitchen table. Magdalena is standing behind, rubbing her bowed back. They can both go to hell.

I do so much! Fiona says. Day after day.

139

Month after month. The head of the green-eyed snake tattoo is just visible from under her long-sleeved T-shirt. Her short hair is tousled from running her hands through it. We've been at it for some time.

Yes, you do. Indeed you do, Magdalena says. Her soothing voice does not match her expression.

And what, exactly, do you *do?* I ask. What have I ever asked you to do? I am inflamed, infused with the power of the injured.

I know it's the disease speaking, but it's still hard. So hard, Fiona says. Her voice is muffled. She has not lifted her head from her hands.

No, it's me speaking. Stop treating me like I'm crazy. I'm forgetful, true. But just because I don't remember where I put my car keys doesn't make me *psychotic.* Don't shake your head at me. I heard you say it. I heard you on the phone. *She's being difficult today. No, beyond difficult, psychotic.* You said those words. Deny it.

Fiona just shakes her head.

The blond woman speaks up. Jennifer, the

140

reason you can't find your car keys is that they don't exist anymore. Your car was sold last year. You are not allowed to drive. You are too ill.

You, too?

Yes, me, too. Everyone, too.

Everyone.

Yes, just ask. Go ahead. Go out in the street. Knock on a few doors.

Then you two have been talking about me, I say. Spreading the word. You're after something. You're after my money. Fiona, you were looking through my papers. I saw that, too.

Fiona raises her head. Mom, I am your financial adviser. You gave me power of attorney. More than two years ago. When you were first diagnosed with Alzheimer's. Remember that?

She gives a snort of laughter and turns to Magdalena. I'm asking a woman with dementia if she remembers. Who's the crazy one?

That's it, I say. Out. Now. And leave the

papers. I want to check them.

Mom, you've never been able to 'check' any numbers. You've said so yourself. You're hopeless with money.

Well, then. Such people can be hired. I will hire one. I will commission an audit.

Fiona lifts her head. An audit? What for?

Why does one do an audit? To make sure everything is in order. Call it a second opinion.

But you've always trusted me. Always.

Be a professional. Do I throw a tantrum every time a patient wants a consult? What kind of doctor would I be if I did?

This is different.

How. How? *What do you have to hide?*

Nothing! Mom, get a grip.

I have a grip. I have a tremendous grip. And I will not be betrayed. Get out. *And stay away.* From this point on, I have no daughter, I say.

I feel a burden rise as I say this. No daughter! No husband! No son! No encumbrances! I will pack my bags. I will depart for parts unknown. I will take leave from work. I am owed the vacation time. I have the willpower.

I remember the statements Fiona was perusing so intently. And I have the money. No one will know where I am going. No one can follow me. No longer a prisoner in my own house. No longer being watched and followed from room to room. Ah, glorious freedom.

Jennifer. You don't mean any of this, Magdalena says. She has completely failed to control her face. There is no doubt of her expression. Secret triumph.

You stay out of this. Actually, you're in it already, aren't you? You're a part of this conspiracy. Okay, you're fired. Both of you, out. I have things to do.

Magdalena puts her hands on her hips. You can't fire me.

What?

You can't fire me. You're not my boss.

If I'm not your boss, who is?

Magdalena gestures to Fiona. She is. Along with your son. They hired me. They signed the agency paperwork. The money comes from them.

No. It's my money. This I know.

It's not your name on the check every month.

A sleight of hand, that's all. Robbing Peter to pay Paul. Besides, you forget. This is my house. I decide who comes and who goes.

Fiona speaks again. Her jaw is quivering. Not for long, she says.

Excuse me?

This won't be your house for long. Mark and I agree.

Since when are you and Mark friends?

We talk. We cooperate. When necessary. And we will not hesitate to have you declared mentally incompetent and put you into assisted living. We have ample evidence. Multiple nine-one-one calls. Emergency room visits. Eye-witness accounts. Not to mention the ongoing investigation.

So you're all in this together.

Yes, all of us, Magdalena says. The whole world! She goes to the stove, puts the kettle on. Time for some tea, she says. Then a walk. We have some shopping to do. Help me make a list. Milk, for sure. And pasta. We'll have pasta for dinner. I'll make my marinara sauce if we can find fresh basil. If not, we'll just grate some parmesan on top. That's something else we need. Also we're almost out of salt. See, here's the list. Anything to add? Anything I forgot?

I take the list. I look at the markings on it. Chicken scratches. Nothing that makes sense. I nod intelligently to show I understand. Something nags at me. The kettle whistles. Tea. Milk. Sugar. What just happened? And why is Fiona wiping red eyes, refusing to look at me?

Yes, that's right. Calm down. It's time to calm down. We'll have a cup of tea and we'll talk and then we'll go to the grocery store. She addresses Fiona. You go home now. It'll be all right. She's already past it. She won't remember any of this tomorrow. Or even in an hour.

But she's never turned on me this way. Mark, yes, but never me.

Actually that's not true. You just haven't been here. The stories I could tell you. The situation is deteriorating.

That's what Dr. Tsien says. He says she's entered the worst stage. The next one will be easier. Much sadder, but easier. It's almost time. Our options are running out.

I listen carefully, I think this is important, but the words disappear into the ether the moment they are spoken.

I accept a cookie from a plate. I bite into its sweetness. I drink the hot wet liquid in the cup that is in front of me. And I ignore the two women who are in my kitchen, two of the multitude of half-familiar strangers who have been intruding, who take such liberties with my house, my person.

Even now, one is leaning over my chair, hand outstretched, trying to pat me on the head. Pet me. No. Stop. I am not a wild thing to be soothed by touch. I will not be soothed.

There is one picture of James that I like and only one. It is James at his most pompous, his most self-promoting, self-gratifying. He could have a crown and a leopard robe about his shoulders and he wouldn't look more ridiculous.

I love it because it is honest. I love it because it is true. In his other photos he appears spontaneous, open, *game.* But that was the pose. In reality, he has too high an opinion of himself to accept most people as equals. That I see this about him doesn't make me love him any less.

I call for Amanda. I close the door behind me, put the key in my pocket. All is quiet. I fumble, find the light switch, flip it upward, and the hallway is flooded with light. Hey there! I say, louder this time. Nothing. Perhaps she is out of town? But she would have told me. Reminded me to water her plants, take in her mail, feed Max.

That reminds me. Max! I call. Good kitty! But no jangling bell, no skittering of claws across hardwood.

Yellow tape has been strung across the

entrance to the living room: POLICE LINE DO NOT CROSS. I walk into the kitchen, which I know as well as my own. Something is wrong. None of the noises of a living household. No electric hum from the refrigerator. I open the door. The inside is dark and rank smelling. The water pipes that give Amanda perpetual insomnia, silent. No squeaking floorboards.

Yet something is here, something that wants congress with me. I do not believe in the supernatural. I am not a fanciful woman, nor a religious one. But this I know: Revelation is near. For I am not alone.

And from the shadows she comes, barely recognizable, so brilliant is her complexion, so golden her hair. She is dressed in a plain blue suit, sheer stockings, low-heeled shoes. I have never seen her attired like this, like a seventies-style junior executive intent on ascending the organizational ladder. Corporate angel. But her face is twisted in pain, and her hands are bandaged. She holds them out to me.

I take hold of her right wrist and gently begin to unwrap the coarse cotton from her hand. Around and under and around until it is revealed: perfect, white, and soft to the touch. The unblemished hand of a good child. I compare it to my own liver-spotted ones. Those of the witch that lures the child into the forest, fattens her up to eat. The hands of a sinner.

Suddenly Amanda and I are not alone. My mother is there with her virgin martyrs. And my father, too, wearing, oddly enough, a motorcycle helmet and jacket, when he was too terrified to ever get a driver's license. And James, of course, and Ana and Jim and Kimmy and Beth from the hospital and Janet and Edward and Shirley from the neighborhood.

Even Cindy and Beth from college and Jeannette from before that. My grandmother O'Neill. Her sister, my great aunt May. People I haven't thought of in decades. The room is full of faces I recognize, and if I don't love them, at least I know their names, and that is more than enough. Perhaps this is my revelation? Perhaps this is heaven? To wander among a multitude and have a name for each.

It is dark here in my house. I bump into something with a sharp edge, bruise my hip.

I put out my hands and feel a wall, a door frame, a closed door. I try the knob. It will not open. I need the bathroom, badly. Where is the light. I want to go home. Home to Philadelphia. I've been here long enough. A prisoner.

What crime have I committed? How long have I been incarcerated? *It's often safer to be in chains than to be free.* Who said that? The pressure in my bladder is too great. I squat. I pull up my nightgown, pull down my pants. Let go. Spatter my bare ankles, my feet. No matter.

The relief! Now I can sleep. Now I can go to sleep. I lie down where I am. There is softness under me, not a bed but acceptable. I hug my body for warmth. If I lie here, still, I will be safe. If I revel in my chains I will be free.

Inside is not safe. Too dark, and the house breathes. It breathes, and strangers appear and touch you. Tug at your clothes. Force open your mouth and fill it with foul pills. Out here it is brighter, the moon and the streetlights conjoining to cast a soothing aura over the sidewalks, the gardens just awakening from the winter.

Everything is where it should be. Even the squat object made of metal and painted bright red is a beautiful sight. It has always been there, in front of the house. It will always be there. There may be things lurking in the shadows, but they come in peace. They let me sit here, unmolested, on this patch of grass.

I can look to the right and see the church at the end of the block. To the left, the Bright and Easy Laundry. And upward, the stars. Bright pinpricks, most staying in their places, but others blinking, transmitting signals as they crawl across the vast darkness.

If only I could interpret this message. I want my friend. She would understand. She is safety. She is comfort. Her features remain constant, her voice does not rise or get loud. She does not reach for the phone. She does not make me drink tea, swallow small round bitter objects. I'm walking now. I'm opening the gate. Down three houses. I count carefully. Three is the magic number, my friend says.

That gate sticks, but I get it open. The brick

path is uneven, so I proceed carefully to the white stone statue of the laughing Buddha that presides over the front garden. Buddha holds the key, my friend says. And you know you are always welcome, day or night.

I take the key from under the Buddha's rotund cheeks and let myself in. I will find my friend. She will explain everything. She knows everything. She knows it all.

It is apparently my birthday today. May 22. Magdalena did the math for me: I'm sixty-five. Fiona and Mark are taking me out to dinner at Le Titi. In the afternoon, my old assistant Sarah stopped by. Remarkable for her to remember. I wouldn't know her birthday under the best of circumstances. Even in my prime. I wouldn't even have asked. Sarah presented me with a gift from the hospital: a three-foot-tall statue of Saint Rita of Cascia. Eighteenth century. A beauty.

You share a birthday, Sarah said.

Technically, the day of her death and of my birth are the same, yes. But we share more than that.

152

That's right — you were often called the doctor of last resort.

You're up on your hagiography.

A natural result of working for you for more than fifteen years. Anyway, everyone felt cheated by not being able to give you a retirement party. You left so suddenly. So we all put our heads together. Here. Here's the card.

I'm honored.

And I was. Extraordinarily touched.

We all felt the same. It was an honor working with you.

I reached out and touched the statue, traced the gilt crown, the lines of the robe from her shoulders to the floor.

Sarah pointed to the statue. Why does she have a cut in the middle of her forehead?

According to the Saint Rita legend, she asked God to let her suffer the same way he did, and a thorn fell off a crucifix that was hanging on the wall and wounded her.

What about the rose she's carrying?

When she was dying, her cousin asked if there was anything she wanted. She requested a rose from her garden. Even though it was winter, a rose was blooming there.

I just love these old legends, don't you?

Some are more interesting than others. I don't find Rita's story particularly compelling. The cruel father, the drunken husband, the disobedient sons. Trite stuff. I like the idea that there's someone you can go to when all else has failed.

Have you ever invoked her? Just curious.

No. No. On those rare occasions when I needed help, there were others I could ask.

You're talking about human intervention. I'm talking about something else.

You mean, a higher power?

I mean . . . your diagnosis. Sarah said this tentatively. We've never discussed this. Officially, no one at the hospital knows why I retired early. Unofficially is another matter, I suspect.

I won't say I didn't hope there was a mistake.

No praying for a miracle?

None whatsoever.

How about just plain hope?

None of that, either.

How can you go on? I don't understand.

What is there to understand? I have a degenerative disease. There is no cure for that disease. That is the condition facing hundreds of thousands of people around the world.

You're so clinical about it. This is your life, not some hypothetical patient.

And whatever choice do I have, my dear Sarah?

I'm sorry. I'm prying. I guess I'm just wondering. How you keep going.

At some point we die. Except under unusual circumstances, we usually get some advance warning. Some of us know sooner than others. Some of us will suffer more than others. You're asking, how do you endure that interval between when you know you're dying and when you actually die?

Yes, I guess so.

I suppose everyone is different. To get her through, Saint Rita wanted the impossible: a rose in midwinter.

And you?

I was stymied. No one asks me such things anymore. They ask me if I want tea. If I'm cold. If I want to listen to some Bach. Avoidance of the big questions.

My deathbed wish?

Well, not deathbed! But do you think you'll stay as practical as time progresses? Or will you ever be tempted to ask for the impossible?

Part of my condition is that the line between those two things is increasingly blurred. I was looking through my notebook this morning, and apparently on some days I still have my parents with me. Magdalena has recorded some long talks I have with them. I don't remember any of this, of course. But I like the idea very much.

So maybe some very impossible requests are being granted.

Perhaps. Yes. And I've been thinking. What you said about how one keeps going.

Yes?

A dear friend of mine just died.

Yes, I heard. I'm sorry.

And amid the grief and the anger, I found myself feeling gratitude — gratitude that it wasn't me. So at some level I still see death as something to be put off. It's not that I don't think about it — and I won't say that on bad days I don't plan for when things are a lot worse. But I'm not ready yet.

Well, that's a good thing! Sarah reached over and gave me a hug before gathering her things together. I waved good-bye from the front door, then closed it, and sat down to examine my present. What a delightful prize. It will get the place of honor in the living room, on the mantel, next to the icon.

Really, I feel utterly blessed today.

No, it's not yet time. Not yet.

We're in front of the television, which seems to be our habit in the evening. This program is easy to follow. I don't need to try to hold anything in my head for too long. A game show, where a motley congregation of contestants possesses a seemingly unlimited knowledge of trivia.

The blond woman loves it. She says things like He's my favorite and I can't believe she didn't make it to the next round. I am having trouble concentrating. I try to do what a new sign in the kitchen commands me: Live in the moment. I have to. There is no other way for me, not anymore. But a young man wearing excessive eyeliner is jumping up and down after demonstrating his superior knowledge of the mating habits of penguins. Do I really want to be in this moment? I get up to leave the room just as the phone rings. I turn back and pick it up.

Mom, it's Fiona.

Who?

Fiona. Your daughter. Can I speak to Magdalena? The nice lady who lives with you?

I hand over the receiver, but I don't leave the room. Conversations are being had about me. Decisions being made.

The blond woman says little but agrees to whatever the person on the phone says. Yes. Okay. Sure. Yes, we'll be there. She hangs up.

And what was that all about? Where will we be?

I am glad to have something to hold on to. Delighted to be able to raise my voice and release this tension.

Calm down, Jennifer. It's no big deal. The police have some more questions. They've asked you to come back to the station tomorrow. Fiona will be there. And your lawyer — remember her?

Why would I need to talk to the police?

About Amanda.

What's Amanda done wrong?

Nothing. Absolutely nothing. The reverse. The

159

police are trying to find out who killed her.

Lots of people would like to.

The blond woman gives a little snort of laughter. Yes. That's what I told them. And then wished I hadn't, because they started asking me a lot of questions.

Now a young woman with implausibly red hair is stumped over a question related to seventies pop music. The TV audience is going wild.

Why would you say that? What do you know about Amanda?

I've been here eight months. That's given me plenty of chances to observe.

Like what?

She always treated you with respect. Deference, even. Even when you were at your dottiest. She never talked down. Always spoke to you as though you were her equal. Or superior. And for the most part, you rose to the occasion. No episodes around her.

That all sounds commendable. What's there not to like?

160

It had its reverse side. She didn't cut you any slack. She'd grow impatient at answering the same questions over and over, and simply stopped answering after a while. Once I heard her say, That was all long ago and far away, in a tone of voice that meant the subject was closed.

You make it sound cruel.

Well, for you a lot of things have been re-opened. Old questions, old wounds, old joys and sorrows. It's like going into the basement and finding all the old boxes of stuff you'd meant to give to Goodwill open and overflowing. Things you thought you'd put away for good. Now you have to go through everything again. And again. Like yesterday. You wanted me to run to the drugstore to get you some tampons. You said it was an emergency.

Perhaps it was.

Jennifer, you're sixty-five years old.

Oh. Yes.

Anyway, Amanda did or said something that distressed you enormously shortly before she died.

What was that?

161

I don't know. I was in the den. I heard raised voices. By the time I got to the living room, it was over. At least the shouting was. But something had happened between the two of you that was still unresolved. Amanda was half out the door. She said one thing before she left.

I will not hesitate for one moment, she said. You were extremely agitated. That evening you had one of your episodes. I had to take you into the ER. You wouldn't take your Valium. They had to inject you with something to calm you down.

I don't remember any of this.

I know you don't. The next morning you wanted to go over to Amanda's — to catch up, you said, because you hadn't seen her in a while. I pretended to call her, hung up, and told you she wasn't home.

And I fell for it?

You did. And it turned out that the previous afternoon was the last time we saw her. She was still alive — they were able to trace her steps around town, to a meeting, to the store. But the next day she stopped taking in her *Tribunes,* and about a week after that Mrs. Barnes checked on her and found the body.

162

Did you explain all this to the police?

Yes, many times.

Why do they want to see me, then? I won't be able to tell them anything.

They're still trying. Ever since they got your scalpel handle and blades. Your lawyer says they're hoping that if they ask enough, and in enough different ways, they'll get a different response.

Didn't someone once say that that is the embodiment of madness? Doing the same thing over and over and hoping for a different effect?

Well, sometimes you do remember things. Surprise us all. Like the other day. Out of the blue, you asked me about my elbow — the one I landed on when I tripped on the sidewalk. That had happened a few days earlier, but you were very clear, remembered that you had examined me and determined nothing was broken or torn. One of the perks of working for a doctor — good thing, too, because my insurance is so lousy.

I don't recall. Things come and go. For example, what is your name?

Magdalena. Look — it's written right here. On this poster.

How long have you been here?

You hired me almost exactly eight months ago. Last October. Just before Halloween.

I love Halloween.

I know. It was the most fun I'd had since my kids were small. You insisted that we both dress up. Witches. The only dignified costume for crones, you said. You decorated the house spectacularly. You bought the kind of candy that kids fight over and won't trade. And you insisted on opening the door yourself and making a fuss over the costumes. You really surprised me. The first of many surprises.

Yes, Halloween excites me. That whole time of year, autumn, I find exhilarating. A passionate season. The others are so bland. In the fall, you see opportunities for change. Real change. Possibilities present themselves. None of the renewal and redemption clichés of spring. No. Something darker and more primal and more important than that.

You paced that night until three AM. You certainly were excited. But not in a bad way. It

164

was the first time I saw you do that. Back and forth, all night. I fell asleep in my chair in the living room. You ended up on the couch. Both of us still in our witch costumes.

I always liked dressing up. Giving out the candy. Assuming my proper guise for a night.

Yes, your costume suited you. The white pancake makeup contrasting with the dark-ringed eyes, the long gray-black wig flowing over your shoulders. The fake mole to the right of your mouth drawing attention to those high cheekbones. A peculiar sort of Sleeping Beauty, but nevertheless a beauty. You opened your eyes to find me studying you. Wicked debauchery, you whispered.

Mark's in a good mood. It doesn't make this mother's heart glad. It makes it suspicious. The euphoria. The fast-talking wit. The notable appreciation of the inferior egg salad sandwich Magdalena presented as our lunch. His inability to recognize that the living room curtains are the same shade of glorious red they've always been. His wanting a heart-to-heart.

How are you, Mom?

How much do you want? I ask.

He doesn't hesitate. As much as you can give me.

Is it that bad?

Worse.

You're being direct for once. Is it because you're high?

Possibly. I find you hard to take under any other condition.

You'll have to ask your sister.

What?

I don't even have a checkbook anymore. Even when I want one. Fiona takes care of everything.

But certainly you can write one check.

I don't have even one to write. Fiona was very thorough.

But you wrote me a check six months ago.

Yes. I found an old checkbook in my bureau. And as soon as it cleared, Fiona went through all my drawers and confiscated it.

The bitch.

A chip off the old block.

You said it.

He taps his fingers on the table in an almost recognizable rhythm. *Dah-dah-dah day-day-dah dah-DAH-dah-dahdah.*

You're sharp today.

Yes.

Interesting how it comes and goes.

Interesting isn't the word I'd use.

We are in the den because the cleaners are here, and they've chased us out of the living room and the kitchen, our usual haunts, and we can hear the approaching roar of the vacuum, the rattle of mops and pails as they work their way toward this final room.

I'm curious. Will you even remember this

conversation tomorrow? Mark is standing by the television, idly clicking through James's DVD collection of classic movies. There wasn't a noir film that James didn't know by heart.

I may. I may not. It all depends, I say. I watch as Mark pulls out *Du rififi chez les hommes,* rejects it in favor of *White Heat.*

So I shouldn't say anything I might regret? He flips open the plastic case, takes out the silver disk, places his finger in the center hole, and spins it around.

It depends on the source of regret. Would you regret it because it was a cruel or otherwise despicable thing to say, or because I would remember you saying it? I ask.

Probably the former. I tend not to have regrets unless there are repercussions. He smiles at this, puts down the DVD on top of the television, and takes a seat opposite me. His jitters seem to be subsiding. How about you? he asks. Any regrets? Although his tone is derisive, I get the feeling he really wants to know.

I was the opposite, I say. I never let the possibility of repercussions influence any decisions I made.

What about your medical decisions? Weren't you concerned that decisions you made could have certain effects? Like, for instance . . . death? His dark face is exaggeratedly solemn. He is waiting to catch me out in something. I won't let him.

Those are outcomes. Outcomes are different from repercussions.

I would have thought they were synonyms, he says.

There are nuances, I say. I am warming to the discussion. Anything is better than another endless chat about nothing over tea with Magdalena. A repercussion has the nuance of being punishing, I say. An outcome is simply a result. You do something, and you have an outcome. An output for an input.

And were you always pleased with the . . . outputs . . . of your actions?

I was not pleased with the outcomes of some of my surgeries, certainly — a small percentage, but nevertheless they existed.

But I made the best decisions under the circumstances. Those were not mistakes. They were decisions that had outcomes.

Mark is silent for a moment. You're on top of your game, certainly, he says. No one could pull a sly one on you today.

That actually makes me smile. He sounds about ten, just having been caught smoking cigarettes with Jimmy Petersen behind the Jewel.

Why? I ask. Did you hope to?

He doesn't answer, instead changing the subject.

Did Amanda talk to you?

About what? Oh. Did you hit her up, too?

Well, I'd gotten a nice check from you. It would have been tasteless to approach you again so soon.

And what did she say?

So, she didn't tell you? Odd. I would have thought that was the first thing she'd do.

No. She liked to keep her own counsel. So

what did she say?

She laughed at me. Told me to stuff it up my nose.

That sounds like Amanda.

It was infuriating. I could have killed her. Mark fidgets in his chair. Oh. I'm sorry. I shouldn't have said that.

Said what?

You know. He looks at me. Or maybe you don't. Never mind.

We sit in silence for a moment. When Mark speaks again, his voice is again one of a small boy.

You haven't asked how I'm doing, he says. How my work is, how my love life is.

I get to my feet. The cleaning crew is coming closer, they'll be here in a few minutes and we'll have to move. I am glad. I am annoyed with the conversation.

I assumed that if you had something to tell me, you would, I say. You're not a child anymore. *Use your words.*

171

Mark stands up, too, and unexpectedly he is laughing. I should have known you wouldn't fall for that, he says. But it was worth a try.

I've never been susceptible to emotional blackmail before, I say. And despite my diseased brain, I have no intention of becoming so now.

Well, let me use my words, as you suggest, and give you a synopsis of my current affairs, Mark says. Tall, dark, handsome twenty-nine-year-old lawyer, with a bit of a substance-abuse problem, looking for love and money in what are apparently all the wrong places. His voice is mocking, but there is a slight sag to his shoulders. I notice his clothes are hanging loosely on his frame, that his jacket cuffs reach too far down over his wrists and that his belt is cinched tight to keep his trousers around his too-slender waist.

I find myself reaching out, and almost touch his right cheek, when he flinches, pulls away.

I like you more the other way, he says. It suits you better. He gestures to the cleaners, who are at the threshold to the den, waiting for permission to enter. Thus ends another visit to dear old Mom's, he says, adding, as he leaves the room, and to use another ironically appropriate expression, let's forget this conversation ever took place.

From my notebook. December 15, 2008. Amanda's name written on top of the page.

Jennifer:

Today we decided to walk to our favorite Middle Eastern take-out place on Lincoln, the one with the sublime hummus, then over to the park for a picnic. Yes, it was that warm! I made you wear your gloves and a hat, because you are still struggling with that cough. Magdalena fussed a bit, but we overruled her. You were clearly itching to get out.

You kept saying how you wished James and Peter could come along. I was unclear at first about why you thought they were missing, and it turned out you attributed their absence to that old man-excuse — work. No matter that Peter had retired more than a decade ago, and James would have retired last year if he'd lived.

Funny how at the end of life things accelerate at a pace beyond our ability to process them. I kept waking up at six to prep for class for three years after I retired. I still can't believe I haven't been in a classroom for a dozen years, haven't had to face a tearful twelve-year-old or an angry parent for that long. *It seems like just yesterday.* How we used to mock our parents and grandparents for using that phrase. And for you it doesn't seem like yesterday, but today. Now.

Anyway, we bought our hummus and baba ghanoush and walked slowly over to the park. We found an empty bench near the zoo. A glorious day. The park bursting with joggers, babies, and dogs.

One ambitious young father had an infant strapped to his back, a dog leash wound around his belt, and was helping his four-year-old fly a kite. You were not as conscious of your state as I've seen you on other occasions. You didn't seem to grasp that you were impaired. Interesting how that self-knowledge comes and goes. But you were operating at a high-enough level for it not to be a problem that day.

Perhaps for that reason, you wanted to dwell in the past. I had an inkling — just an inkling — of how it must feel when you asked, *Do I use this?* and held up a plastic spoon with the plastic container of tabbouleh.

We talked about Peter and James, nothing much, did our usual complaining about their foibles. What women do when they're bored and have nothing to say really but like the sound of their voices responding to each other. First me, then you, then me again. As satisfying as a good tennis volley.

For once I didn't set you right. I usually won't indulge you — it's the thing I really argue with Fiona about — but I had to keep correcting myself when I slipped into past tense. *Yes, James was a bit of a dandy. No, Peter wasn't that hard to live with.*

One moment was out of step with the rest of the lazy good feeling of the day. At some point one of the animals in the zoo let out a cry. I don't know what it was — an elephant? A big cat? It was really more of a mournful wail, over quickly, but you got upset.

Give that child back her blanket! you yelled loudly, startling everyone around us.

You certainly startled me, and I dropped my soft drink and soaked my pants. You seemed to have forgotten your outburst as soon as it was out of your mouth. I was reminded of what Magdalena says about how you can change so suddenly. It's not something I had ever seen before. You are either in a slightly better or slightly worse state.

I know there have been what everyone refers to as *episodes.* I tell Magdalena and Fiona to call me when they need help. So far they haven't. I think there's some sense of possessiveness, some rivalry there.

If nothing else, the day reminded me of how we gradually inure ourselves to tragedy. For it is a tragedy, my old friend, what is happening to you.

I am very selfish: I am more concerned about myself than you in this regard. You'll get past this stage of awareness, and the disease will be its own pain-management regime. But me. These little outings remind me of how much anesthesia I'm going to need. Like the topical sedative that goes in before the big needle, everything I've done to prepare myself is going to be too weak to withstand the pain of separation that's looming.

The end of my marriage is nothing compared to the end of our friendship — if that's what you want to call it. It's enough to want to burn the bridge and leave you on the other side. Too many good-byes lie ahead. How many times have you had to endure the death of James? How many times will I have to say good-bye to you, only to have you reappear like some newly risen Christ. Yes, better to burn the bridge and prevent it from being crossed and recrossed until my heart gives out from sheer exhaustion.

I am performing a complex brachial plexus procedure where the total plexus lesions have permeated all the nerve roots. The patient is under general anesthesia. His (her?) face is covered.

Things are not going well. I am attempting an intraplexual neurotization using the parts of the roots still attached to the spinal cord as donors for the avulsed nerves. But I miscalculate and hit the subclavian vein. Horrifying quantities of blood. I put pressure on it and call for the vascular surgeon, but it is too late.

I think about the faces of the family members in the waiting room. I also cannot help thinking, ashamedly, of the lawyers, of the internal hospital investigation that will inevitably follow. The tediousness of the paperwork that accompanies blunders large and small.

Then the room undergoes a sort of seismic shift and I am no longer in the OR. No patient anesthetized on a table. Instead I am gazing down at a bed with rumpled floral sheets. I am still perspiring, there is still an irregular drumming in my chest, but my hands are no longer encased in rubbery gloves, they no longer hold sharp implements. It's a large bed with an oak frame. A matching dresser. An ornate red Oriental carpet. Nothing familiar.

I want the OR back, the soothing green walls, the steel instruments reflected large in the steel cabinetry. Everything placed just so. But this. This richly furnished, unsterile environment. It makes me uncomfortable. I want to wash my hands, suit up, try again. I close my eyes, but when I open them I am still in the same room.

Then I hear voices. With difficulty, I find the doorway to the room. I must scrutinize every inch of every wall before it finally materializes. Outside the doorway, a long hallway, painted a deep crimson, hung with photographs. And at the end of that, the way down. Soft plush material under my feet on top of polished wood, patterned with blue and green intertwined flowers.

I walk carefully, watching my feet and holding on to a long smooth piece of wood. I go down and I count. Twenty times I extend my right foot, place it on a lower surface. Twenty times I pull my left foot down until it is level with my right. And then again. The voices grow louder as I descend. There is laughter. I hear my name. I will proceed carefully.

There are two of them, a man and a woman, sitting in the living room, on the mission oak sofa. The woman has shoulder-length yellow hair, clearly dyed. It does not suit her. She is heavyset. Her pants are too tight to be comfortable, I can see the top button cutting into her belly.

The man stands up when he sees me. An older man. An old man. He opens up his arms. Jenny! he says, and without waiting, his arms envelop me. He smells good. His plaid shirt feels soft against my check, but his beard scratches. Snow-white hair with a bald spot on top. A gray, not white, beard. It looks dirty in contrast, gives him a slightly disreputable look.

Aren't you glad to see your old friend Peter? asks the blond woman.

Oh yes, I say, and smile. Peter. How are you? I infuse my voice with warmth. I even force myself to take his hand. One must be cunning. One must play along.

Quite well, he says. Enjoying the sunshine. As you know, I was never a fan of Chicago winters. Although this one seems to finally be over. Here, sit down, sit down. Over here. He pulls over a beige chair, and I sink into its softness. He takes my hand again. It's been too long, Jen.

How long has it been? asks the blond woman. She doesn't wait for an answer. Your ears must have been buzzing! she says. Peter's done nothing but talk about you!

She smiles. He smiles. I smile too.

Yes, they have been, I say. Indeed they have.

There is silence, rather awkward. Then the man speaks again, less heartily, more gently.

You don't really remember me, do you? he

180

asks. But he doesn't have that pleading, hurt look that people generally have when they ask me this. That look that begs me to lie, to reassure them.

I immediately like him better. No, I say. Not a glimmer.

I'm in town to wrap up affairs, he says. I was here for the funeral, but everyone thought it best not to bother you. Unfortunately, things are a little tangled. Amanda never updated her will after the divorce. The estate has to go into probate. It's going to take months to resolve, to find the next of kin who will inherit the house. That was really her only asset. But even in this market, it'll be a substantial sum. For now, my hands are tied.

What divorce? I ask. What funeral?

He pauses. Well, I'll just remember for both of us, he says, smiling. Then he turns sober. I understand you're in a bit of trouble, he says. I wanted you to know that I believe in you. Without reservation. You clearly don't know what I'm talking about. You probably won't remember this. But on the chance that some things stick, I wanted to say it.

The blond woman makes as if to get up

from the table.

No, no. There's no need for you to go, he says. This isn't a private conversation. It's just something I wanted to get on the table. For myself, mostly, as it turns out. Otherwise, I would like to talk about good things, he says. Maybe it will spark something.

I'll be the secretary, says the blond woman. I'll write it all down. That way she can read it over when she's in better shape. It might make more sense to her that way. She leaves the room, comes back with a large leather book, opens it to a blank page, picks up a pen. She writes something at the top of the page, pauses, and looks at the man expectantly.

Where shall I start? asks the man. Once upon a time. Yes, that's the way to handle it. A myth-making event. Filled with archetypes.

I am interested. Go on, I say.

Once upon a time there were six people. Four adults and two children. Two married couples. One couple, older by about a decade, childless. The younger couple had a girl and a boy. The girl was very small, maybe two. The boy seven. Although not close in age, the two couples are close in friendship. He stops and thinks. What shall I tell you about them? No generalities. But one specific event. And he continues.

One day they decide to go to the beach. They pack some ham sandwiches, some hard-boiled eggs, apples, pears, and bottles of wine for good measure.

They decide to drive out of the city. Far north. To a state park on the lake that features large sand dunes that are mostly deserted on beautiful summer Sundays like this one.

There is a reason for this, of course. A huge nuclear power plant looms over the sand dunes, spills its excesses into the shallow water. It casts a pall on the scenery for anyone faint of heart. Which the adult members of these two families definitely are not. They joke about the relative warmth of the lake water, about mutant fish and the oversized shore-birds.

The two-year-old, relieved of all her clothes except her diaper, is taken to the edge of the water by her mother to wet her toes. The boy takes his shovel and bucket and begins dig-ging random holes in the sand. The older woman and the two men settle themselves on beach chairs and talk. All is calm. An uneventful day at the lakeside. When they start feeling hungry, they break out the food, eat a few sandy mouthfuls, wash it down with red wine. An idyllic afternoon at the beach among dear friends. Everything is perfect. More perfect than it will ever be again. He stops, apparently in a reverie.

The blond woman is writing furiously. What a lovely gift, this story, she says. Jennifer will enjoy reading about it later. But I am getting a glimmer. More than a glimmer, a Technicolor movie. It comes in bursts of images. Invoking all the senses. I speak quickly before it dissipates.

Yes. The sandy ham that crunches between our teeth. The acidic wine. The power plant looming overhead. The grown-ups perhaps drinking a little too much. Voices are raised. Laughter comes easier. The older man abstains: He is the driver but continues pouring. The other three drink past the point of pleasure. Past the point of honesty. To somewhere more primal.

That's right, says the man. He opens his mouth as if to continue, but I push on, following the movie in my mind. I can feel the heat of the noonday sun on my bare arms. The sand against my thighs. Hear the cries of the mutant birds.

The older woman starts it. She asks the younger man if he has noticed anything different about his wife.

Different how? the younger man asks.

Her hair. Her clothes. A general glow.

I can't say that I have. She always looks terrific. And he gives his wife an affectionate smile, gestures to the older man to top off her glass of wine.

The younger woman is startled. Something is happening that she has not expected.

You didn't think, for example, that perhaps she has reason to celebrate? asks the older woman. That something has happened that she considers a good thing? Perhaps not news that every woman would welcome. But she isn't an ordinary woman.

The younger man doesn't miss a beat. He is a lawyer with a growing reputation. This is what he is like in the courtroom, in the boardroom. There is no curveball he cannot catch, no supposed revelation that he does not appear to have intimate knowledge of beforehand.

My wife is no fool, he says.

But you might be, the older woman says. She takes a sip of wine but doesn't take her eyes off him.

I don't follow.

Power is a strange thing.

It is. But what does that have to do with this conversation?

They say knowledge is power, says the older woman.

And that ignorance is bliss, says the younger man, derisively.

Does that mean you want this conversation to end?

The younger man considers. No, he says. I want to see where you are going.

The younger woman speaks up: Me too, actually.

The older man is the only one not getting it. The other three are facing off. The kids are squabbling over sand toys.

The younger man is the first to break the silence. So she knows. I haven't exactly been discreet. If she'd asked I would have told her. It's not important. Nothing can touch what we have.

The younger woman relaxes. She is relieved by his reply, and the tension dissipates from her shoulders. She shrugs indifferently. There was nothing I wanted to ask. Nothing that was worth the bother of asking. I did a little checking on my own. Found out what I needed to know. A trivial liaison, soon to end. That was the end of it.

The younger man smiles, an odd, almost proud, smile. Yes, our marriage isn't so fragile.

It most certainly is not.

Ah, says the older woman. But this is not about the trivial. Not in the least. Sex is banal. I didn't want to talk about sex. I wanted to talk about the thing that either holds families together or tears them apart. Something much more powerful than sex or even love. Money.

The younger woman stiffens again, her features becoming rigid. Don't do it, she says.

The older woman addresses the younger man. You lock your office door. You lock your desk drawer inside a locked room. You keep your wife out. Why is that?

The kids, of course. There are important documents in there. I can't have evidence of confidential memos scribbled over with a red crayon.

Because of the kids?

Because it's standard protocol when taking sensitive documents out of the office.

But what would someone find if they managed to circumvent your locked doors and locked drawers? the older woman asks. What if someone knew you well enough to know where you would hide the keys?

They wouldn't find anything that would interest anyone outside corporate financial litigation, says the younger man.

The older woman raises her right eyebrow. It seems like a practiced gesture somehow, a dramatic device used to control others.

The younger woman interrupts. Now, that's not quite true. She seems incensed by the younger man's dismissive tone.

The younger man meets her eyes. And so?

And so, says the younger woman, and repeats, knowledge is power.

Seems like you relinquished a little of that power. To your good friend here. Why on earth would you do that? Cracks are appearing in his equanimity.

Seems like I did, the younger woman says, without looking at the other woman. Seemingly foolishly.

So? asks the younger man, addressing the younger woman. So what? What are you going to do? Turn me in? That would be against your own interests.

Absolutely, says the younger woman. It was a struggle, but I decided to not disturb the status quo. Not to confront you. This discovery was just a little curiosity I took out of my pocket and looked at every once in a while. As my dear friend here says, it was a power thing. It made me happy.

This was always about us, not just me, the man says. He is gulping his wine. He reaches over and takes the bottle from the older man, who is frankly bewildered, and pours himself another full glass. What I took will not be missed. I made sure of that. I didn't hurt anyone, didn't rob children and orphans. Only institutions have standards. Small amounts siphoned off over time. They added up. But no harm done to any human. This will never come to light. And it's for you as well as me.

I believe that, says the younger woman. I believe that you tell yourself that and mean it sincerely.

And for the kids.

I believe that, too, says the younger woman. She turns to the little girl, brushes sand from her forehead, smooths her hair. The boy is still engrossed with his shovel and pail. He is digging a hole to China. The discussion is over as far as the younger woman is concerned. She is ready to move on. But the older woman doesn't agree. She stands up.

But this is not just between you. It is a question of morality. This . . . activity, must stop. Right here and now. No more juggling of books. No more victimless crime.

No one doubts that this is an absolute order. And no one doubts that the repercussions of disobeying it would be severe.

I pause the movie. Come back mentally to the world. I ask the old man, Why would Amanda do this thing? What was her motive?

Peter seems resigned to the direction the conversation has taken. Who knows? he asks. One never knew with Amanda. Revenge? Mischief? Perhaps she thought she was doing the right thing: preventing a serious crime. Or saving her friends the humiliation of being caught, incarcerated. But you haven't finished the story.

I no longer need the film to guide me. The rest has formed itself in my mind.

Back at the beach, I say. The older man is

upset. His world is being shaken.

Apologize! he tells his wife. Apologize for your appalling behavior. I don't care how drunk you are, you don't wreck lives for the fun of it.

But the younger woman interrupts him, addresses the older woman directly. No apologies are necessary because no apologies will be accepted. None would be acceptable. You betrayed my trust.

You see? the older woman says. Trust does matter. Betrayal is a serious act.

The younger woman considers this. Fair enough, she says. She picks up a hard-boiled egg. But seven hundred years ago I would have taken stronger measures.

And what would they have been? the older woman asks. She is amused.

I would have buried this under a waning moon in your yard, as medieval women did with their enemies.

And . . . ?

You would have commenced to rot. The younger woman pauses. Of course you are already rotten in mind and spirit, she says. Both men, the older and the younger, sit up and pay attention. This is serious. These are words that can't be unsaid.

This would pertain to the body. It would start inside. With the heart. Then the other organs. You would start to stink out. The decay would reach your outer epidermis. It would start to disintegrate. And the scavengers would take care of the rest. Your eyes. Your genitalia. Your extremities — your ears, toes, and fingers.

The older woman laughs at this. She seems delighted. I always forget you studied medieval history before medical school. What a potent combination!

This is not an anecdote, the younger woman says. It's a warning. You would be well served to pay attention to it. And she begins to put the picnic things away, as if a reasonable conversation between reasonable people has just concluded.

Magdalena is no longer writing. The notebook and pen lie in her lap.

What about the men? And the children? What were they doing while these things were being said? she asks.

They are the audience. The necessary audience. For these women are nothing if not expert dramatists.

But the children!

Yes, the children. Exactly.

But what happened next? she asks.

Nothing. Absolutely nothing. The effects of the wine wore off, they drove home together in one car, crowded elbow to elbow. The little girl was too young to have taken it in. The boy kept his own counsel. No adverse effects.

They arrived home, unpacked the car. The women kissed each other, kissed each other's husbands. The husbands shook hands. They went into their respective houses. And continued as if nothing had happened.

So your marriage wasn't over, says Magdalena. It is not a question.

Peter speaks.

It may have suffered a temporary hiccup. But no one moved out. No one served papers. The younger man and woman continued to exhibit the same respectful camaraderie. If it was an act, they performed it well. No one ever saw a crack in it.

What happened to the money? I take it that the . . . theft . . . or whatever it was, stopped, asks Magdalena.

Yes. There was never any scandal, no trial, no prison. But the couple ceased going on expensive trips, buying costly furnishings, rugs, artwork. Still, they continued to live seemingly happy lives.

And what about the two women? asks Magdalena.

The same. It was as if the day had never happened. As if a group memory had been erased. A *folie en quatre* dissipated.

The bearded man speaks up. And you remember, he says to me. Of all things, this story survives. He sighs heavily. It'd be best if this conversation hadn't taken place, he says.

He gets up to leave, and something about the way he stands, favoring his right leg, causes something to spark. You're Peter, I say.

He sits down again. That's right, he says. That's right. He smiles. It is a lovely smile.

Peter! My dear, dear friend! I lean over and hug him. No, hold him. I have trouble letting go.

It's been years! I say. What made you stay away so long?

Actually, it's been just eighteen months since I left. But it's seemed like a long time. I didn't have much reason to come back here. Not until . . . recent events.

You mean Amanda being murdered?

He gives a short laugh. Yes, that.

How are you holding up?

Not great. Thanks for asking. It's funny — well, not funny, but naive — for people to think that just because there's been a split all emotional connection is broken.

I know. I saw it all the time at the hospital. The divorced couples had the most touching scenes in the recovery room.

Magdalena touches my arm. I flinch and draw away. It's time to get dressed, she says.

I look down and realize I am still in my nightgown. I blush. Of course, I say. I'll be right down.

But something happens. At the top of the stairs I lose my bearings. There was an idea in the back of my mind. Some intent. Now gone. Just a dim hallway, lit only by light coming from open doors.

Through them I glimpse neatly made beds, sun streaming through windows. I feel a vein throbbing in my neck. I cannot get enough air. I reach my arms out straight, touch a wall, make contact with a rectangular plastic plate. I know this. The light switch. I flick it on. Royal blue walls. Photographs of smiling people. How can so many people be so happy all the time?

I flip down the switch, plunge everything into shadow. Up, illumination, down, despair. Up down. The satisfying, familiar click. I know what this is. I know what it does. My body begins to feel comfortable again, my breathing evens out. I continue what I'm doing until the blond woman comes and leads me away.

Some things do stick. I do what my neurologist friend Carl suggests and scan my memory. Just see what pops up, he says. See where it leads you. Exercise those neurons.

Surprising things. Not what I expected. No weddings, no funerals. No births, no deaths. Small moments. My cat, Binky, up a tree when I was five. A pair of my underwear blowing off the clothesline in the wind and into Billy Plenner's yard next door when I was in seventh grade — something that he never let me forget. Finding a five-dollar bill on the floor of the roller-skating rink and feeling rich. Rolling in the grass in Lincoln Park with Fiona, nine years old.

The day after my fiftieth birthday, after a party James had thrown for me. Wondering if things were shredded for good this time.

It had been an evening of joy. People crowded in the living room, overflowing into the kitchen, some sitting on the stairs. Drinking the excellent wine selected by

James. My colleagues from the hospital. Dear Carl, and my assistant, Sarah, and, naturally, the orthopedics team: Mitch and John. Cardiovascular was there in force, as was Psych. And my family. Mark, fifteen, looking his most handsome, wrapping his arm around my shoulder, leaving it there as he guided me to the table laden with bottles and wonderful treats. Hugging me before pouring me a glass of wine. Buddies. Fiona darting among the partyers, emerging occasionally to touch my arm. And James. Thrilling to know he was in the room. We sometimes met in the crowd. Each time he gave me a quick hard kiss on the lips. As if he meant it. Bliss.

But then, the downward plunge, the slide into hell. I was looking for James, he had disappeared. I searched the kitchen, the living room, dining room, even knocked on the bathroom door. No James.

Suddenly the room felt too crowded, too hot. I opened the front door and escaped to the stoop, to feel the cool May evening air. But then I heard sharp voices. Peter and Amanda. So intent on each other that they didn't notice me.

You crossed the line, Peter was saying. He

199

was speaking in a low tone but was clearly enraged.

But I did nothing . . . Amanda's voice was cool and controlled.

Nothing? You never do nothing. Never. And now, a lie. On top of such cruelty. Like I said, you crossed the line.

The moon was bright enough to see their faces. From both, righteousness shone. A battle between two avenging angels.

It is time James knows, time he understands that his little family has some anomalies, some . . . unconventional antecedents. That he has a cuckoo's egg in his nest. That he is in fact a cuckold. That he was not the only one who had wandered. He was holding Fiona's hand. He had been joking about how she was a changeling, so different from himself. It was the perfect opportunity, one I have been waiting for. An opportunity to be seized. The truth must out.

And you were simply truth's vehicle?

I didn't say anything. I just looked. Just gave a look. That was all James needed. He was ninety percent there. How could he not be?

So you were lying when you said you did nothing.

Peter was having trouble modulating his voice and was breathing heavily. I had never experienced him like this. Usually so slow to anger, the sleeping giant.

I never lie. I didn't say a word, after all. Not a word. So no. I never lie.

Except *in extremis,* that's true.

What's that supposed to mean?

It means that when it's important enough to you, when it comes to protecting yourself against some intolerable consequence, you're like the rest of us mortals.

Name one time I lied. Just one. Other than this supposed incident.

I have to go back fifty years. But it happened, and I have a long memory. Peter was calmer now, in control. He spoke deliberately. The philosophy test in 1966, he said.

Silence. Amanda didn't move. I heard nothing but the cars streaming down Fullerton.

201

How did you know about that?

I was a research assistant for Professor Grendall. I was waiting outside his office. The door was half open. And you denied everything. That you'd cheated, plagiarized. You lied then.

Of course I did. It was necessary.

And then, after you left, Professor Grendall walked out, saw me, shook his head, and said, What a woman. What ruthlessness. She'll go far.

And you said?

Be careful. That's my future wife you're talking about.

So when you approached me in the quad that year?

I'd already decided.

There was a silence. Amanda took a step back, put her hand on the iron railing surrounding the front garden, and wrapped her fingers around one of the iron spikes.

Well. You certainly know how to win an argument.

I wasn't looking to win.

The Peter I knew began to appear again. The tension left his shoulders, and he put his hand to his head and stroked his hair — a gesture of appeasement often used when with Amanda.

No, you never are. I saw her fingers slowly unwind from the gate. She, too, touched her hand to her head, but as if it were aching.

So why did you do it? Peter asked. Make him aware of Fiona's . . . ambiguous . . . paternity. About Jennifer's single instance of straying, about what everyone else has known for nine years. As I said, you never would lie unless you were *in extremis.* What is going on?

Again, nothing but the sound of traffic.

Peter was speaking slower now, working it out.

The party. It's something to do with the party. But what? We're celebrating — that's a happy thing. And honoring your best friend. You helped James organize it. And it's gone splendidly. I've seldom seen Jennifer so delighted. She's so difficult to please. But you pulled it off. You must have seen that. Jennifer and James so openly affectionate. Mark so proud of his mother, a kind of miracle at his age. Fiona taking brave forays out into the crowd before running back to Jennifer or James for safety. So what?

Amanda was rigid. She was not going to help him.

Peter stopped stroking his hair, his hand resting on the back of his head. He raised his other hand and extended it toward Amanda. Almost pointed but at the last second closed it into a loose fist.

That's it, isn't it. Too much happiness. You're envious. A foul-weather friend.

That's when I quietly turned and went back into the house, into the warmth and light. James was not to be found. I smiled and nodded until my face and neck muscles ached and the last guest had left. I put Fiona to bed and kissed Mark good night. Then lay sleepless in my own bed until morning.

The next day, James declined to go to the park with Fiona and me. He took Mark to the zoo. He rejected the idea of a family dinner, and he and Mark went to McDonald's. For a month after that, he bit his words back into his throat every time I addressed him. He showed his back in bed. He turned his cheek when Fiona attempted her good-night kiss.

And then, after a month or so, the trouble passed. As it always did between James and me. You learn, you grieve, you forgive, or at least you accept. That's why we've lasted. That's how we've endured. The secret of a happy marriage: not honesty, not forgiveness, but acceptance that is a kind of respect for the other's right to make mistakes. Or rather, the right to make choices. Choices you can't be sorry for, because they were the right ones. So I never apologized. And so the matter died between us, but with it something else. Not enough to bring down the tree of our marriage, but a bough did fall that didn't grow back.

Mark and Fiona felt it, of course. As children do, they acted out. Mark was sullen and rude to James. Me he treated with distance. But Fiona — it was hardest on her. She would sit on the couch between James and me as we watched a movie, placing her hand on each of our arms, as if she could be a conduit. Of what? Affection was still there. Delight in each other's company, if slightly dampened. But respect — yes, that was the problem. There was now the taint of distain when James talked to me, a roughness in his embraces. In bed he was insistent and aggressive. Not necessarily a bad thing, for me. But Fiona took the change in our household very hard. She swung wildly between attempts at reconciliation and fits of rage. When she was good, she was very very good. But then the episodes. Too early to blame on adolescent hormones. Although as she got closer to puberty, they increased in intensity. She spent a lot of time with Amanda. When I couldn't find her in the living room or her bedroom I would walk the three doors down to retrieve her. Amanda standing at the door, waving in a way that was both a beckoning and a farewell. Fiona, a recalcitrant and obstinate stranger. Then, after hours behind her closed door, the other Fiona would appear, offering to do the dishes, to help Mark with his math homework.

Those were strange, difficult years. I took on extra shifts, accepted new patients I didn't have time for. Published articles. Began working at the free clinic. Busied my mind and body but emotionally descended into despair. It was Amanda, of course, who noticed and slowly patched me together again. The inflictor and healer of my pain, both.

I open the door, and there they are. My two children. The boy and the girl. Older, looking more careworn, especially the boy. I pull them both close, one arm around each, my cheek resting halfway on my daughter's shoulder.

Why did you ring the bell? I ask. This is your home! You're always welcome. You know that!

They both smile in unison. It looks almost choreographed. They seem relieved. Oh, we didn't want to sneak up on you! says my son, my handsome, handsome boy. Even before his voice changed, the girls started calling.

Well, come in! I say. My friend and I just made some cookies. The blond woman has come up behind me. She smiles at the young man and woman.

We settle ourselves around the kitchen

table. The blond woman offers coffee, tea, cookies. They both decline, although the boy accepts a glass of water. The blond woman takes a seat, too. There are undercurrents.

How have you been? the boy asks me.

Quite well, I say.

The boy looks at the blond woman. She shakes her head slightly.

Are you sure? You seem a little . . . excited. Overwrought, even.

This is from the girl, my daughter. The snake wrapped so tenderly around her delicate bones. Oddly enough, she takes after James. For all his height he is somehow insubstantial. Always ten pounds too thin. He doesn't see it that way, of course. Always running, always swimming, always moving. On days he can't go out because of excessive rain or snow or cold, he runs up and down the stairs for an hour at a stretch.

I consider her question. I weigh my options, my choices. And make up my mind.

This is a talk we had to have sooner or later,

I say. I've been putting it off. But since you're both here, now is as good as anytime.

The girl nods. The boy looks at me. The blond woman keeps her eyes on the table.

Your father doesn't know. Not yet. So please don't mention it to him.

We won't, says the boy. You can count on that. He gives a wry smile when he says this.

It started a while ago. Months. I noticed I was forgetting things. Little things, like where I'd put my keys or my wallet or the box of pasta I'd taken out of the pantry. Then these gaps. One minute I'd be in my office, the next in the Jewel frozen foods section with no recollection of how I'd got there. Then words started to go. I was in the middle of surgery and I forgot the word *clamp*. I remembered it afterward, driving home. But at the time I had to say, *Give me that shiny thing that pinches and holds.* I saw my residents exchanging glances. Humiliating.

The boy and girl don't look shocked. This is good. The hard part is yet to come.

I'll even make a confession, I say. I don't

know your names. My own children. Your faces are clear — for that I'm grateful. Others blur beyond recognition. Rooms are sealed without doors, without any way in or out. And bathrooms have become extraordinarily elusive.

I'm Fiona, says the girl. And this is your son, Mark.

Thank you. Of course. Fiona and Mark. Well, to make a long story short, I went to the doctor — to Carl Tsien. You know Carl, of course. He asked me some questions, sent me to a specialist at U of C. They have a special clinic there. They call it, without a trace of irony, the Memory Unit.

They ran some tests. You may or may not know, but there is no conclusive way to diagnose Alzheimer's. It's mostly a process of elimination. They ran a number of blood labs. Made sure there were no low-lying infections. Eliminated hypothyroidism, depression. Mostly, they asked a lot of questions. And at the end of it all, they didn't give me much room for hope.

Both my children nod calmly. They're not crying. They're not noticeably distressed. It's the blond woman who reaches over and covers my hand with hers.

Perhaps I'm not being clear, I say. This is a death sentence. The death of the mind. I've already given notice at the hospital, announced my retirement. I have started keeping a journal so I have some continuity in my life. But I won't be able to live on my own for very much longer. And I don't want to be a burden on you.

The girl reaches out and takes my other hand. This is not comforting, this is awkward, having both my hands held captive by these nameless people. I disengage from both, place my hands safely in my lap.

That must be very scary for you, the girl says.

The boy gives me a half smile. You're a tough old bird, he says. You're going to wrestle this disease to the ground and break its arm before it takes you.

You don't seem surprised.

No, says the girl.

You've noticed?

A little hard not to! says the boy.

Shh! says the girl. Actually, this kind of brings us to why we came here today, Mom.

Not only are we not surprised, says the boy, in fact it's gotten so bad that it's time to make a change. Sell the house. Move into a more . . . suitable . . . living situation.

What do you mean, sell the house? I ask. This is my home. This will always be my home. When I walked into it twenty-nine years ago — pregnant with you, by the way — I said, at last I found the place I can die in. Just because I mislay my keys every once in a while . . .

It's not just the keys, Mom, says the boy. It's the agitation. The aggression. The wandering. Your inability to use the bathroom, take care of basic sanitary needs. Refusing your medications. It's too much for Magdalena.

Who is Magdalena?

Magdalena. Right here. See? You don't even remember the woman who lives with you. Who takes care of you. Wonderful care. You don't even remember that Dad is dead.

Your father is not dead! He's just at work. He'll be home — what time is it? — very shortly.

The boy turns to the girl. What's the use? Let's just do what we planned. We have all the documentation we need. It's the right thing. You know it is. We've considered all the options — including you moving in here to help Magdalena. That idea was lunacy.

The girl nods slowly.

We could have a trained nurse. Start using the locks we installed on the doors. But that upset her so much, it did more harm than good. And she's deteriorating so fast. It's just not safe for her to be in anything but a closely controlled environment.

The girl does not answer. The blond woman abruptly gets up and leaves the room. Neither the girl nor boy seems to notice.

I don't understand the boy's words, so I concentrate on his expression. Is he friend or foe? I think friend, but I am not certain. I feel uneasy. There is a trace of hostility in his eyes, tenseness in his shoulders, that could be remnants of old injuries, old suspicions.

I am sitting at a table with two young people. They are getting up to leave. The girl had retreated somewhere, was no longer mentally present. Then she suddenly comes back.

Mom, I hope you'll forgive us. There are tears in her eyes.

Fiona, she won't even remember. This conversation was pointless. I told you that.

The girl is pulling on her sweater, wiping her eyes. And then there's Magdalena. She's been so important to us over the eight months. That is hard, too.

The boy shrugs. She's an employee. It was a business relationship. A quid pro quo.

Ass, says the girl. Then a pause. I'm still glad we came, she says. Funny, I never knew how she felt when she realized what was happening to her. How she figured it out. That part was always a mystery.

Well, she's never exactly been one for sharing feelings.

No, but I feel . . . honored somehow.

She has squatted down beside my chair.

Mom, I know you've checked out. I know you

won't remember this. And it's all so very sad. But there have been moments of grace. This was one of them. I thank you for that. Whatever happens, know that I love you.

I've been listening to the rise and fall of her soft voice, paying attention to the cadence. Wondering who she is. This brightly colored bird in my kitchen. This beautiful girl with the face of an angel who is leaning over to brush her lips against my hair.

The boy is looking amused. You've always been sentimental, he says.

And you've always been an ass.

She gives him a little push as they walk toward the door. The end of an epoch, I hear the boy say as he closes it behind him.

The end, I echo, and the words hang in the now-empty house.

■ ■ ■ ■ ■

Two

■ ■ ■ ■ ■

The woman with no neck is screaming again. A distant buzzer and then the muffled sound of soft-soled shoes on thick carpet hurrying past my door.

Other noises emerge from other rooms on the floor. The calls of incarcerated animals when one of their own is distressed. Some recognizable words like *help* and *come here* but mostly cries that swell and converge.

This has happened before, this descent from one circle of hell into the next. How many times? The days have morphed into decades in this place. When did I feel the warmth of the sun? When did a fly or mosquito last land on my arm? When was I last able to go to the bathroom at night without someone materializing at my side? Tugging my night-gown down around my hips. Gripping me so hard I look for the bruise after.

The screaming, although subdued, hasn't stopped, so I get up. I can stop this. Prescribe something. One of the benzodiazepines. Or perhaps Nembutal. Something to relieve the anxiety, stop the noise, which is now coming from all different directions. I'll order a round. Drinks are on me! Anything to prevent this place from descending into true bedlam. But arms are pulling at me, not gently. Heaving me to my feet before I am ready.

Where are you going. To the bathroom? Let me help. In the dim light I can barely make out the speaker's face. Female, I think, but I find that increasingly difficult to tell. Unisex white scrubs. Hair short or tightly pulled back from the face. Impassive features.

No. Not the bathroom. To that poor woman. To help. Leave me alone. I can get out of bed myself.

No, it's not safe. It's the new meds. They make you unsteady. You could fall.

Let me fall then. If you're going to treat me like a child, then treat me like an actual child. Let me pick myself up when I fall.

Jen, you could really hurt yourself. Then I

would get into trouble. And you wouldn't want that, would you?

It's Dr. White. Not Jenny. Absolutely not Jen. And I wouldn't care if you were fired. Another would just take your place. You're interchangeable enough.

Dozens of people come and go, some lighter, some darker, some speaking better English than others, but all their faces blending into one another.

Okay, Dr. White. No problem.

She doesn't let go of my arms. With a grip that could subdue a 250-pound man she pulls me to a standing position, puts one hand on the small of my back and the other at my elbow.

Now we can go together and see what's happening, she says. I bet you could be of service to Laura! She sure needs it sometimes!

Still holding on to my arm, she walks me into the hall. People are milling aimlessly, as if after a fire drill.

Oh good, see, all over! Would you like to go back to bed now or have some hot milk in the dining room?

Coffee, I say. Black.

No problem! She turns to a girl, this one in an olive smock. Here. Take Jennifer to the kitchen for some hot milk. And make her take her meds. She refused at bedtime. You know what will happen tomorrow if we don't get them into her.

Not milk. *Coffee,* I say, but no one is listening. That's the way it is here. People will say anything, promise anything. You can ignore the words, even on the days when you can retain them, because you need to keep your eyes on their bodies. Their hands most of all. The hands don't lie. You watch what they are holding. What they are reaching for. If you cannot see the hands, that is the time to be concerned. The time to begin screaming.

I study the face of the girl walking me to the dining room. My prosopagnosia, my inability to distinguish one face from another, is getting worse. I cannot hold on to features, so when a person is in front of me, I study them. To try to do what every six-month-old child is capable of doing: separate the known from the unknown.

This one strikes no chords. Her face is pockmarked, and her head brachycephalic. She has an overbite and her right foot is slightly intoed, probably due to an internal tibial torsion. Enough work there for many expensive medical specialists. But not for me. Because her hands are perfect. Large and capable. Not gentle. But this is not a place where gentleness thrives. Natural selection takes care of that, for both the caring and the cared for.

It's a much-used word here, *care*. He needs long-term care. She is not qualified for home care. We are currently hiring more caregivers. Take care of her. Be careful with that. The other day, I found myself repeating the word over and over until it was meaningless. *Care. Care. Care.*

I asked one of the male attendants for a dictionary. The man without the beard yet who is not clean-shaven, the one whose face I remember because of the hemangioma on his left cheek.

He came back later with a piece of paper. Laura looked it up online for you, he said. He tried to hand it to me, but I shook my head. That was not a reading day, very few of them are anymore. He held up the paper

223

and haltingly spoke, stumbling over the words. He is from the Philippines. He believes in the Holy Spirit, the Lord and Giver of Life. He makes the sign of the cross in front of the statue of the haloed woman on my dresser. He has asked me several times about my Saint Christopher medal and clearly approves of me wearing it.

Care: a burdened state of mind, as that arising from heavy responsibilities, he read. Watchful oversight. Assistance or treatment to those in need.

He paused and frowned, then laughed. That's a lot of definition for such a short word! It sure makes my job sound hard!

It is hard, I said. You have the hardest job. I like this one. He has a face I approve of, in spite of — or perhaps because of — his birthmark. A face you can remember. A face that makes my anguish over my prosopagnosia dissipate a little.

No, no! Not with patients like you!

Stop flirting! I told him. But he got a smile out of me. Something this girl with the good hands is not going to do.

We reach the dining room, and she deposits me in a chair, leaves. Another will take her place. And another.

As with my patients at the free clinic I volunteer for every Wednesday: I focus on the symptoms, ignore the personalities. Just this morning I saw a case. If not for the puffiness around the hands and ankles, I would have simply diagnosed a mild case of depression. He was irritable. Unable to focus. His wife had been complaining, he said. But the inflammation made me suspicious, and I ordered tests for endomysial and anti-tissue transglutaminase antibodies.

If I'm right, a life of deprivation to follow. No wheat. No dairy. No bread, the staff of life. Some self-dramatizing, self-pitying people would see being diagnosed with celiac as a death sentence of life's pleasures. If only they had known what lay in store for them, what would they have done differently? Indulged more? Or restrained themselves sooner?

My milk arrives, along with a small cup of pills. I spit into the milk, hurl the pills so they scatter under tables, into corners.

Jen! someone says. You know that's against

the rules!

People start bending, going down on their hands and knees to retrieve the red, blue, and yellow pills. I resist the urge to kick the one closest to me in the backside and instead head back to my room. Yes. I will break every rule, transgress every line. And I prepare myself for battle as reinforcements begin arriving.

Something nags. Just out of reach. Something to be shuddered at. Something bloody but unbowed by my resistance. This dark shame. A pain too lonely to bear.

Visitors come and go. When they head toward the exit, I always follow, I quietly move in, ingratiate myself with the person or persons leaving. When they pass through the door, I will too. It's that simple. No matter that I've always been stopped. One day it will work. No one will notice. No one will realize until mealtime. Then I will be long gone. I will eventually make it. Next time for certain.

◇ ◇ ◇

There is a woman here who is always surrounded by people. Visitors, night and day. Beloved by all. She is one of the lucky ones. She doesn't know where she is, she doesn't always recognize her husband or children, she wears diapers, and she's lost many of her words, but she is sweet and serene. She is descending with dignity.

The Vietnam vet, on the other hand, is alone. No visitors. He continually and loudly relives his glory days or his nightmares, depending on the day or even the hour. He either did or did not participate in a massacre, one of the famous ones. Some of the details ring truer than others. Heaving a goat carcass into a well. The way blood mists when slicing a vein. Like me, he understands that he is incarcerated for crimes past.

James has come home today from one of his trips. From Albany this time. A tedious case, he says. His schedule is as draining as my own.

Like me, he hasn't slowed down with age.

227

Still as urgent, as engaged as when we were in graduate school. And for me, always that thrill, that sense of discovery, no matter how brief his absence. Not a conventional sort of good looks. Too sharp, too angular for most tastes. And dark. Where Mark got his darkness, darkness within as well as without.

James starts to sit down, then changes his mind and strides across the room, straightens my Calder where it hangs. Then comes back. Finally settles in the chair, but is not relaxed. On the edge of his chair, his foot tapping. Always in motion. Putting people on edge, wondering what he will do next. An extraordinarily useful weapon in the courtroom and in life. In a world where people usually behave as expected, James is exploratory surgery: slice and probe, and you discover things. Sometimes a malignancy. But frequently something that delights. Today he is unusually quiet, however. He waits a few moments before speaking.

You look like crap, he says. But I imagine that's just a shadow of how you feel.

You always call it like it is, I say. And because his features are fading into the early morning gloom, Can you turn on the light?

228

I prefer it this way, he says, and falls silent. He is fiddling with something in his hands. I lean forward. It is some sort of engraved medallion on a chain. It is somehow important. I hold out my hand, palm up, in the universal gesture of *give me.* But he ignores that.

You forgot about this, he says. He holds it up by one finger, the medallion swinging slightly back and forth. It could be a problem, he says.

I am trying to remember. There is a connection I must make. But it eludes me. I reach again for the medal, this time intending to take rather than ask. But James swiftly pulls back his hand, denying me. And suddenly he is gone. I feel a sharp sense of loss, the prick of tears on my eyelashes.

People come and go so quickly here.

Mark sits with me in the great room. He pleads. Please, Mom. You know I wouldn't ask for it if it weren't important.

I am trying to understand. People are

watching us. A scene! The television is off, they are hungry for drama. And here it is, with Mark and me as the central characters. Yet I still don't comprehend what he is saying.

Mom, it's just until the end of the year. Until we get our bonuses.

His hair wants cutting. Is he married yet? There was a girl. What happened to her? He looks so terribly young, they're all so terribly young. I've asked Fiona but she says no. Mom, can you understand me? Mark at ten. My tender boy. Fiona even younger, but watching over him. He has broken the Millers' garage window with his baseball bat on a dare and it's Fiona who knocks on their door and offers to cut their lawn for six weeks to pay for it.

You shouldn't have done that, I tell him. You should have taken responsibility.

Mom? Stay with me here.

And you came home drunk last night. I caught Fiona mopping up the vomit on the living room rug. Fiona watches out for you.

Yes, always Fiona. You don't know how sick

that makes me.

What have you done that even your little sister won't cover for you?

Mom, I swear, I promise, this time will be the last. Now he is getting angry. You have more than you need. You'll be giving it to me and Fiona anyway, eventually. What's a little in advance?

More people are stopping and staring. Even the Vietnam vet pulls up a chair. Entertainment! Mark's voice continues to rise in impotent fury.

If you just told Fiona that you agreed, she would give me the money. Why won't you do this for me? Just this one last time.

I was a reluctant mother. And Mark was difficult to love, I remember trying to cuddle him when he was three or four and crying about some playground injury, and I felt frustrated by the awkwardness of it all, the sharp elbows and bony knees. Yet he is my boy.

Mom? He has been watching me closely.

Yes.

You'll do it?

Do what?

Give me the money?

Is that what you wanted? Why didn't you say? Yes, of course. Let me just get my checkbook.

I get up to go to my room for my purse, but Mark stops me. Holds out a notebook and a pen.

Mom, you don't have a checkbook anymore. That's in Fiona's hands. All you have to do is write a note here saying you'll lend me the money. Just those words: I will lend Mark $50,000. No, you need a couple more zeros on there. That's right. Now sign it. Great! Wonderful! You won't regret it, I promise you. I'll show you that I can make things right.

He's halfway to the door before collecting himself, turning back, and kissing me on the cheek. I love you, Mom. I know I'm a son of a bitch sometimes, but I do. And it's not just the money talking.

Show's over, I tell the people who have gathered around. Go to your rooms. *Shoo.*

They scatter like cockroaches.

Love, love is everywhere. People are pairing off, two by two, sometimes three. Couplings that last perhaps an hour, perhaps a day. Junior high for the geriatric set.

The woman with no neck is utterly promiscuous. She will be intimate with anyone. Here that means holding hands. Sitting in the lounge side by side. Perhaps a hand on a thigh. Very few words spoken.

Husbands and wives show up, are looked at blankly. Some of them cry, all are relieved. A burden lifted. But these lovers. To be eternally seeking, to be besotted, to retreat to and be stuck at the most ignoble stage of life. God preserve me from ever going through that again.

I was that foolish just twice. There was James. And then there was the other. It ended badly, of course. How could it not? His young, aggrieved face. His sense of entitlement.

He would be close to fifty now — how odd

to think that. A decade older than I was then. I never cared to see how he fared after leaving. I assume he did well, things are easy for the beautiful ones.

But it wasn't his beauty that attracted me. It was his feeling for the knife. I thrilled at that. His grip on the handle as if grasping the hand of a beloved. Still, to have that passion, that desire, but not the talent. I pitied him. And then pity turned into something else. I never used the word *love*. It couldn't compare to what I felt for James. But it wasn't like anything else either. And that counts for something.

When thinking over one's life, it's the extreme moments that stand out. The peaks and the valleys. He was one of the highest peaks. In some ways looming larger than James. If James was a central mountain in the landscape of my life, then this other was a pinnacle of a different sort. Higher, sharper. You couldn't build upon its fragile precipices. But the view was spectacular.

There is colored tape on the rich carpet — somewhat spoiling the effect of luxury they work so hard to maintain here, but useful.

This is a linear world. You go straight. You make right turns or left turns.

Following the blue line takes me to my bathroom. Red leads to the dining room. Yellow to the lounge. Brown is for the circumference walk, which takes you round and round the perimeter of the great room. Round and round. Round and round.

Past the bedrooms, past the dining room, the TV room, the activity room, past the double doors to the outside world with EXIT painted seductively in red letters. And on you go, in perpetual motion.

Something nags. Something that resides in a sterile, brightly lit place where there is no room for shadows. The place for blood and bone. Yet shadows exist. And secrets.

An extraordinarily clean place, this. They are constantly scrubbing, vacuuming, touching up the paint. Dusting. Fixing. It is pristine. And luxurious. A five-star hotel with guardrails. The Ritz for the mentally infirm. Plump cushy armchairs in the great room. An enormous flat-screen television in the TV lounge. Fresh flowers everywhere. The scent of money.

They keep us clean, too. Frequent showers with strong antiseptic soap. Harsh wash-cloths wielded expertly by rough hands. The indignity of a vigorous scrubbing of the belly, the buttocks.

Why bother exfoliating? Let the dead cells accumulate, let them encase me until, mummified, I am preserved as I am. No more deterioration. To stop this descent. What I wouldn't pay. What I wouldn't give.

I am sitting with a well-groomed woman with feathered gray hair. We're in the dining room, at the long communal table. It has been freshly set for a dozen or so diners, but we are the only ones eating.

I have some sort of long pale strings of matter swimming in a thick red liquid. She has a piece of whitish meat. We both have a mound of white mush with a brown liquid poured on it. Through a sort of haze I recognize a fellow professional. Someone I could respect.

What is that? I point to something she has to the right of her food, something I don't have.

That's a knife.

I want one.

No, you don't need one. See, your food is soft, easy to break into bite-size morsels. You don't need to cut it.

But I like that one. Most of all.

That makes sense.

How long have you been here? I ask.

About six years.

What did you do?

What do you mean?

To get sent here. What did you do? Everyone here has committed a crime. Some worse than others.

No, I work here. My name is Laura. I'm the resident manager. She smiles. She is tall and broad-shouldered. Strong and sturdy. And what crime did you commit? she asks.

I don't like to say.

That's all right. You don't need to tell me. It's not important.

How long have you been here?

Six years. My name is Laura.

I like your necklace, I say. A word comes to me. Opal?

Yes. A present from my husband.

My husband is out of town, I say. Somehow I know this. In San Francisco, at a conference. He travels.

You must miss him, then.

Sometimes, I say. And then suddenly the words come more easily.

Sometimes I like rolling over in the bed, to find a place where the sheets are still cool. And he can take up a lot of psychic space.

But it seems that you have great affection for him. You talk about him a lot.

What is that you are holding?

A knife.

What is it for?

To cut.

I remember that. Can I have one?

No.

Why not?

It's not safe.

For whom?

For yourself, mostly.

Just mostly?

There is a concern.

That I might hurt others?

Yes. There is that.

But I am a doctor, I say.

And you've taken a solemn oath.

I am gifted with a vision. A framed script hanging on a wall. I quote what I see written there. I swear by Apollo, Asclepius, Hygieia, and Panacea, and I take to witness all the gods, all the goddesses . . . the image leaves me before I can finish.

Impressive words. Frightening, even.

Yes, I've always thought so, I say.

And of course, there's the part everyone knows, about never doing harm, the gray-haired woman says.

I've always fulfilled that oath, I say. I believe I have.

Believe?

There is this thing that nags.

Oh?

Yes. It has to do with the thing you're holding.

The knife.

Yes, the knife.

The woman leans forward. Are you remembering? No. Let me rephrase that. If you are remembering, keep it to yourself. Don't tell me.

I don't understand, I say.

No, not today. It is not your day to understand. But you might remember tomorrow. Or the day after. Memory is a funny thing. It might be a good thing not to try too hard. That's all I'm saying.

And with that, she leaves, taking the lovely shiny sharp thing with her. *Knife.*

One living creature still trembles at my command. A small dog, a mutt that has somehow become attached to me. I've never been fond of dogs. The opposite, in fact. The children's pleas counted for nothing.

At first I kicked the thing away. But it persevered, haunted me morning until night. The other residents attempt to entice it away at every turn, but it always returns to me after devouring a treat or being subjected to a trembling petting session.

I'm unclear who it belongs to. It wanders

the halls at will and is a general favorite. But I am the one it pursues relentlessly. Despite the fact that it has a bed in the television lounge, bowls of food and water in the dining room, it sleeps with me. Shortly after I go to bed I feel a thump, a rustle of bedclothes, and a small hot body nestling up. A tongue rasps at my hand. The smell of dog that I always hated. But gradually I have found comfort in it, have enjoyed being so adored.

Other residents are jealous. They try to steal Dog away. Several times I have awakened from deep sleep to find a dark shape bending over my bed, attempting to grab the whining wiggling body. I always let it go without comment, and the thing always returns to me. My familiar. Every crone needs one.

The only thing that helps is the walking. What the people here call *wandering.* They've set up a kind of a trail. A labyrinth for the mentally deficient.

On any given hour, there might be two or three of us traversing the loop. If someone tries to wander more randomly, they are stopped and firmly put back on the trail.

I remember the Chartres labyrinth, the children fascinated with it, following its mesmerizing lines to the center. Where pilgrims hoped to get closer to God. Where repentant sinners who suffered the stony path on their knees finally arrived, bloodied and weary, their penance fulfilled.

How I would love to experience once again that sense of freedom that follows punishment, that release that children feel once they have confessed and paid for their trivial crimes. But I — I have no choice but to keep wandering.

We have a visitor, Jen. Aren't you glad we had a bath? Look how nice your hair looks!

It is a face I have seen before. That's what I am reduced to now. No more names. Just characteristics, if they are idiosyncratic enough, and knowing whether a face is familiar or unfamiliar.

And those are not absolute categories. I can be looking at a face that I have decided is unfamiliar only to have its features shift and reveal a visage that is not only known but beloved.

I didn't recognize my own mother this morning, disguised as she was. But then she revealed herself. She cried as she held my hand. I comforted her as best I could. I explained that, yes, it had been a difficult birth, but I would be home soon, the baby was doing well. But where is James? I asked. Mom, Dad can't be here right now. Why are you calling me Mom and him Dad? More tears.

And then my mother was gone.

Now this one. A different sort altogether.

I am Detective Luton. We've spoken on a number of occasions.

Who performed your thyroidectomy? Was it Dr. Gregory?

My what? Oh — and her hand goes to the scar on her throat. I actually don't remember his name. Why?

He always had a good hand with the needle. Your scar healed nicely.

So I've been told.

Has your dosage been titrated correctly?

Ma'am?

When was the last time your T3 and T4 levels were checked?

O, perhaps a year ago. But that's not why I'm here.

It's not my specialty, I know. But it's something I would ask your endocrinologist. I find that eighty percent of the people with chronic thyroid conditions aren't adequately monitoring their levels.

Okay, well I appreciate that. But I actually came here on another matter. I know you don't remember, so I'll just fill you in real quickly. I'm with the police. I'm in charge of an ongoing investigation into the death of Amanda O'Toole.

She pauses as if waiting for something.

Is that name familiar?

There's someone on my street of that name. But I don't know her well. We've only just moved into the neighborhood, and I have a new baby and a very busy practice. So I'm very sorry to hear it. But we were not more than acquaintances.

I'm glad. Because it was very upsetting to the friends and family of this woman. The sudden death, but also the way her body was treated after death.

Go on.

We believe, due to the violence with which her head hit the table, that it was not an accident. And then, sometime after death, the fingers of her right hand were cut off. No. Not cut. Surgically removed.

An interesting modus operandi. And why are you telling me this?

Because I want your brain. I need your brain.

I don't quite understand.

We think you know something about this. But that you don't know what you know.

How did you know that?

Just a hunch. You see a lot in my line of work.

Yes, I've been worried. My memory. It's not

what it used to be. Just this morning, I told James — my husband — that we were going to have to start eating more fish. You know, for the omega-three fatty acids. He wasn't enthusiastic. It's hard to get good fresh fish in Chicago.

Right. So you know what I'm talking about. So I'm wondering if you'll humor me. Talk to me about your work, the memories you do have of Amanda O'Toole. Play some word games. I want to try and trigger a reaction from that very large brain of yours.

I'll cancel my appointments for the morning.

The woman nods gravely. I appreciate that.

She takes out her phone. Do you mind if I record this? I have a bit of a memory problem myself. So, do this: Think about Amanda. Here's a picture if it will jog your memory. No? Well then, don't worry about what she looks like. What do you think of when I say the name Amanda?

I think of someone tall and straight and unyielding. Someone with dignity.

How would a dignified person meet death?

247

It's a silly question. The only good death is a swift one. Dignity has nothing to do with it. Whether you suffer a heart attack or die due to a head trauma, it doesn't matter. As long as there's little or no suffering it's a good death.

But you do hear of people who die with honor. Not just soldiers. You know what I mean.

It's drugs. Drugs get most people through. Without drugs our own families wouldn't wait for a more natural end. The drugs are as much for them as for us.

You're a doctor, so you're closer to death than most people. But then you don't often deal with fatalities in your line of work, do you?

No, not many deaths due to hand trauma. I permit myself a smile.

But amputations?

Yes, a fair number.

What are the reasons you would amputate, say, a finger?

Infection, gangrene, frostbite, vascular compromise, bone infection. Cancer.

Is there ever any reason you would amputate all the fingers and leave the rest of the hand intact?

Yes. In cases of extreme frostbite or meningococcemia, there's the possibility of gangrene, and you might well need to remove all digits.

And what, exactly, is gangrene?

A complication of necrosis, or cell death. In effect, a part of your body dies and starts to rot. Amputation is eventually required.

Have you ever had to perform an amputation due to gangrene?

Yes, occasionally. In this climate, you get some frostbite cases. It doesn't usually get to the point where amputation is necessary — when it does, it's unfortunately mostly among the poor and homeless.

But you wouldn't see homeless people, would you? Not at your practice?

I do pro bono work at the Hope Community Health Center over on Chicago Avenue, and most of my work of this kind takes place there. And occasionally you get cases of what is called wet gangrene, which is due to infection. That's more serious. If you don't do an amputation in those cases, the gangrene can spread and eventually kill the patient.

So, in other words, you cut off body parts to keep the rot from spreading?

Yes, that's one way of putting it. For the serious type of gangrene.

But there would be no reason to amputate after death.

No, of course not.

None?

None whatsoever.

Then why would someone do such a thing? In your opinion.

I'm not a psychiatrist. Certainly not privy to the deranged or criminal mind.

No, I realize that.

But it seems to me it might have symbolic value.

How would that work?

Well, if an amputation stops rot from spreading, then someone who was guilty of using their hands to do wrong — if their hands were, say, corrupted by unclean activities — that might be a way of sending a message. You know what Jesus says at the Last Supper: Behold, the hand of him that betrayeth me is with me on the table.

But why the fingers, not the hands?

That could be symbolic, too. A hand without fingers can't easily grasp, can't easily hold on to things. It could be a message for someone perceived as greedy, mercenary. Or someone who won't let go emotionally. After all, without fingers, a hand is just a paddle of bone covered with soft tissue. Good for very little.

The woman nods. She stretches, gets up, and starts walking around the room.

I've noticed a certain number of religious things around the room, she says. And your ability to quote the Bible. Are you, in fact, a religious woman?

I shake my head. I was raised Catholic, but

now I just like the accessories. It's hard to avoid some degree of biblical scholarship when you choose medieval history to specialize in for a graduate degree.

The woman stops in front of my statue.

I notice you brought this from your home. Who's this? The mother of Jesus?

Oh no, that's Saint Rita of Cascia. See the wound on her forehead? And the rose she's carrying?

Who is she?

The patron saint of impossible causes.

I thought that was Saint Jude.

Yes, those two saints have very similar missions. But the feminist in me prefers Rita. She was not a passive vessel like so many of the virgin martyrs. She took action.

Yes, I can see how you would be attracted to that. Is that her medal you're wearing around your neck?

This? No. This is Saint Christopher.

Why are you wearing this?

252

It's a joke. Amanda's idea.

What kind of joke?

Saint Christopher is not a real saint.

No?

A fraud. No, that's not right. An implausible and unprovable legend. A fantasy of the devout. He was evicted from the host of accredited saints some time ago. But I loved him as a child. He was a protector against many things. One of them is a sudden, unholy death. The patron saint of travelers. You'll still find people with statues of him on their car dashboards.

More accessories.

Yes.

So what does this have to do with Amanda?

She gave it to me. On my fiftieth birthday. I had just ended a tough decade.

Tough in what way?

On many fronts. So many losses. Of a very

personal, rather self-involved narcissistic kind. Loss of looks. Loss of sexual drive. Loss of ambition.

That last one surprises me. You were at the top of your game when you retired.

Yes. But ambition is not success. It's something else. It's a striving, not an achieving. By age fifty I had gotten where I wanted to be. I didn't know where else to go. In fact, there was nowhere I wanted to go. I didn't want to be an administrator, join boards. I wasn't ambitious in that way. I didn't want to write textbooks or advice books. I didn't want — didn't need — more money.

And then?

Amanda helped, in her way. She told me to volunteer at the New Hope Community Medical Clinic, on Chicago Avenue, to give back to the world. Insisted on it. She had her reasons for knowing that I would comply. But the experience turned out to be extraordinarily gratifying on a number of levels. I had to become a generalist again. Think of the human body beyond the elbow. It was difficult.

And Saint Christopher? Sudden death?

Yes. *If thou on any day Saint Christopher you see / Against sudden death you will protected be.* In my case, death of the spirit. Against my fear, my despondency, that everything important had come to an end. The medal was Amanda's way of saying don't panic just because of the current darkness. That there was a way out. That by paying for past . . . transgressions . . . my mind would be at ease. That brighter things lay ahead. So she thought.

So the medal represented vanquishing spiritual trouble — nothing to do with friction between you and Amanda.

I wouldn't say that. No. There was friction there.

She leans forward, asks, May I? and takes the medallion in her hand. Her face tightens. There's something on the medal, she says. A stain. Do you mind if I look closer?

I shrug, reach behind, and pull the chain over my head, hand it over. She studies it.

It's dirty, she says. Let me take it away and clean it. I'll bring it back, don't worry.

There is a pause. I say, Is there anything

255

else? Because I have patients waiting. I'm surprised my nurse hasn't interrupted us. She's got instructions to keep me on schedule.

I beg your pardon. Yes, I've taken up too much of your time already. Do you mind if I stop by again?

Just make an appointment at the front desk. I hold office hours Mondays, Tuesdays, and Fridays. Wednesdays and Thursdays are my surgery days. I should see you in three weeks, to follow up on this consultation.

Yes. Thank you. You've been very helpful.

She leans down, pushes a button on her phone, and puts it in her briefcase.

Yes, she says. I am sure we'll be talking again, quite soon.

Fiona is here. My girl. Her green eyes are slightly reddened. She has three moon earrings arcing up the outside of her right ear.

What is it? I ask. I'm still in bed. I can't seem to find a clock to see the time.

What do you mean? she asks, but she is palpably upset. She sits down on the chair beside my bed, stands up, sits down again, takes my hand, and pats it. I pull it away, struggle to sit up.

You seem agitated, I say.

No. Well, yes. She stands up again, starts pacing. Isn't it time for you to get up? It's nearly nine o'clock.

I push myself up to a sitting position, throw off the bedclothes, lift my legs, and put my feet on the floor, steady myself. She pushes her chair back, stands to help me. I shake her hand off.

Are you okay? she asks.

New meds, I say. Or, actually, more of the old ones. They upped the dosage of both the Seroquel and Wellbutrin. They've also been slipping me Xanax when they think I'm not paying attention.

Yes, I know. They told me.

I look more closely at her face. The nose slightly reddened in addition to the eyes. Limp hair around her ears from tugging at it. Signs of distress. I know my girl.

Tell me, I say.

She searches my face for something, appears uncertain. Then makes a decision.

We closed on the sale today, she says. I just came from signing the papers.

You bought a house?

No, she says. Well, yes. But that's not what happened today. Today I sold one.

I didn't know you owned a house. I thought you had that apartment in Hyde Park. On Ellis.

I moved, about three months ago, she says. That apartment was so small. I bought a house right off campus. A brownstone, hardwood floors, exposed brick.

Her face becomes less haggard, as if reliving a fond memory, before clouding over again. No, it was the house in Lincoln Park, on Sheffield, that we sold, she says.

That's where my house is. I love that neighborhood.

Yes, I know. I loved it too, Mom.

Her eyes begin to tear up. Mark, too. We were both born there. We've known nothing but that house. It was really, really hard. We took sleeping bags and spent last night over there. We stayed up all night talking and remembering. You know how long it's been since Mark and I have spent that much time together without fighting? When I first called he wouldn't pick up. But I kept trying and eventually he relented.

Wait a minute. You're saying you sold my house?

Yes. Yes.

My house?

I'm so sorry.

But my things. My books. My art. The tapes of my surgeries.

Mom, we cleaned it all out months ago. You packed yourself. You decided what you would take with you and what would go.

But what about when it's time to go home?

This is your home now.

259

This is a room, I say. I am furious.

I gesture around at the four walls. Point to the stainless-steel bathroom without a bathtub, only a shower. At the windows shuttered against the view of a parking lot.

Yes, but look. All your things are here. Your statue of Saint Rita. Your Renoir. Your Calder. And your most beloved of all, your Theotokos of the Three Hands.

There were others. Many others. Where are they?

Safely stored.

My furniture?

I took the little oak secretary desk, Mark the Stickley mission oak sofa and rocker. The rest, sold.

I swing my legs around, get up from the bed. My hands are clenched.

I'm having some trouble absorbing this, I say.

Yes. Mom, I'm sorry. I wasn't going to tell you.

Then why did you?

Because I'm heartsick. Because you'll forget. Because there's no one else to tell.

Cry me a river, I say. I pull my nightgown over my head. Sit there in my underpants. Not caring.

Mom, please, don't do this. Get dressed. She goes to the chest of drawers, starts pulling out clothes, hands me a bra, a dark blue T-shirt, a pair of jeans.

Don't what? I drop the clothes, put my hands over my eyes, try to still the rising fury. No. Not at my girl. Hold steady.

Please don't cry. We talked about this at length. You knew we had to do it. It was time. Please. I hate to see you cry. Look, I'm crying, too. She picks up the clothes, puts them on my lap. Here. Please. Get dressed. Please don't cry.

I take my hands away from my face, show her my dry eyes. I'm not crying. One doesn't cry over things like this. You get mad. You take action.

Fiona runs her fingers through her hair, rubs her eyes. I just don't get you, Mom. You never crack. Not through any of this. Not

through Dad's death. Not even when Grandmother died.

That's not true, I say.

Which wasn't true? Dad or Grandmother?

What your father and I had was private. I
grieved in my own way.

What about Grandmother? I was only nine,
but I remember you coming home from Philadelphia. It was right before dinner. I was doing
my homework at the kitchen table.

You know, I seem to recall this.

Yes. You came in, changed your clothes, sat
down, and ate a huge meal. Roast chicken
with mashed potatoes. Amanda had made it,
and she and Peter came over and ate with
us. Dad was off somewhere on one of his
business trips. Mark was at football practice.
And we sat and talked about nothing. Your
recent surgeries. Amanda's wayward students. My math scores. And your mother had
just died.

About which I could do nothing.

But it was your mother. Your mother! Wouldn't

you expect someone to grieve even a little bit?

Of course. Unless one were a monster.

But you didn't.

You don't know, I say. You just don't know.

My voice is raised. A woman in lavender, a badge attached to her shirt, passes by the open door to my room, glances in, sees Fiona, hesitates, then passes on.

I was there, Mom. Unless you're saying you got it all out on the two-hour flight between Philadelphia and O'Hare.

But I didn't lose my mother that day.

I start getting dressed. It takes concentration. These are the pants. First one leg, then the other. This is the shirt. Three holes, the largest one for the head. Pull it down to the neck. There.

The day before then.

No. I had lost my mother years before.

I find my shoes. Slip-ons. I stand up, still

holding on to the bed. I test the floor, find it steady, and stand up straight. Fully dressed. Where is my suitcase. The discharge nurse.

Here, fix your hair. She hands me a comb. You mean . . . ?

My mother was long gone by the time she died. Her mind had rotted out. She spent the last eight years of her life among strangers.

I walk around the bed, looking but not finding.

Oh. Yes, I see. Now I know what you're talking about. Now I know.

No, I don't think you do. I don't think you could. Unless you've experienced it yourself.

Fiona gives a little half smile. And how do you experience it, Mom?

As termites eating away at my emotions. Nibbling at the edges at first, then going deeper until they destroy. Robbing me of my chance to say good-bye. You think, Tomorrow, or next week. You think you still have time.

But all the while the termites are doing their work, and before you know it, it's no longer possible to feel the loss honestly or spontaneously. Most people start acting at that point. I'm not capable of that. Hence, no funeral. Hence, no tears.

I can't imagine that.

Believe me, it happens.

Maybe to you. But not to me.

You think not. But you don't know.

I do know. I do. I still feel. Everything. You have no idea.

Yes, well. Apparently not. What's that expression? *Other people's troubles are easily borne.* I'm sorry. I'm sorry for you and your pain. But I've had enough of this morbid talk. I want to go home. Let's go.

I start looking again for my suitcase. I had put it here. Next to the bed.

No, Mom.

What do you mean, no? I'm ready — I

packed last night.

Mom, you pack every night. And every morning the aides unpack you.

Why would they do that?

Because you live here now. Because this is your home. See? Look at your things. Look at your photographs! Here's one of all of us on Mark's high school graduation.

Yes, I miss the children. They left one day.

Mom, we went to college.

It was more interesting when they were around. I tried not to mind, but I did.

Well, you have plenty of people to keep you company here. I saw lots of them in the dining room, eating breakfast. Laughing and talking. It's time for you to get over there yourself. Eat something. You'll feel better.

Yes, but it's time to go home. I'll eat breakfast there.

Not quite yet. You don't want to insult your hosts, do you?

What an utterly ridiculous question. You

don't keep guests against their will. What kind of host would do that? Let's just go. They'll understand. I'll write a thank-you card later. Sometimes you just have to dispense with the niceties.

Mom, I'm sorry.

What are you sorry for? I'm ready.

Mom, I can't. You can't. This is where you live now.

No.

Mom, you're breaking my heart.

I give up on the suitcase and make for the door.

If you won't take me, I'll get a cab.

Mom, I have to go now. And you have to stay.

She is openly crying, goes to the doorway of the room, waves her arm, flags down the woman who had passed through before. I need some help here.

Suddenly there are others in the room. Not anyone I know. Unfamiliar faces. They are pulling at me, preventing me from following Fiona out the door, telling me to be quiet. Why should I be quiet? Why should I take this pill? I close my mouth tight against it. Struggle to free my arms. One is being held behind my back, the other straight out. A prick, a sting on the inside of my elbow.

I fight, but feel the strength ebbing from my body. I close my eyes. The room is spinning. I am pushed onto a buoyant surface covered with something warm and soft.

She'll be out for a while.

Good thing! Man, she's strong. What caused this?

I don't know. Her daughter visited. Usually that's a good thing. Not like when that son comes around.

Why do we put up with it?

Friends in high places. She used to be some muckety-muck doctor.

I try holding on to their words, but they evaporate. The chattering of creatures not of my species. I lift my right arm, let it flop back down. Do it again. And again. It reassures. It hypnotizes. I do it until my arm is too heavy to lift anymore. Then, blessed sleep.

I open my eyes. James. A very angry James. How unusual. Usually he expresses dissatisfaction by refusing to eat the rare dinner I've cooked or by strolling in late to one of our children's birthday parties. Once he threw my favorite pair of broken-in tennis shoes outside into the garden — the ones I used for my longest and most delicate surgeries. I found them later, covered with mud and infested with earwigs.

What is it? What happened? I ask now.

But he isn't paying attention to me. It isn't me he's angry with.

Who let her in? he asks. He is speaking to the other woman in the room, one wearing green scrubs and a name tag. Ana.

We had no reason to know, she says.

I gave explicit instructions that no one could see my mother except those on the list I gave Laura.

Laura doesn't screen everyone who comes to the ward.

Who does?

No one person does. Whoever is on duty. It's very secure. They have to sign in. They have to show ID. And they can't get out until we let them out. It's a locked ward, as you know.

Who was on duty that day?

I don't know. You'd have to ask Laura.

I will. You bet I will.

Mr. McLennan? A tall woman with gray hair waved back off her face has come into the room. She is wearing an auburn blazer that matches the carpet, and a knee-length black skirt. Sensible shoes. The way I used to dress when not in scrubs.

Laura, James says.

I understand you are upset by what you perceive as a breach of security.

Yes, he says. Very much.

She was a police officer pursuing an investigation. She showed her ID. She signed in and signed out. It was all properly done.

Did she read my mother her rights?

That I couldn't tell you. I'm sorry.

James's face reddens. We are about to witness something uncommon: James losing his temper. He almost always stays in control. Even in the courtroom, he prefers to keep his voice low. It makes for good theater. People have to lean close, strain to hear. I've never seen a jury so rapt as when James is lovingly murmuring all the reasons they should acquit.

But before things erupt, James notices I'm awake. Mom, he says, and bends down and gives me an awkward half hug. He is dressed oddly, for James. Not his casual clothes of jeans and a T-shirt. Not business attire either. No suit. Tan-colored cotton trousers and a white shirt. Black sneakers. But he is young and vibrant and handsome as ever.

Why are you calling me that? James, it's me. Jennifer. How glad I am to see you!

James's face softens. He sits down on the

271

edge of the bed, takes my hand. And how have you been?

Well. Very well. Missing you. How tired you look. They work you too hard. How was New York?

New York was good, he says. I tripped the light fantastic. Went out on the town. Painted it red. He pats my hand.

Now you're patronizing me, I say. I have a temper, too. Stop talking to me like I'm an imbecile. What happened? It was the Lewis case, wasn't it? A tricky deposition? Did it not go well?

I'm sorry, Mom. You're absolutely right. I was being patronizing. And you probably get enough of that here. He glances back at the gray-haired woman. I'll come talk to you later, he says.

There is an ominous tone in his voice. There is something wrong with his face, too. Some trick of light. It is fading away, and the features are rearranging themselves, transmogrifying into someone who is not-James.

James? Why are you calling me that?

Mom, I know Fiona shines you on, and that's

okay, but it's, well, it's not my way. I am Mark. You are my mother. James is my father. James is dead.

Mr. McLennan, the gray-haired woman interrupts. She is still standing by my bed.

I said I'll come to your office. When I'm done here.

James! I say. My anger is dissipating. Turning into something else, something unsettlingly like fear.

If I can make a recommendation, Mr. McLennan . . .

No. I can handle this on my own, thank you.

James!

Shhh, Mom, it's okay.

Okay, the gray-haired woman says. She does not look pleased. If she becomes too agitated, push the red button there.

The door closes behind her.

James, what was that about?

Not James, Mom. Mark. Your son.

Mark is a teenager. He just got his driver's license. He took the car out last week without asking, and now he's grounded for a month.

Yes, that happened. But many years ago. Not-James smiles. And it wasn't a month. Dad relented, as he always did. I think I had to stay inside for three days. You were furious.

He was always able to charm his way out of anything. Just like you.

Not-James sighs. Yes, just like me. Like son, like father.

James?

Never mind, he says. He reaches over and takes my hand, holds it against his cheek.

These hands, he says. You know, Dad used to say, All our lives are in your mother's hands. Be careful of them. I didn't understand what he meant. I'm still not quite sure, completely. But something about how you were the center. You were it.

He takes my hand from his cheek, clasps it between both of his.

He was very proud of you, you know. Whatever else may have happened. When I was small, and you were late coming home from the hospital, he used to take me into your office. He'd show me all your diplomas and awards. These are the credentials of a real woman, he'd say. It scared the hell out of me. Small wonder I haven't married.

You're nobody's fool.

No. Whatever I am, I'm not that.

He is fading fast into the shadows. I cannot see his face anymore at all. But his hand is warm and substantial. I grasp it and hold on.

Do me a favor, he says.

What's that?

Talk to me. Tell me about what life is like for you right now.

James, what kind of game is this?

Yes, call it a game. Just tell me about your life. A day in the life. What you did yesterday, today, what you'll do tomorrow. Even the boring stuff.

A silly game.

Humor me. You know how it is. You think you know someone, you take things for granted, you lose touch. So just talk to me.

What is there to tell? You know it all.

Pretend I don't. Pretend I'm a stranger. Let's start with the basics. How old are you?

Forty-five. Forty-six? At my age you don't count so carefully anymore.

Married, of course.

To you.

Right. And how are the children these days?

Well, I already told you about Mark.

The charming, intelligent, delightful one. Yes.

My daughter is another matter altogether. She was a gregarious, outgoing child. But she's closed down now. They say girls do. And that you get them back, eventually. But right now we're in the middle of the dark years.

It's a mother-daughter thing.

I suspect so.

I can promise you that it does work out.

You have psychic powers?

Something like that.

Well, that would be something to look forward to.

You say that so mournfully. Yet you have a very rich, very full life.

The forties are a hard decade for women. I'd be the first to admit it. Lost hair, lost bone density, lost fertility. The last gasp of a dying creature. I'm looking forward to getting on the other side. A rebirth.

That sounds like something Amanda would say.

It does, doesn't it? Well, we're close. You pick things up.

You were a formidable pair. When I was small, I thought all women were like you and Amanda. God help anyone who didn't treat me the way you thought I should be treated! Avenging angels.

She is one of a kind.

She was, indeed. He pauses. Did the detective ask about her?

What detective?

A woman here earlier this week. Did she ask about Amanda's enemies? Whether there was anyone that wished her harm?

Oh, lots of people did, I would imagine. How could they not? She is difficult. Like you just said, an avenging angel. That is her genius — spotting the carcass before it has begun to rot. She out-vultures the vultures.

A nice way to talk about your best friend.

She'd be the first to admit it. She senses weakness and goes in for the kill.

Whereas when you saw weakness you chose to heal.

I wouldn't say that's why I chose surgery. Not exactly.

Did you and she ever fight?

Once or twice. Almost breached our friendship. We would declare a truce almost immediately. The alternative was too horrifying to contemplate.

What would that horror have been, if a breach had occurred?

For me, loneliness. For her I can't guess.

It sounds like an alliance rather than a friendship. Like the treaties between heads of state, each with powerful armies.

Yes, it was a bit like that. Too bad she doesn't have children. We could have arranged marriages between our two houses.

Created a dynasty.

Exactly.

I have some other questions, but you look tired.

Perhaps. I had a long day of surgeries. One particularly difficult one. Not technically difficult. But it was a child with meningococcemia. We had to take off both his hands at the wrist.

I never did understand how you could do what you did.

279

The father was distraught. He kept asking, But what about the kitten? He loves the kitten. It turns out he wasn't worried about eating, writing, or playing the piano, but about the child losing the soft feel of fur against a certain part of the body. Trying to reassure him that other areas of the epidermis were equally sensitive to the feel of fur didn't do any good. We had to medicate him almost as much as his son.

Sometimes that's how you grieve. In the small ways. Sometimes those are the only ways open to you.

I wouldn't know.

Oh?

My losses have been minimal. Containable. Small enough that they don't need to be broken down any further to be processed. Except when I lost my parents, of course. My dear father. My exasperating mother. There I managed to compartmentalize, to shut off the particular horrors that way.

You're lucky, then.

I forgot your name.

Mark.

You look familiar.

Lots of people tell me that. I have that kind of face.

I think I am tired.

I'll go now, then.

Yes. Shut my door behind you, please.

The good-looking stranger nods, leans down to kiss me on the cheek, and leaves. Just a stranger. Then why do I miss him so much?

Wait! Get back here! I call. I command.

But no one comes.

When I have a clear day, when the walls of my world expand so that I can see a little ahead and a little behind me, I plot. I am not good at it. When watching the heist movies that James loves, I am impressed by the trickery the writers think up. My plots are simple: *Walk to the door. Wait until no*

one is looking. Open the door. Leave. Go home. Bar the front entrance against all comers.

Today I look at the photo I picked out. Labeled clearly: *Amanda, May 5, 2003.* My handwriting?

In the photo, Amanda is dressed simply but severely in a black blazer and pants. Her thick white hair is pulled back in a business-like bun. She has just come from a meeting, something official. The expression on her face is a mixture of triumph and bemusement. The memory tickles, then slowly returns.

I had heard a story about her, told to me by one of my colleagues at the hospital whose son attended a school in Amanda's district. One of many such stories that had been whispered over the years in the neighborhood. But this one was different, more extreme. It concerned an eighth-grade history teacher. A plausible rogue. Stocky and shorter even than some of the students, he nevertheless charmed. A thick mop of ragged black hair and dark eyes to match. Refined features and a low, thrilling voice with which he told delightful stories about authority subverted, injustices corrected, wrongs revenged. Even Fiona, as world-weary as she was at thirteen, had been enthralled when she was in his class.

Parents watched him carefully, especially around girls, but there was never a hint of impropriety. He always left his door open when with a student, never contacted one outside of school by phone or by e-mail. Never touched a student, not even a casual hand on the arm.

Why had Amanda disliked him so much? Perhaps only because he took the easy way out as a teacher, choosing popularity over her more rigorous and less appreciated pedagogical methods. And then, acting on an anonymous tip, the police raided his classroom, found pornography on the computer. A terrific scandal ensued, but the fact that it was a school computer, left mostly unattended in an unlocked room, made the police hesitate to prosecute. He still quit. My guess was that he couldn't bear his students looking at him as anything but a hero. But soon after he left, the rumors began. That he had been set up, that it had all been engineered. That someone powerful wanted him out. No one actually said

Amanda's name.

I asked her about it. I remember that day, the day of the photograph. She'd stopped by to say hello, was waiting in my vestibule to be asked in. I kept her waiting.

Did you have anything to do with Mr. Steven's ouster? I asked.

To my surprise, she looked uncomfortable. Extraordinary, really. There was a pause before she answered.

Do you believe I would do such a thing? she asked, finally.

That's not an answer.

There was another pause.

I don't think I'll give you one, she said. After all, whoever actually put the pornography on that computer would face federal charges. I think I'll take the fifth.

She started to smile, but then stopped. What are you doing? she asked.

Getting the camera.

Why?

To capture the expression on your face.

Again, why?

It's an unusual one. One I've never seen before. There. Done.

I'm not sure I'm pleased about this.

I'm not sure I care, I said. And now, if you don't mind, I've got some paperwork to do.

And I closed the door on her face — not something I had ever dared to do before. As I recall, we left it at that. We never referred to it again, as was our way. But I thought the interchange significant enough to print the photo and put it in my album. *Amanda, accused.* I might have added, *Jennifer, marginally victorious. For once.*

Dubuffet. Gorky. Rauschenberg. Our eclectic tastes in art amused the people around us. But James and I were always in absolute agreement. We'd see a print or lithograph and would know without even looking at each other that it must be ours.

It was an obsession that grew with our

285

means, became an addiction. And sometimes there was the pain of withdrawal. There was that Chagall we saw in a Paris gallery: *L'événement*. Love and death, love and religion. Our favorite themes. We talked about it for years, I even dreamed about it, became the bride in the chicken's belly, was seduced by the tunes played by the levitating fiddler, drifted in a glorious world of deep blues and warm reds. So far above us, yet like spoiled children, we longed for it.

They tried, of course, to conceive, Peter and Amanda. My guess is that no egg was tough enough to implant itself into her impenetrable womb. For she was hard through and through. *A tough old bird,* I overheard a neighbor say at a party. *A prize bitch,* was the response. But not always. No. There was how she treated Fiona. She took her role as Fiona's godmother seriously. Even though it started as a joke.

Fiona was never baptized, we had no intention of ever doing such a thing, heathens that we were. Yet the day after I brought Fiona home, and Amanda and Peter came over with a bottle of champagne, I announced that I wanted Amanda to be Fiona's godmother.

A fairy godmother? Peter had teased.

I dipped my fingers into my champagne glass and sprinkled some of the bubbles onto Fiona's tiny wrinkled red forehead. She awoke and let out a piteous wail.

Amanda was taken aback by these developments.

And what if my christening gift turns out to be a curse? She did an imitation. On your sixteenth birthday, you will prick your finger . . .

We all laughed. No, give her a real blessing, James urged.

Well then, Amanda said, and cleared her throat. Became solemn, to all of our surprise. Serious she was frequently; solemn, never.

Fiona Sarah White McLennan. You will inherit the many strengths of both your mothers, she said. Both your birth mother — she raised her glass to me — and your godmother. Here she toasted herself, took a sip. And you will have the love and support of both of us no matter what happens. Nothing except death can or will separate us from you. Never forget that.

For good measure, Amanda threw another sprinkle of champagne on Fiona.

And now comes one of those moments. A shift in perception, a wave of dizziness, and an awareness. It comes to me. What Fiona was going through. Amanda already gone. Me slipping away. Every day a little death. Fiona at three days old being told she could never separate, that she would always re-member. A curse indeed.

A red-haired woman sits opposite me. She knows me, she says. Her face is familiar. But no name. She tells me but it evaporates.

How are you? she asks.

Well, I don't tell many people this, I say, but my memory is shot.

Really? That's terrible.

Yes, it is, I say.

So I'm curious, the woman says. What do you

remember about me?

I look at her. I feel I should know her. But there is something wrong.

I'm Magdalena, she says. I changed my hair color. Just felt like it. But it's still me. She tugged at her hair. Now do you remember?

I try. I stare at her face. She has brown eyes. A young woman. Or youngish. Past child-bearing age, but not like me yet. A melancholy face. I shake my head.

Good, she says.

That surprises me. Pleasantly. Most people are distressed or get angry. Aggrieved.

I need an ear, the woman says. I want to say something, and then I want it to vanish. A kind of confession. But I don't want it in anyone's brain, even if they are sworn to secrecy. And I don't want a traditional confession, to do penance for it, because I've already finished with that. No one has suffered more for this than I have. And I don't even have to ask you not to tell it. That's the beauty of it all.

I have no objections. It is a sleepy heavy day. The kids are at school. I don't have any

289

surgeries scheduled. I nod to continue.

She takes a deep breath. I sold drugs. To kids. I took my grandchildren to the playground at the middle school. I sold lots of stuff. Pot, of course. But also Ecstasy, speed, even acid.

She stops and looks at me. No shock, she says. That's a good beginning.

She continues: Then, one day, one of my grandkids got into my stash. Swallowed some LSD. She was just three years old. Three! I didn't know what to do. I couldn't take her to the hospital. So I didn't. I just sat with her in a dark room and held her hand while she screamed. Screamed and screamed. Hours of it.

The red-haired woman covers her eyes with her hands. I am patient. I will hear this out.

She was calmer when my daughter came to pick her up, but not enough. My daughter was already suspicious. She knew I had been a user. She knew I had friends, still. And so that was the end. She didn't turn me in. It was close, but she didn't. She said I needed to get help, get off the stuff, and if I did she wouldn't report me. But she also wouldn't speak to me again. So I did it. Went to rehab. But despite that, lost my family anyway.

I don't say anything. At the clinic, strung-out teenagers are a dime a dozen. And occasionally we get children. Mostly children who had gotten into their parents' bottom drawers. Behind the socks or underwear. Occasionally one that had been given the stuff on purpose. I treated everyone, let the staff deal with the legal and moral issues, which didn't concern me.

But why tell me this? I ask.

I've needed someone to pass this on to. Someone who wouldn't be shocked and wouldn't wince at the stink of me. You've got a practical and resilient kind of morality. You forgive trespasses.

No, I say. I wouldn't call it forgiveness.

No? What is forgiveness but the ability to accept what someone has done and not hold it against them?

But to forgive, something has to touch you personally. This hasn't touched me. That's why I stopped believing in God. Who could worship someone that narcissistic, who takes everything anyone does as a personal affront?

You don't really believe that. I know you don't. She gestures toward the statue of Saint Rita. You have faith. I've seen it.

What is your name?

Magdalena. And do you remember what else I've told you?

I pretend to think, although I already know the answer. No, I say finally. I wait for the exclamations, the reminder, the subtext of blame. But it doesn't come. Instead, relief. No, something more. Release.

Thank you, she says, and takes her leave.

A man is in my room. Hyperactive. Hopped up on something. Eyes dilated, jittery, moving around too fast. Fingering my things, picking them up, and putting them back down again. My comb. The photo of the man and woman and boy and girl. He grimaces at the latter and puts it down again.

He is wearing black trousers, a pressed white and blue shirt, a tie. He does not look completely comfortable.

We were apparently in the middle of a conversation, but I have lost the thread.

And so I told her, it's time for a truce. No more squabbling. After all, we used to be so close. And she agreed. But with reservations, I could tell. Always so cautious. Always playing it safe.

What are you talking about? I ask. I see, with alarm, that he is tracing his finger around the edge of my Renoir, his fingers coming perilously close to the young woman's red hat.

Oh, never mind. Just babbling. Trying to keep the conversation going. So. You do your part. You tell me something. He's now opening and shutting the top drawer of my bureau, sliding it in and out, in and out.

Like what? His movements are making me dizzy. Now he is on the move again, flitting from one object to another, examining everything with great interest.

He seems especially fascinated by my paintings. He moves from the Renoir to the Calder, from the left side of the room to the right, and then to the center, where my Theotokos of the Three Hands glows from its place above the door frame.

There is some connection here, something that tickles about this man and this particular piece. History.

Tell me what you did today. He sits down briefly on the chair next to my bed, then quickly stands up again, continues pacing.

I can more easily tell you about what happened fifty years ago, I say. I struggle out of my bed, holding on to the rails for support. Wrapping my gown around me in some semblance of modesty, I sit myself in the chair he has vacated.

So tell me. Something I don't know.

And who are you again?

Mark. Your son. Your favorite son.

My favorite?

That was just a joke. Not a lot of competition for that honor.

You do remind me of someone I know.

Glad to hear it.

A boy living in the graduate dorm at Northwestern. Dark like you. Restless like you.

The man stops. I have his attention. Tell me more about him, he says.

Not much to tell, really. A bit of a ladies' man. More than a little of a pest. Always knocking on my door, trying to entice me to put down my books and come out to play.

Which I am sure you would not do. This was when you were in medical school?

No. Before that. When I still wanted to be a medieval historian. I smiled at my words, so implausible.

What changed your mind? The man has settled down, is leaning against the door frame, his fingers drumming against his chest.

My thesis. The conflict in the medieval medical community between applying traditional folkloric remedies and following the precepts found in Avicenna's *Canon of Medicine.*

Whew. Glad I asked.

I had a double undergraduate degree in history and biology. My thesis was a way of combining both my passions. But I fell in love with the *Canon.* I spent more and more time at the medical school, interviewing professors and students, observing. The dissections especially captivated me. I wanted a scalpel so badly. One of the students noticed. He allowed me to shadow him, took me down into the lab after hours, showed me the procedures he was learning, put the knife in my hand, and guided my first incisions.

Dr. Tsien?

Yes. Carl.

Is that how you met? I never knew.

My first mentor.

I've always wanted to know, was there anything between you? Anything romantic, I mean?

No, never. He just recognized a fellow addict. He was the first person I told that I was quitting the PhD program to apply for medical school. My biggest supporter when I chose orthopedic surgery. The medical establishment was not exactly friendly to the idea of a woman in that role.

And what about that guy, that party animal in your dorm? The man is smiling wryly.

Oh. Yes. Him. Another unexpected detour. My life was full of surprises around then. By that I mean I surprised myself. So many about-faces. So many disruptions of well-laid plans.

You and Dad didn't talk much about your early years. I got the impression that both of you spent them in a bit of a daze. Him in law school, you beginning medical school. And by all accounts completely besotted with each other. Dr. Tsien spoke about it sometimes, with a bit of envy, I always thought.

Yes. It was that.

You don't seem inclined to talk about it. Neither was Dad.

I'd rather not.

Because . . . ?

Because some things shouldn't be scrutinized too closely. Some mysteries are only rendered, not solved. We found each other.

And never regretted it the way others do their own youthful couplings.

The young man is picking up his soft leather satchel, leaning over me, brushing my cheek with his lips.

Bye, Mom. I'll see you next week. Probably Tuesday, if work allows.

Yes, definitely a familiar face, one resonating on numerous levels. Later, after dinner, I finally get a name to attach to the face. *James!* I say, startling the Vietnam vet so that he spills his water into his bread pudding.

It is somewhat later that I realize my icon is missing. I keep my own counsel, for now.

They are telling me something, pointing to their heads. Pointing to my head. Tugging at my hair. I push their hands away.

The hairdresser. The hairdresser is here. It is your turn.

What is a hairdresser, I say.

Just come on, you'll look and feel so much better!

I allow myself to be pulled to my feet, guided step-by-step down the hall, passing stuffed armchairs positioned strategically in little groups, as if conversing with one another. Tables laden with fresh flowers. What kind of place is this.

We enter a large room with shiny tile floors. Along one wall, tall cupboards containing plastic bins filled with yarns, colored paper, markers. A long counter along the opposite wall with a sink in the middle. Tables and chairs have been pushed to one side, and a clear plastic tarp has been laid out on the floor, a single molded plastic chair on the middle of it. A woman dressed in white, standing by.

Would you like to wash your hair before your cut? she asks, then answers herself. Yes, I see that would be a good idea.

I am turned around, and propelled gently but firmly over to the sink, and bent over. My hair and neck are ignominiously scrubbed, rinsed, then scrubbed and rinsed again. Led back and pushed into the chair, where the woman tugs a comb through my hair.

And what shall we do today? Another woman's voice breaks in. Short, I think. Very short. We're having some problems with grooming.

The woman in white agrees cheerfully. Very well! Short it is!

I try to protest. I've always been complimented on my hair, its thickness, color. James calls me "Red" when he's feeling especially affectionate. No, I say, but no one responds. I feel the pressure and coldness of steel against my scalp, hear the clip clip clip of the shears. Shorn like a sheep.

Other people are gathering around, looking. She looks like a man, one woman says loudly and is shushed. I wonder about that. Man. Woman. Man. Woman. The words have no meaning. Which one am I really?

I look down at my body. It is thin and spare. Androgynous. Sunken chest, chicken legs, I can see the femoral condyles and patellas through the material of my slacks. My malleoli without socks translucent and delicate, ready to snap if I put too much weight on them.

You look beautiful, says the woman doing the cutting. Like Joan of Arc. She holds up a hand mirror. See. Much better.

I don't recognize the face. Gaunt, with too-prominent cheekbones and eyes a little too large, too otherworldly. The pupils dilated. As if used to seeing strange visions. And then, a secret satisfied smile. As if welcoming them.

Something is worrying at my ankles. A small furry thing. Dog. This is Dog. What is that joke. About the dyslexic atheist insomniac. I have turned into that joke.

I have managed not to swallow my pills this morning, so I am alert. Alive. Before depositing them under my mattress, I examine them. Two hundred milligrams of Wellbutrin. One hundred fifty milligrams of Seroquel. Hydrochlorothiazide, a diuretic. And one I do not recognize, oblong and pale beige. I make a point of crushing that one between my fingers and letting the dust fall onto the rug.

I do three laps around the great room,

301

deliberately ignoring the brown line. I step over it, around it, never on it. *Step on a crack.* Around and around. I count the doors. One. Two. Three. Four. Only twenty in total, and four are unoccupied.

On my third pass I pause at the heavy metal doors at the far end of the long hallway. I can feel hot air wafting in through the crack, see the relentless sunshine beating onto the cement walkway outside through the small, thick windows. I remember those Chicago summers, heavy, oppressive, and stultifying, keeping you a prisoner in your house and your office as much as the bitter winters did.

James and I talked about escaping when we retired. Fantasized about a Mediterranean climate. Moderate temperatures, somewhere near the sea. Northern California. San Francisco. Or farther down the coast, Santa Cruz, San Luis Obispo. Lotus land. Or perhaps even the Mediterranean itself. James and I spent a month on the island of Mallorca after Fiona left for college. To forestall the empty nest blues that never came.

After that, there was idle talk of an

eighteenth-century finca with a large garden. Growing our own tomatoes, peppers, beans. Living off the land. Solar panels on the roof, our own well. Out of sight. Our own desert island. Who were we fooling? We were going off the grid in any case, each in our own way.

A hand touches my elbow.

Hey, young lady! A man's voice. He has a pleasant enough smile, but his face is marred by an eggplant-colored hemangioma in his right upper quadrant. Inoperable.

I am finishing up my lunch when someone pulls out the chair next to mine, sits down heavily. A face I recognize, but I am in a stubborn frame of mind today. I will not ask. I will not. This woman seems to understand that.

Detective Luton, she says. Just here for a short visit.

I am not going to make it easy for her. So I take my napkin off my lap, fold it, and place it across my empty plate. Push my chair back to rise.

No, wait. I won't be here very long. Just sit with me for a moment. A young man in scrubs approaches, offers her the coffeepot, and she nods. He puts a cup in front of her and pours. She raises it to her lips and gulps it, neat, as if it were water.

I was on my way somewhere. My annual pilgrimage. And suddenly found myself driving here. One of those urges. I used to have more of them. I used to be more spontaneous. Here she smiles. One of the hazards of growing older.

I nod. I don't understand, but my impatience is ebbing. This is someone in pain. A state I can recognize.

So how are you doing today? the woman asks.

We seem to have taken a step backward, I say. From words that mattered to socially appropriate but meaningless questions.

Instead of appearing upset by my rudeness, the woman looks pleased.

In good form, I see. Glad to see that.

So why are you here? I ask.

304

As I said, I was on a pilgrimage. I guess you could say this is part of it.

In what way?

I was on my way to the cemetery.

Anyone I knew?

No, not at all. You and I aren't connected in that way. Our relationship is a . . . professional one. She motions for more coffee. Well, mostly.

Are you my doctor?

No, no. A member of the police. An investigator.

She stares at her hands, pressed tightly against her coffee cup. Seconds tick by. I find I am now curious rather than annoyed or impatient. So I wait.

She finally speaks, slowly.

My life partner had Alzheimer's. Early onset. She was a lot younger than you — only forty-five.

I am having trouble following her now. But

I sense the emotion and nod.

People think it's just forgetting your keys, she says. Or the words for things. But there are the personality changes. The mood swings. The hostility and even violence. Even from the gentlest person in the world. You lose the person you love. And you are left with the shell.

She stops and pauses. Do you know what I'm talking about?

I nod. My mother.

The woman nods back. And you are expected to go on loving them even when they are no longer there. You are supposed to be loyal. It's not that other people expect it. It's that you expect it of yourself. And you long for it to be over soon.

She reaches over and takes hold of my wrist, gently raises my arm into the air a little. It is a sorry spectacle, no muscle tone, as thin and desiccated as a chicken's leg. We both gaze at it for a moment, then, just as gently, she lowers it down into my lap again.

It broke my heart, she says. And, somehow, you're breaking it again. Another pause.

Then, as suddenly as she had arrived, she is gone.

A dark night. Figures emerging and diverging from shadows, moving just out of my range of vision. A very dark night and I need to get up, to *move,* but I am restrained, my arms and legs tied down tightly to the bed.

I retreat into myself. I use all my will to get myself away from here to somewhere else. A dial spins in my head and I hold my breath and wait for what might happen. The pleasures and risks of a time traveler.

And so I find myself walking in the door to my house, greeted by the shrieks of a young infant in pain. I know immediately when and where I am. I am a mother for the second time. I am forty-one, she is one month old. She has been crying for half her life. Every day from 3 PM until midnight. Colic. The unexplainable screaming of a young child. The Chinese call it one hundred days of crying, and I have eighty-five days left.

A particularly bad case, the pediatrician

says. The noise assaults me every night after a long day of surgeries. When I come home, the nanny, Ana, hands me the child and literally runs from the room. James and Mark are already hiding behind closed doors.

I am marking my calendar, as I did before my first child was born. We've tried all the latest drugs and theories of modern medicine. I have cut out dairy and wheat from my diet, filled her bottle with catnip and ginger teas, dissolved Hyland's colic tablets in milk pumped from my breasts. But nothing has worked, nothing eases her and our pain.

To save my family, every night I put the baby in the car seat and drive. I stop for gas, for a cup of coffee, and when I enter the convenience store or the café with my wailing bundle, all conversation ceases, and I am hustled to the front of the line.

Tonight is typical. I pack a thermos of coffee, put the baby in the car, and head out. I prefer the expressways, the long thin ribbons of concrete that stretch out in all directions except east, turning Chicago into a great spider.

I take the Fullerton ramp onto the Kennedy heading north, past Diversey, past Irving Park, past the Edens split and north to O'Hare. All the while the baby screeches, taking no noticeable breaths.

The noise. The noise. Sometimes we park at O'Hare and walk among the crowds there, moving in our own little bubble, everyone on their way to parts unknown, rushing a little faster now because of us.

But this night we continue north of O'Hare, proceed northwest through Arlington Heights and Rolling Meadows and farther until we hit country. The numbing ugly flatness of the Illinois landscape that I've never quite adjusted to.

The baby has not stopped her wailing. It is only 9:30 PM. Two and a half hours to go. All moisture has long ago been expelled from her tear ducts, and she's now into the dry heaves, her little motor revved to high. It will not stop until the clock strikes midnight. When the world turns right side up again.

Then, up ahead, flashing lights, a crowd of people. An accident. It looks serious. I stop, put the baby into a pouch that I buckle around my neck and waist, and go to investigate.

People scatter as I approach, Fiona's cry as painful as any siren. Above her and the expressway noise, I shout, I am a doctor! How can I help? A motorcyclist is down, a compound fracture of his leg, the bone protruding, his face as white as the bone, his eyes closed against the pain.

I stoop down, the weight of the baby making me sway a little off balance. Everyone moves away from us, even the paramedics retreat. I examine the young man, who by now is barely conscious. An open femoral shaft fracture, he will need antibiotics, an irrigation and debridement, and an intramedullary rod.

I probe his other limbs: arms and other leg, all is well, but he is growing paler. His breath is coming quicker, he is clearly distressed, he is going into shock, and so I turn to the paramedics and say, Get him to the nearest trauma center, but first administer ten milligrams of IV morphine sulfate to help control the pain.

All the while the baby continues to wail, and everyone is moving farther and farther away from us except the prone motorcyclist who manages to sort of gesture with his hands.

One of the EMS technicians seems to understand this and shouts something to me that I cannot catch because at that moment the baby emits a particularly loud burst of misery. The technician opens his mouth again, shuts it, cups his hands around his lips, and forces out words.

You've been very helpful, he begins. He takes one step toward me, hesitates, and then retreats two. But now could you do us all a favor? Absolutely! I shout back. What do you need? He hesitates a moment. We're very appreciative! he yells, and takes a deep breath. But would you please please just leave?

I turn to go but cannot move and suddenly I am back in the softness of my bed, the straps hard around my legs and arms. A small warm body is still next to me, but it is silent and furry and odorous. Dog. The silence is welcome. But I wonder. How long do I have? How long before things come full circle and I descend to that state of inarticulate rage and suffering, the state Fiona started her life in? Not long. Not long now. I open my mouth and begin.

I like tactile things. A carved wooden candlestick, from a beautiful grain, I guess mahogany. A string of prayer beads with the Turkish evil eye hanging off as a pendant. A porcelain teacup patterned in royal blue curlicues.

And there is a scarf. A plain cream-colored woolen scarf. But long. Long enough to reach from the head of my bed to the foot. Perfect for wrapping around my head and lower face to protect against the Chicago winter.

I remember winters. Once we lost heat for a week and the water in the toilet bowl froze. We had to move out. James insisted on the Ambassador East. It was a frivolous choice, as the children were still young and the luxury was wasted on us. We all slept in one bed, the baby crawling among us, her breath tickling our cheeks. That golden time! James let Mark shave, smeared menthol shaving cream all over his six-year-old face, carefully pulled the razor across his fuzzy cheeks. I painted the baby's toenails a bright magenta. We ate at the Pump Room every night, the kitchen made macaroni and cheese for the kids, and James and I ate lobster risotto and veal chops, and eggs Benedict in the mornings. The tangy half-cooked yolks, the creamy hollandaise, the asparagus that delicately scented our urine for days. Ana would show up as breakfast was ending so James and I could go to work. I'd put on layers of clothing and that woolen Irish scarf, and head off to the hospital.

All this evoked by a simple article of winter clothing. Something I won't need again. For winter doesn't exist here. No seasons at all. No heat. No cold. They've even banished darkness. They said, *Let there be light,* and there is, perpetually. A temperate climate for intemperate people.

There is a young man interested in me. A teacher crush. How we used to laugh when it happened, we women. For the men, it is no laughing matter, however. They are tempted. They fall. It is a serious thing. But for us, amusement only.

Yet this one. The way he watches me. And he is beautiful. Does that matter? Yes. He comes to my office after lectures on various pretexts. Once he pretended not to understand the basics of tendon transfer surgery. Another time he asked me about skin grafting, that most basic procedure.

Once he posed a riddle and I answered it, not realizing he was joking. What do you say when someone tells you, Doctor, it hurts when I do this? I absentmindedly replied, Tell them not to do it. He laughed and I looked at him for the first time.

It makes you feel *young*. It makes you feel *old*. You feel *powerful*. You are vulnerable.

It was none of those things. I felt no guilt. I felt no shame. And not because of James's own behavior. I simply wanted to take it as far as it could go, to run it into the ground. This was a new experience.

For the most part you leave doors open. Bridges unburned. You don't accept hopeless cases. You make sure to have an exit strategy. There was none in this case.

Hello, old friend.

A balding man, Asian American, with a strong Bronx accent, is standing by my chair. He is smiling familiarly at me. That is, he is smiling as if he expects to be familiar to me. He is not.

Do I know you?

I say this coldly. No more pretense. No more smiles for strangers.

Carl. Carl Tsien. We were colleagues. At Quicken St. Matthews Medical Center. I was Internal Medicine, you were Orthopedics.

That sounds plausible, I say.

Ah, you're being cautious. Not committing yourself. He smiles as if he has just said something witty.

So, you say we were colleagues? I ask.

Yes.

Why were?

I am testing him, not just for knowledge but for truthfulness. Trustworthiness. He hesitates for a moment, then speaks.

You retired.

A nice euphemism.

Yes. To his credit, he looks a little chagrined. Well, that's what you called it at the time. So you're aware of your disease?

On good days like this, yes, I am completely

aware of how far I've sunk.

Is my face at all familiar?

No. And I can't tell you how boring it is to get asked that all the time.

Then you won't hear it from me again, old friend.

Glad to hear that, stranger. So, why are you here?

He again looks uncomfortable. Shifts a little in his chair.

As an . . . emissary. From Mark. And as I look enquiringly at him, Your son, he says.

I have no son.

I know you're angry with him. But let me make a case on his behalf.

You don't understand. I have no recollection of any son. And I'm not inclined to play along. I used to, you know. Nod and pretend. No more.

He is silent.

Well, let's talk hypothetically. Say you did have

316

a son. And say that he had gotten himself into a bad situation. Made some mistakes. And imposed on you — or tried to.

Imposed in what way?

Borrowed money, repeatedly. Asked for more. Hassled your friends, as well. Even stolen, for example, your icon. He got a substantial sum for that.

I'd say, To hell with him.

Yes, but suppose he's cleaned up his act. And wants to reconcile.

I'd want to know why.

Well, you're his mother. Isn't that enough?

Since I don't know him, I don't know why it would matter one way or another to him.

It's just the idea of it. And the fact that he can't get through to you. Either you're furious at him, or you don't remember him. Either way, he's lost his mother.

How old is he?

Maybe twenty-nine, thirty.

317

In other words, old enough to survive without a mother.

That's the person who doesn't know she has a son talking.

In other words, a rational person. I've noticed that people with children do irrational things. Anything to protect their young.

As you have.

How is that?

It means that you yourself have protected your young on occasion. Even beyond what a rational person would do.

And how would you know that?

Jennifer, we've known each other for nearly forty years. Longer than most marriages survive. There's little I don't know about you. What you've done. Or what you're capable of doing.

Sounds tedious. Like most marriages. Once you know everything there is to know about someone, it's usually time to move on.

Well, there is affection.

Perhaps.

And that irrational thing that's even stronger. Love. People do strange things in the name of love.

What exactly are we talking about here? We seem to have strayed from the subject.

Back to the subject, then. Will you forgive Mark, your hypothetical son? Under the circumstances I just described?

I give it some thought, try to conjure up an emotion beyond bemusement at being asked to forgive and forget when I've already forgotten.

No, I say, finally. You can ask me again when I know who we're talking about.

But that may not happen. As you yourself said, today is a good day.

No, it may not happen.

At the very least, can you not do anything that will harm him in any way?

That implies I have power over him.

You do. More than you know at this moment.

319

As I'm unlikely to remember this conversation either, what's the point?

Sometimes things stick. Promise?

Hypothetically I promise not to harm this person I don't remember. *Do no harm.* If you're really a doctor, you took that oath, too. So this is an easy promise to make.

A vision. My young mother, sporting a Peter Pan–like haircut. She who always wore her dark hair long, pulled back in a ponytail during the day, loose and flowing and beautiful at night, even throughout her long decline.

She has her hands cupped around something precious. She is not wearing her wedding ring. Perhaps she is not even old enough to be married yet, although she met and married my father when she was eighteen. He was twenty-seven, and both sets of parents complained but were powerless to stop them.

But this image is so much more vivid than anything in my present life. The colors vibrant, my mother's rich chestnut hair, her milky clear complexion, the white softness of the skin on her arms, shoulders. I feel so calm looking at her. Hopeful. As if she held my future in her girlish hands and that the smile on her face was an assurance that my story would have a happy ending after all.

Never felt guilt. Never felt shame. Until I was brought to this place. Trussed like a chicken. Denied the right to move my bowels in private. *Purgatory* I heard one of the other residents call it. But no. That implies that heaven is within reach once you have paid for your sins. I suspect this is a station on the one-way road to hell.

I was fifteen, spotted with acne and smitten with Randy Busch. I was a young mother with an ever-present child at my side — Mark clung tenaciously to me until he was ten — and then I was an older pregnant woman being tested to ensure I wasn't carrying a mutant. I was a reluctant host, during that pregnancy. I pushed Fiona out and went to sleep. I had to be nudged to take her to my breast. I simply endured those first six months, the colic, the sleepless nights, those months so critical to bonding.

I went back to surgeries within two weeks. A cold vessel indeed. But somehow attachment grew. Fiona hated our nanny, Ana, so beloved by Mark, by us all. It was only me she cried for, when I left and when I returned. And so reluctantly I took her on.

Someone came in this morning and brought photographs. Lovely full-color photographs. I sit in the great room and study them.

One woman sidles over, then screams. Others come over. Others recoil. My lovely lovely pictures. One shows the excising of a tumor in the olecranon fossa. Another, a hand reattachment. I feel the twinge of muscle memory. Contrary to what people might think, the knife is not cold, the blood on latex gloves is not warm. The gloves separate you from the heat of the human body.

From the moment I opened up the arm of a cadaver and saw the tendons, the nerves, the ligaments, and the carpal bones of the wrist, I was in love. Not for me the heart, the lungs, or the esophagus — let others play in those sandboxes. I want the hands, the fingers, the parts that connect us to the things of this world.

The straps are too tight around my legs. I can move my arms an inch perhaps. My head from side to side. There is an IV in my arm. A bitter metallic taste in my mouth.

Someone is sitting at my bedside. It is dark. Through the blinds a dull gleam illuminates the lower part of her face. She has the mouth of a ghoul, thin-lipped and grotesquely long. If she opened it she could swallow the world. What is this. She is taking my hand. No. She is raising it. No. Help me. She will bite into a vein, she will suck out what remains of my life.

Stop. Please stop. They will come if you don't stop, the ghoul says.

She is placing something in my hand, closing my fingers around it.

What is this. A holy relic. Did they give this to you. Why am I being so honored.

It is a plastic bag containing a small metal

disk, engraved. I can feel the protrusions. On a long chain. The bag is cold against my palm. I shake my head. I continue shaking it. The movement feels good.

Do you know your name?

I strain against what binds me. I do not answer.

Dr. White. Jennifer. Do you know where you are?

I do, but it is in pictures. No words. I am on a porch, sitting on the top step. A brisk morning in late October. The trees are golden. There is a line of pumpkins on the porch gazing at the world with horrified expressions. A daddy pumpkin, a mommy pumpkin, and a baby pumpkin. All agape at some terrible vision. That was my idea.

I am sixteen. There is a young man coming. I am ready. My dress is short, cut square, boldly colored with blue and red geometric shapes. My boots reach just below my knees. The step is rough against my bare thighs. These boots are made for walking. Any moment now, he will be here. I am quivering with excitement.

Dr. White?

The young man will come. I am beloved.

Dr. White, this is important. That medallion. It tested positive for type AB blood. Amanda O'Toole's blood type.

We will be charging you with first-degree murder. You will go through a mental competency examination, plead not guilty for reason of insanity, and that will be it. But I'm not happy. Because I don't understand. And I like understanding.

Amanda.

That's right, Amanda. Why did she die?

Amanda, she knew.

Knew what?

She never dyed her hair. Never wore a scrap of makeup. But vain, regardless.

Vain about what?

A seducer. Not for sex. Secrets. She knew everything. I never figured out how. A dangerous woman.

Yes, I can see that. I can indeed. Would you like some water? Here let me pour you some — and here is a straw so you can drink. That's right. Don't strain, I'll hold it.

I am . . .

Yes?

Frightened.

Yes.

What will happen next?

You will be examined. Declared mentally incompetent to stand trial. The judge will dismiss the case on the condition that you are committed to a state facility. Where you will likely end your days.

What are the alternatives?

Her face is becoming clearer. Not a ghoul at all. A plain, doglike face. A face you can count on.

Untie me?

I believe I will. I believe you are calm enough. Here — and I feel the pressure around my arms, then legs, slacken. I pull myself up to a sitting position in the bed, drink some more water. Feel the blood start flowing back into me.

Yes. My illness is getting worse.

And it will get worse still.

The woman is silent for a moment. Then, I want to know why Amanda died, she says.

I believe I could. Kill. There is that in me.

Yes. There is that in many people. I have a recurring dream that I have killed my sister. I am overcome by shame. And afraid. Not of the punishment. Of having people know what I really am. I think that's why I became a cop. As if the trappings of good would keep me safe from that nightmare.

I pause and try to clear the thickness from my throat. It is hard to talk.

The knife in my hand always felt right. The first incision, to get inside the body, that playground beneath the flesh. But those guidelines. To know what is acceptable. Stay within parameters.

The woman stands up, stretches, sits down again.

Jennifer. I want you to help me.

How?

You know something. I want you to try. She takes the plastic bag away from me, holds it up. Do you recognize this? A Saint Christopher's medal. With your initials engraved on the back. Can you think of any reason Amanda's blood would be on that medal?

No.

Did you wear the medal?

Sometimes. As a reminder. A talisman.

And do you have any ideas about who killed Amanda?

I have ideas.

The woman leaned forward.

Are you protecting anyone? Jennifer, look at me.

No. No. It's better this way.

The woman opens her mouth to talk, then looks hard at my face. What she sees there convinces her of something. She lays her hand on mine before she leaves.

I am sitting in the great room. Although there are clusters of other residents in the vicinity, I am alone. I want to be left alone. I have much to think about. Much to plan.

The door to the outside world buzzes, and a woman enters. Tall, brown hair cut smartly to her jawbone, carrying a suitcase made of buttery leather. She comes straight over to me, holds out her hand to be shaken. Jennifer, she says.

Do I know you? I ask.

I'm your attorney, she says.

Is this about our wills? I ask. James and I just redid them. They're in the safe-deposit box.

No, she says. This is not about your will. Can we move over here? Good. Let me help you. Much better.

Dog trots over, settles himself at my feet.

How cute. Look how he loves you. She makes herself comfortable in her seat, sets her briefcase on her lap, and opens it up. This is not a happy visit, I'm afraid. It's about your being a so-called person of interest to the police in an investigation. I have some bad news. The DA's office has decided to charge you. In one sense, this is just a formality. You will be examined, be found mentally incompetent.

None of this makes sense, but her face is serious, so I make mine serious too.

The bad news is you won't be able to stay here after that. You'll be committed to a state hospital. I'm trying to get you into Eglin Mental Health Center here in the city. But the DA is pushing for the Retesch facility downstate, which is substantially more restrictive.

She stops, looks at me. I don't believe much of this is getting in.

She sighs, then continues: I'd hoped you'd be in good enough shape today. To understand. Legally, your son has power of attorney. But I prefer to get my clients to sign, as well. Here. Here's a pen.

She puts something in my hand, guides it

to a piece of paper, and touches its surface.

You're petitioning for acquittal for reasons of mental incompetence. The DA is not going to fight it. As I said, the only point of contention is where you'll be sent. I'm sorry.

Her face is mobile, expressive. Makeup expertly applied. I always wondered how to do that. I never bother myself — it rubs off, streaks my surgical mask, my glasses during surgery.

The woman is now telling me something else that I can't follow. She sighs, pats Dog absentmindedly. I'm sorry, she says again.

She gives the appearance of waiting, perhaps for a response from me. That she considers her words bad news there is no doubt. But I have no intention of letting them touch me.

We sit like that for several minutes. Then she slowly puts papers back in her briefcase and snaps it shut. It's been a pleasure working for you, she says, and then she is gone. I try to remember what I have been told. I am a person of interest. Of course I am. I am.

◇ ◇ ◇

I am cunning. I get rid of Dog. I do this by kicking him in front of one of the aides. Then I pick him up and make as if to throw him against the wall. Shouts ensue. Dog is taken from me, forcibly. Taken off the ward at night, forbidden to come into my room. I miss him. But he would ruin my plans.

Mom?

I turn to see my handsome son, aged considerably but still recognizable. Someone visited this morning, a stranger to me, left abruptly when I didn't recognize her. When I wouldn't play along. A brash, unreasonable woman.

How were your exams? I ask.

My what? O, yes, they were good. They went well.

I'm not your professor. You don't have to be afraid I'll flunk you.

I'm a little . . . nervous . . . when I visit. I never know how you'll greet me.

You're my son.

Mark.

Yes.

Do you remember my last visit?

You've never come to see me here. No one
has.

Mom, that's not true. Fiona comes several
times a week. I come at least once. But last
time you told me you never wanted to see me
again.

I would never say that. Never. No matter
what you'd done. What have you done?

Never mind that now. I'm glad it's forgotten.
You weren't exactly . . . sympathetic. But all is
well now.

Tell me.

No. Let's move on. Glad to see you're in good
form today. I wanted to ask if you remembered
something.

Remember what?

Something that happened when I was around
seventeen. Certainly older than sixteen,

because I was driving. I'd borrowed your car to take my girlfriend out to the movies. Remember Deborah? You never liked her. You never really liked any of the girls I dated, but Deborah, my girlfriend throughout high school, you really hated. Anyway, you had a bunch of boxes filled with stuff. Deborah began rooting around in them. Just curious, or maybe it was a malicious kind of curious, because when she found it she was positively gleeful. A plastic flowered pouch filled with what Deborah said was very expensive makeup.

Makeup? Among my things? Seems unlikely, I say.

Well, I don't know the names of all of it, but I did recognize mascara, lipstick, a powder compact. Various brushes. Deborah said it was all well used. She showed me a tube of magenta lipstick, half worn down. I nearly swerved off the road. I'd never seen you wear any makeup. Not a scrap. And yet here was this tube of magenta lipstick.

Magenta is for people with no taste. I would have been, what, fifty at that time? This is sounding increasingly implausible, I say.

Yes, I thought so. It totally disconcerted me. Like finding Dad prancing around in one of your dresses. I realized you had secrets. That there was this side of you that none of us knew about. Where you wore mascara and magenta lipstick and needed to please in that way — a desire we'd never have attributed to you.

Oh. Yes.

Now you're remembering.

Yes, I say, and am silent. There was only one time I tried to please in that particular way.

Well?

How old were you?

Like I said, probably seventeen.

Yes. That was around the time I shifted offices — they built the new facilities on Racine and I cleaned out my filing cabinets, my desk, threw everything in boxes and into my car. Probably all sorts of odd things in there from previous lives.

Is that all you're going to say?

Yes, I think so. Just history. Prehistory, as far as you are concerned. Nothing to be said about that. Now I've come up with something. My turn. I'm also going back to around that time. When you were seventeen. Same girlfriend. Deborah. The peddler's daughter.

Yes, that was your charming name for her. Because her father owned a gourmet cookware distributorship. And I know exactly what you are going to say.

No, I don't think so.

You caught us. In flagrante delicto.

Well, it would have been hard not to! Right in the middle of the living room, clothes everywhere, the noise! But that wasn't what was important. What interested me was that when you heard my footsteps, you turned around, almost as if expecting me. You had a look of intense satisfaction on your face that quickly changed to disappointment, before the more expected embarrassment.

Your point being?

You'd hoped for a different witness. My guess is your father.

Now why would I want that?

I don't know. Something happened between you around that time. Something after you'd interned for him when you turned sixteen, just before your senior year. You were so close until then. Then, trouble. You came home from work together one night that summer not speaking. And it lasted for years.

I'd rather not talk about it.

Even now?

Even now.

If it had something to do with a woman, you don't have to worry about telling me. I knew it all. It didn't change anything between your father and me.

Well, maybe you weren't the only one affected.

What's that supposed to mean? Who could it matter to but me?

There were two other members of our family. Two other people who were betrayed.

No, honestly. Why would it matter to you? He was still your father. There was no

337

betrayal there.

No, not there.

Stop being so mysterious.

Oh, come on, Mom. Even you had to admit that the peddler's daughter was pretty hot. Did you think Dad wouldn't notice? And once he noticed, what he would try to do?

So he made a pass at your girlfriend. He made passes at everyone.

Forget it.

Or is the problem that he succeeded?

I said, forget it. I should have known better than to try to have a conversation with you. I'm actually sorry you won't remember this one. Because I want it to stick.

How angry you are. You seemed to come here in a conciliatory frame of mind. And now you're burning bridges?

They'll be rebuilt. And reburned. The never-ending cycle.

Just be careful.

Why? Because you might just remember this time?

Yes. At some level, I believe you do remember these things.

He gets up and dusts something off his pants. His face changes, grows crafty. His voice is now quieter and more measured.

I think you do remember. Fiona does, too. Like what happened to Amanda.

I don't answer.

You do know, right now, don't you? That she is dead?

I nod.

He lowers his voice, comes even closer. Almost touching.

And do you know more than that? What do you remember?

Get out, I say.

Tell me, he says. He is so close I can feel the warmth of his body.

I said, get out.

339

No. Not until you tell me.

I reach for the red button above my bed. He sees what I am fumbling for and his hand shoots out, grabs my wrist.

No, he says. You're going to deal with this.

I struggle to free myself, but his grip is strong. I give a sudden twist to my hand, free it, and slam the button. He gives a little shout of anger and grabs my wrist again, holds it against his hip. It hurts.

You know you're guilty, right? You know there's no way out. A confession won't do any good at this point. It won't do anyone any good.

We hear running outside the room. He releases my wrist, stands back.

Out, I say.

Good-bye then, he says. And he's gone.

My door is closed, but I am not alone. Although it is dim, I can see a shape flitting around the room. Dancing, even. As my eyes grow accustomed to the light, I can see that it's a young girl, thin, with spiky auburn hair, bending and shimmying, barely avoiding the furniture. Her arms are raised above her head, and her fingers are wiggling. She is clearly in high spirits. Manic, I would even say. But not a healthy state. Someone agitated beyond her ability to control it.

Hello? I ask.

She stops twirling and is suddenly at my bedside. She takes one of my hands but remains standing despite the chair next to her.

Mom! Oh Mom, you're awake! She stops and looks at my face. Mom, it's Fiona. Your . . . oh, never mind. I stopped by to say hi. Her words come out staccato — even now she can barely control her limbs, she is in such a state, waving and gesturing as she speaks. I'm sorry I haven't been here this week — it's been midterms. But now I have some time off. And I'm going to take a little break. Only a week, then classes start again. But I'm flying out this afternoon. Five days in paradise! Don't worry, I'll be in touch. I know you don't talk on the phone anymore, but I'll check in with Laura twice a day. And Dr. Tsien has agreed to keep an eye on you while I'm gone.

She is trying to keep a somber face as she tells me this, but the edges of her lips keep tugging up. Still, I would diagnose her state as one of fevered, rather than healthy, excitement.

I believe I should call in a consult, I say. I'm concerned. But your condition is not in my area of expertise.

The young woman gives off a little shriek of laughter. Borderline hysterical.

Oh, Mom, she says. Always the clinician.

Then she takes a breath, runs her hands down the sides of her body, smoothes out her dress. She sits down next to me.

I'm sorry, she says. It's a combination of excitement and relief. Some time off to enjoy the fruits of my labors, which as you know I very rarely take. But it hit me yesterday: Why not? And so I booked a trip to the Bahamas. You and Dad took us to New Providence a couple of times, remember? I'm not going back there. I've been doing a little too much revisiting of the past. And the future is so grim. You. Mark on the verge of going under. I don't want to think about these things. So it's five days of now. Which is something you should understand.

I'm having trouble holding on to her words. Her face is slipping away.

Yes, just go back to sleep. It's late. I didn't mean to wake you, just wanted to say good-bye. And it's only a few days. I'll be back next Wednesday and will come by Thursday. They have my contact info here.

She gets up to go, still electric with energy.

Bye, Mom. I'll see you again before you even realize I'm gone. She gives a little snort of laughter as she says it, and then the door bangs and my room is empty.

I need to get to the hospital. I was paged. Where are my clothes. My shoes. I just have time to splash some water on my face, I'll grab a cup of coffee at the Tip Top diner on Fullerton. Now. My purse and car keys.

Jennifer? Why are you up? It's three o'clock in the morning. My goodness, you're dressed oddly. Where are you going?

No time to chat. There's a trauma coming in.

A young woman, in light green scrubs speaks soothingly. No need to hurry. We've got everything under control. The emergency has been taken care of. I'm not convinced. Her name tag reads simply ERICA. No letters after it, no credentials. A bit slovenly, rubbing sleep from her eyes. Asleep on the job? It hardly seems possible. Still some of the urgency is dissipating. I am beginning to wonder why I am standing here, with a red skirt over my nightgown and a wool scarf around my head and neck.

I heard a noise, I say.

Did you? The only thing I heard was you thumping around.

No, it was outside. A car door slamming.

There isn't any downstairs here, sweetie. Just the one level.

Dr. White.

Excuse me?

It's Dr. White.

I'm sorry. I don't mean anything by it. You're really a sweet lady, that's why!

It was Mark, I think. He keeps coming by. Asking for money. I don't know why he'd come over now, in the middle of the night. Only to leave again without saying anything. I tried to wake up James, but he sleeps so soundly. When I went to the window, all I saw was a figure heading down the street, walking quickly.

Dr. White, you were having a dream.

No. I heard the door slam. The footsteps. The figure.

I know. Now time to go back to sleep.

I can't. I'm up now.

Dr. White, there's nowhere to go.

I need to walk. If I can't walk, I will scream. You will regret it.

Okay, okay. No need for that. Just behave yourself. Don't get me in trouble.

No, I just need to walk. See? Just walk.

And I begin to make my nightly rounds, to walk until my ankles can't support me any longer.

◇ ◇ ◇

I sit in the great room, tears streaming down my face. Dog is trying to lick them off, but I push him away. This is what I remember: my son Mark on the table, his chest open. Flatlining. Everyone has left the OR, the lights have been turned off. I can barely see, but I know it's him. A coronary artery bypass grafting gone awry, a simple procedure, but one I am not qualified to perform. This was not a dream. I have not been asleep. That I have done something terribly, terribly wrong is beyond a doubt. The gallery is full of people, no one I recognize. All sitting in judgment. All in possession of knowledge beyond my reach.

◇ ◇ ◇

My pills sit untouched on the bedside table. I will not take them. Not today. I want to see clearly. I have a plan. I awoke with it fully formed in my mind. It grows stronger as the day progresses.

At breakfast we are reminded that the Girl Scouts are coming today and we will stuff cambric squares with lavender to make sachets. *Your clothes will smell so nice!* the gray-haired woman says encouragingly. I am

346

remembering today. I recall Girl Scouts, their fresh faces and forced smiles. How they enunciate. They are at the cruelest age. They do not call Fiona. They do not invite her to their parties. They do not know how much I hate them for this. How I want revenge.

A little later, the painters arrive. Not just a touch-up. All the walls in the great room are being redone, painted the inevitable green. The door opens and closes as they bring in equipment, buckets of paint, tarps. They set up a barrier of tape, WET PAINT signs hanging from it.

This does not prevent incidents. A new arrival to the floor plunges his cupped hands into a bucket of paint, begins drinking it like water. Attendants run toward him, emitting cries of dismay. There are calls for the doctor, and the man is grabbed by the arms and hustled toward the front desk. I see my chance.

I go to my room. I put on my most comfortable shoes. Is it summer or winter? Hot or cold? I don't know, so I struggle into an extra shirt just in case. If it is winter it will be hard, but I will make it. I will go home. My mother and father are worried. They always worry.

I wasn't allowed to have a driver's license. I had to learn secretly during college. Even though I was still living at home, my boyfriend taught me in the parking lot of St. Pat's, and took me to the testing facility. When my mother went through my purse looking for contraceptives, she found the license. A greater betrayal, in their eyes, a worse sin against them, such an unexpected rebellion. Honor thy father and mother. I did, I do. I must get back to them. I hurry back to the scene, where the painters are all standing around in confusion. None of them speaks English. They are waiting for something, someone. I edge toward the door, hidden among the workers. There is a banging on the door. An attendant runs over, punches the code, and the door swings open wide, admitting a man dressed in white like the others, except clean, not spattered with paint.

I catch the door with my foot just before it closes. I take one look back. The man in the clean clothes is talking to a tall gray-haired woman, gesturing with his hands. Old people are crowding around them, attendants trying to entice them away. I open the door wider, feel the rush of hot air. I won't have to worry about frostbite, at least. One more step, and I am through. I let the door fall behind with a click.

■ ■ ■ ■ ■

THREE

■ ■ ■ ■

The sun is blinding. How long since you were so bombarded with unfiltered light? Overpowering heat, the air thick and foul-smelling from the fumes of softened asphalt under your feet. It gives as you step, makes a dark, sucking sound with each move. Like walking on a tarry moon.

You tread carefully over the sticky black surface. Sweat trickles down your neck, your bra is already soaked. You pause to take off your sweater but then are confronted with the problem of what to do with it. You hang it carefully on the antenna of a small blue car parked nearby and keep walking. There is some urgency to move, some sense that there are conspiracies afoot, that lightning will strike multiple times if you stand in one spot.

You are in a lot filled with cars of all makes, models, and colors. Which one is yours.

Have you been here before. Where is James, he has the keys. And your purse? You must have left it at the hospital. Your phone. It should be embedded in your flesh so critical is it to your ability to function.

Fiona once threw your pager down the toilet and flushed. Mark, not nearly as competent, merely buried it in the back garden, and you heard it chirp at dinner. You didn't punish either of them, understood that they were merely playing out their Darwinian destinies. Who will inherent the earth? Not any scion of your flesh.

You are nearly at the street. Placards everywhere, VIOLATORS WILL BE TOWED. A gate, a gatekeeper adjusting a waist-high sign, LOT FULL. He nods to you.

The sidewalks are crowded with people, mostly the young, dressed in as little as possible. Girls in short summer dresses with spaghetti straps holding insubstantial fabrics against small breasts. Young men in oversize shorts that reach below the knee, falling from their slight hips. Sidewalk cafés, umbrellaed tables encroaching upon the sidewalks, forcing people out into the street. Cars honking. Planters that trail flowers too bright and perfect to be real. Yet you see a woman pick off a blossom and put it in her hair. Waiters hefting trays over their heads. Colorful red and pink and blue cocktails in large v-shaped glasses. People sipping from small white cups. Enormous salads.

Everything as it should be. Everything in its place. Where is your place. Where do you belong.

You realize that you are impeding the flow of traffic. People are politely navigating around you, but you are inconveniencing them. One man bumps your elbow as he passes and stops briefly to apologize. You nod and say, not at all, and begin moving again.

Summer in the city. How exciting when your mother and father allowed you to begin coming here by yourself, away from the row houses of Germantown, the concrete schoolyards and industrial storefronts, the glazier shops and printing presses. Away from the grime-colored house with the trains running through the backyard. Your mother and her gypsy charm. Black Irish, full of magic.

In your teens you turned yourself to stone to withstand her. You vowed to never rely

355

on trickery to bind others to you. Not a difficult vow to keep, as you had no such tricks at your disposal. Your charm nonexistent. Your beauty minimal.

Whatever power you had to attract was of a colder variety. *Touching nerve-terminals / to thermal icicles.* Who told you that? No matter. As it turned out there were some who appreciated it. Enough of them, yes.

You have been walking for miles. Hours and hours. South, judging from the sun, which is setting to your right. This endless street of endless festivities. You cannot see beyond it, an eternal pleasure fair. And nowhere to sit.

You realize you are hungry. It is long past dinnertime, your mother will be worried. You are suddenly tired of the gaiety, and you would settle for the quiet kitchen, the dried-out pot roast and soft brown potatoes, the boiled carrots. You realize you are beyond hunger, indeed famished. But why are you hesitating? You are surrounded by bounty!

With some trepidation you approach the

nearest restaurant. Italian, its name unpronounceable, written in fancy neon script over a flowery bower. Outside, perhaps a dozen tables covered with white tablecloths, full of diners.

The din is tremendous. You can't see inside the restaurant, it is dark and the entrance is overflowing with people laughing and talking, at least a dozen men and women holding glasses filled with red and white wine lounging against the railings of the outdoor seating area, toasting one another. You try to get closer to see inside.

Just one, ma'am? This is a man in jeans and a white shirt. Is he talking to you? You look around, but no one else is there.

My husband is parking the car, you say. This must be true. You do not eat alone in restaurants.

The wait is at least fifty minutes. Would you like me to put you on the list? Unless you'd like a seat at the bar.

He seems to be waiting for an answer, so you nod. It seems expedient. He beckons and you follow him through the path he clears in the crowd. He leads you to a high

357

stool, places a menu in front of you, and a menu in front of the empty bar stool to your right.

I'll show your husband here when he arrives, he says. You nod yet again. Gestures seem to take you a long way. You are relieved, as words seem evasive, unreliable. It seems like months since you have had congress with anyone. You have been a wraith weaving through the streets of revelers, unseen and unheard.

You open the menu, but cannot make sense of it. *Penne all'Arrabbiata, Linguine alle Vongole, Farfalle con Salmone.* But the words are evocative, make your mouth water. How long has it been since you've eaten? Days and days.

People sit elbow to elbow, some with plates of food in front of them, others with glasses of different shapes and sizes filled with colorful liquids. Some are watching a television mounted on the wall, surrounded by shelves and shelves of bottles that reach to the ceiling.

On the screen, beautiful girls in evening gowns are pointing to appliances — refrigerators, microwave ovens. It is a pretty, even spellbinding sight: the girls in their bright dresses flashing across the screen, the light flickering over the bottles.

The noise is high but not unpleasant. You feel as though you are in the belly of a live organism. The camaraderie of productive bacteria, the kind that sustain life.

The bartender approaches. He is a heavyset man with thick black glasses. Young, but he will need to monitor his cardiovascular health, his ruddy complexion is not due to sun or overexercise. A stained white apron tied around his ample waist.

And how-a can-a I-a help-a you, my-a beauteous one-a? he asks in a mock accent that you assume is meant to be Italian. You point to one of the menu items, the one with the shortest name.

Ah, the Pasta Pomidoro. A specialty of the house-a! And to drink? You are thirsty but cannot think of the right word. Something in a liquid state. You point to the bottle he is carrying. You test out your voice.

That, you say, and are grateful that it comes out only slightly rusty.

Jack Daniel's? He drops his accent and gives a spontaneous-sounding laugh. This day has been full of surprises! Straight? You nod. He laughs again. Very well, a straight whiskey it is. I don't suppose you want to follow that up with a beer chaser?

You try to judge from his expression what the right answer is. You nod again. What'll it be? he asks. We got Coors, Miller Lite, Sierra Nevada on tap.

Yes, you say. Something changes in his face. He gives you a look that worries you. Watchful. You have seen that look before. You never could fool anyone. You always got caught. That is what keeps you on the straight and narrow. Not a conscience. No. But the knowledge that you are no good at cheating, that no bad deed goes unpunished.

He shrugs and turns away, busies himself at some machinery with complicated handles, and then places a tall frosted glass filled with something frothy and yellow in front of you. What is this. Where am I. You suddenly have a revelation. You are Jennifer White. You live at 544 Walnut Lane, in Germantown, in Philadelphia, with your beloved mother and father. You are eighteen years old and have just started classes at the

University of Pennsylvania. A biology major. Your life stretches out in front of you, a clear path, no encumbrances to speak of. There is a cold beer in front of you. Your first in a restaurant! You have never ordered a beer on your own before. You have every reason to be lighthearted. Suddenly you are.

You notice another glass at your elbow. This one is smaller, not cold. Filled with a rich amber-colored liquid. You pick it up and swallow. It burns going down, but it is not distasteful. You drink again, and it is gone.

Another? asks the man. You are startled. You did not realize he was still there, still watching. You nod. You test out your voice again.

Certainly, you say.

He gives a short laugh and again you catch that look. He places another small glass on the counter, pours, pushes it in your direction. You leave it there, turn your attention to the tall cold glass, and take a sip. This goes down easier. Beer, yes.

Your father always pours a small amount into a teacup for you whenever he opens one for himself. This one quenches your thirst in a way the other one didn't. You drink deeply. You are starting to feel good — you hadn't noticed how on edge you had been. That edge is dissipating. Slow, pleasurable warmth. A heaviness of limbs. Colors are brighter, the noise subdued. You have traveled into a private space within the organism, a private pocket of comfort. You love it here. You will come back every night. You will bring your mother and father and let them work their considerable magic on these delightful people, your comrades.

The bartender puts a napkin and some silverware in front of you. You pick up the knife. There is something about this. Something that is familiar yet strange. You have a sense of anticipation. You press the sharp edge of the knife against the wooden counter, press and pull it toward you. A white line appears in the wood, straight and true.

If you could press harder, split open this dark matter, what would come out? What would be revealed? O the excitement of exploration! You pick up your beer again and drink some more. Good. You had not realized how tight your shoulders were, the tension in your neck.

Waiting for someone?

The voice is from a girl to your left. She is about your age, you estimate. Perhaps a little older. Twenty. Twenty-two perhaps. Very pretty. Her hair cut so that it hangs longer on one side of her face than the other, and fringed unevenly at the edges. It is not unattractive. She has a nice smile. Her eyes are ringed with blue, mascaraed to bring out their size and brilliance.

Am I? You consider this. You want to answer, but you do not yet trust that the words will match your intent. You try.

No, you say. I'm alone.

You are heartened that she is not disconcerted. You try again. I was hungry, you say. This looked nice.

Oh, it's a great little place. We love it. She gestures to a young man on the other side of her. He watches the television. And Ron takes good care of everyone. She smiles at the man behind the counter. He leans forward to you and speaks confidentially.

If this young lady gives you any trouble, just let me know. I'll take care of her, he says. The pretty girl laughs.

A plate of noodles covered with thick red

sauce appears in front of you. It smells fabulous. You are ravenous. You pick up the fork and begin eating.

So, let me guess. You're a professor. This is the young man to the girl's left. He has forsaken the television, the beautiful girls, and now seems to be addressing you.

Excuse me? You wipe your mouth. The food is as good as it looks. The noodles al dente, the sauce rich and aromatic with spices. So much better than what you could do. James is the real cook, the children's faces fall when they come into the kitchen and find you there.

The girl interrupts. Oh, it's just a game we play in bars. Guessing who people are, what they do. He thinks you look like a college professor. I can see that. But I need to think about it before I guess. There's a lot at stake! Winner has to buy everyone a round of drinks. She puts her hand to her forehead, acts as if she is thinking hard. Definitely someone professional, she says. You weren't just a house-wife.

The young man hits her playfully on the arm.

Okay, okay, I shouldn't say that. It's just that you look like you've been out in the world more.

The young man hits her again.

Oh, did I say something else stupid?

No, you say. The words come out smoothly. You are saying what you mean to say. Relief. The path between your brain and your tongue is open.

And, yes, I am most definitely not a housewife, you tell her.

You realize your voice sounds contemptuous. James always warns you about this. You wrap another length of pasta around your fork. You take another bite. You have not been this hungry in a long time. There were only five women in my program, you explain.

What type of program was that? No, let me guess. The young man is enthusiastic. I'm good at this. You'll see. My guess is . . . English literature. Medieval poetry.

The girl rolls her eyes. How sexist can you be? A woman, she must be an English major,

365

must be poetry.

Well, what would you guess, Einstein?

The man behind the bar breaks in. Given the way she throws back her drink, I'd say something a little tougher. Engineering. You built bridges, right?

No, no. You are laughing. It has been so long since you have enjoyed yourself so much. These fresh young faces, their ease, no trepidation around you. You realize, suddenly, that you have been frightening people. That thing you see in their eyes, it is fear. But what have they to fear from you?

What's your guess, Annette? The young woman pretends to think hard. I'm going to go out on a limb here and say lawyer, she says. I bet you defend the poor and defenseless of the world against unfair prosecution.

No, no, you say. Never a lawyer. Words have never been my forte. That's my husband.

See? I was close!

Well, I wouldn't exactly call him a friend of the underprivileged, you say. The thought makes you smile.

Then what would you call him? asks the girl.

The last resort of the rich and powerful. And he's very good at what he does. He always gets them off. He's worth every one of the considerable pennies he charges.

Something closes down in the girl's face. And you? she asks.

You realize that you have erred. That you have forgotten the hyper-sensitivity of the young. Fiona and Mark were inured to it early. The cynical joking about it around the dinner table. During Mark's teenage years, he insisted on opening up every meal with a particularly egregious lawyer joke. He was hoping to get to James, but that wasn't the way. He'd bring his own to the table.

How can you tell the difference between a dead skunk and a dead attorney on the road? Then, after a pause, he'd triumphantly bring out the punch line: The vultures aren't gagging over the skunk.

The girl is still waiting for your answer.

I'm a doctor, you tell her. An orthopedic surgeon.

That's bones, right? the young man asks.

Yes. It's more than just the bones. It's everything to do with injuries, degenerative diseases, birth defects. I specialize in hands.

Annette does hands, too.

The girl laughs. He means I read palms. I took a Learning Annex class in psychic skills. Most of us were there as postmodern cynics. But I learned some things.

Chiromancy, you say. You'd be surprised how many believers there are. There's been a considerable amount of research into palm creases and fingerprint whorl variations published in medical journals.

Really? The girl leans forward. She turns slightly and it's her turn to hit the young man. See? I told you! She turns back to you. Like what?

For a long time scientists have been interested in exploring whether phenotypic markers can diagnose genetic disorders.

Can you say that in English?

Certainly. Doctors have always been interested in whether they can use the lines in your hands and the length of your fingers and even your fingerprints as a way of diagnosing illness.

Like what kind of illnesses?

Mostly genetic. For example, there turns out to be a strong correlation between a single palmar crease and aberrant fingerprints and Cri Du Chat syndrome.

Cri Du Chat? Cry of the cat? the young man asks.

Yes, because babies born with this defect mew like cats. They are usually severely mentally impaired. Then there's Jacobsen Syndrome. Also diagnosable by the hands. Very similar to Down.

Are there any happy diagnoses you can make with the palm? Annette likes telling people they have long lives and will come into riches some day.

Unfortunately, most of the deviations from the normal in hand characteristics point to problems, often severe ones. But one researcher claims to have found a strong correlation between different ratios of finger lengths and exceptional musical ability. You pause. Of course, that's just statistically speaking. Look. You hold out your right hand. See how my index finger is just as long as my middle finger? That's statistically abnormal. Yet I don't have any genetic defect that I know of.

Let me see your hand, the girl says, somewhat abruptly. You hesitate, then let her take it. She leans over your palm, frowning.

How's my life line? you ask.

Oh, no one believes that one anymore. Good thing, too. According to your life line, you had a very short life. You're dead, technically. But otherwise, you are intellectual rather than materialistic. You have the power to manipulate, but you choose not to exercise it. And your life has not been especially fortunate.

You're using past tense, you say. Is that because I'm technically dead?

I'm sorry?

You didn't say, your life will not be especially fortunate, but that it has not been.

The girl blushes. I'm sorry. I didn't mean to

imply that your life is over. You don't act old.

You are puzzled. Why should I? you ask.

You're right, I'm stereotyping. Blame it on the beer.

But how old do you think I am? you ask.

Oh, I'm terrible at this. Don't ask me.

I would guess we're about the same age. Or that I'm slightly younger.

The girl smiles. I deserved that. You know, I took that Internet test, the one that is supposed to tell you your real age, and I scored sixteen. All my friends scored older — thirty, thirty-two. Jim here is an old soul. His real age is thirty-five, according to the test. In actual years, he's only twenty-four, of course.

I'm eighteen, you say.

Good for you! Forever young!

Not forever, you say. Although it certainly seems that way sometimes.

If I were really thirty-five, I'd want to slit my wrists, says the young man.

The girl rolls her eyes. Here he goes again, she says.

Why on earth? you ask.

I mean, if I were thirty-five and were in the position I am now. Stupid job. Not getting on with anything. Not having written my novel. Things like that.

Are you working on a novel? you ask. It seems like this is information that a lot of people divulge in bars, on examining tables.

No. That's the point. Here I am, still in my twenties, so I have an excuse. But at thirty-five you don't have any more. Excuses, I mean.

You'd be surprised, you say. Mark will have plenty of excuses when he's that age. Just wait and see.

Who is Mark?

You are confused. Who is he?

Just someone I know, you say. I think he might be my nephew.

You think? The girl starts to laugh and then

looks at your face and stops.

An image rises up in front of you. A distraught face. Slight shoulders shaking. Someone in deep distress. Her face is familiar.

Fiona, you say slowly. Fiona is someone else I know, someone I admire very much, who seems to have gotten herself into some trouble. Mark, on the other hand. You pause to think. Mark has always been in trouble.

The girl looks confused. Fiona?

Fiona is someone who always knows exactly what she wants and how to get it, you say slowly. But sometimes that is not the best thing. No.

I find I don't really like those kind of people very much, the girl says.

No. You would like Fiona.

The girl nods politely. She has lost interest in talking about people she doesn't know. She whispers something to the young man next to her and he smiles in return. He has turned his attention back to the television. It's now the national news, all bad. Catastrophes natural and manmade. Money lost by millions, upticks in flooding, natural disasters, murders committed and unsolved.

You have finished the food on your plate, and both glasses, the tall and the short one, are empty. The heavyset man is at the other end of the counter, talking to another man in a suit.

Do you know where the bathroom is? you ask. The girl points. There. Near the door where you came in.

You get off the stool, stumbling slightly. You feel your way across the crowded room, using the backs of chairs and sometimes people's shoulders, as guides. You are unsteady and feel intense pressure on your bladder.

The door marked TOILET is locked, so you wait, shifting from one foot to the other like a small child. You hear the toilet flush, water being run in the sink, and the click of the door as it finally opens. A woman emerges.

You stumble past her and barely make it to the toilet to relieve yourself. Even so, there is a wet patch on your pant leg. You take a paper towel and rinse it out, making it more prominent than before. At least it's not as bad as blood. You think of all the times you locked yourself in public bathrooms like this, scrubbing at pants to rid them of bloodstains from tampon overflows. For a doctor you've had remarkably little insight into your own body. You secreted tampons everywhere: in your purse, in the glove compartment of the car, in your desk drawer, and yet you were continually caught short. Your body was always betraying you.

It got worse as you got older. There were days in your forties and early fifties when you hesitated to schedule surgeries because of brief, intense episodes of hemorrhaging that could happen any time. Your body defeated you in ways it had never in the past. You wore double tampons and pads underneath that. You'd go into the surgery wearing adult diapers, waddling slightly when you walked. But once the gushing started, there was no stopping it. You learned to live with the humiliation. Blood in the OR. You kept extra clothes in the office, in the car. Two years of that. You thought you might mourn the loss of fertility, but the trauma of perimenopause made you welcome it.

You look in the mirror as you wash your

hands. What you see there startles you. The very short crinkly white hair. Your face covered with red blotches, liver spots on your forehead, and the slack skin over the jawbone. Too much sun.

You never did listen to the dermatologists, felt their cautions were old lady-ish. Now you are an old lady. Your life should be discussed in the past tense. You are suddenly tired. It's time to go home. You exit the bathroom only to stop, disoriented.

Where are you? A crowded restaurant. Overwhelming smells of heavy garlicky sauces. The noise makes your head ache. Bodies press up against you, propel you back into the open door of the bathroom. As if from far away, you catch sight of a door marked EXIT. You start to make your way toward it.

Voices are shouting behind you. Hey! Lady! A man holding menus nods, opens the door for you. Stop her! The man sings a cheery Good evening! Evening? you ask, and then you are outside, a warm breeze caressing your face.

When did day turn to night? The heat into deliciousness? The streetlights are on, all

the shops and restaurants are lit and welcoming, and bright lights shine amid the
leaves of the trees, which are in full bloom.
People everywhere, holding hands, linking
arms, the warmth of human bodies in
harmony. It is a party. It is a fairyland. You
plunge deep into the festive night.

You have not lived until you have seen fish
striving for the moon. By the dozens they
burst out of the water, their silvery bodies
flashing as they rise. The perfect shiny arc
as they peak. The downward trajectory is
lyrical: perfect dives back into the blue gray
depths.

The air is balmy and tropical, but the lake
water frigid. How it numbs your feet and
ankles. Still, there are others who would not
be dissuaded. You see heads just above the
water, arms reaching up and slicing through
the water, a long line of heads attached to
shoulders and arms. Bursts of water from
the feet, those tiny motors.

The park is nearly as bright as day — the
automatic streetlights haven't switched on.
Celebratory howls emanate from the zoo.
All the benches are occupied, the pavements

crowded. And dogs everywhere, running, rolling, chasing balls and Frisbees, frolicking in the shallow waves. The fish continue to jump and splash.

Ma'am? A young man is running up behind you. He is holding something in his hand.

You forgot your shoes! He is out of breath. He stops and holds out a pair of new-looking white sneakers. He has the look of someone who expects gratitude, so you try to infuse your voice with warmth.

Why, thank you, you say. He is still extending the shoes, so you take them, but the minute he turns his back, you drop them on the grass. Who needs shoes on a night like this? Encumbrances. They just separate your flesh from this goodly sphere, the earth.

To your right you see a young couple vacate a bench. You sit down, not because you're tired but because you want to watch the parade.

And what a parade! Musicians: drummers and horn players and trombonists. You have to strain to hear them because the crickets are so loud. Then come the entertainers, the tumblers and acrobats and men on unicycles and women on stilts, all dressed in the most outlandish costumes.

Some are naked. You have to laugh at the men's fully extended penises, aroused by the night air and the proximity of so much beauty. You are almost aroused yourself.

You think of your young man. He is late. He is always late. You are always waiting. Your father says that a woman who waits must contain all and lack nothing. You think he was quoting, but you were never able to discover what. He is full of surprises, your father. Barely an eighth-grade education, yet he would correct your college English papers.

But your young man, your beautiful young man. He wears green to match his eyes. He is not stupid, but he is not smart enough to hide his vanity. You discovered foundation makeup in his locker, yet not for a moment did you think he was cheating. Not that he wasn't capable of that. But he was so full of guile as to be guileless.

But you? Hook you up to a polygraph and you would flunk every question. Did you love him? Yes. No. You would have been tagged a liar for either answer. Sometimes.

Maybe. Only when hooked to a machine calibrated to detect ambivalence would you pass.

After the entertainers, the animals. But such animals! Not any that God created. Fabulous creatures with the heads of lions with large child faces mounted on them. A herd of cats, goose-stepping in the moonlight.

You are reminded of the wonderful and terrible books of your childhood. There was one where a boy was given the power to read into the hearts and souls of creatures by feeling the shape of their hands. Thus the hands of kings and courtiers often felt like the appendages of cloven beasts, and the hands of honest workers were soft like those of the highest royalty.

The idea that you couldn't tell the nature of the creatures around you, human or otherwise, without such a gift was terrifying. In bed you would hold your own hand to determine what you were. Human or beast?

Across the path from your bench is a low stone wall separating the grass of the park from the sand of a narrow beach. There is writing on it. A sacred script. Thick strokes in black paint outlined in red. Punctuated by a face that grins. It is sending a message. But what is it?

The parade is over. People are leaving for other festivities. The dogs have vanished, the children lifted onto shoulders and taken to bed. Silence descends. You close your eyes to revel in it.

You wake up with a start. There is a hand on your arm, moving down it. You are startled to see it is still night, but a night so bright that you could read by it. The hand belongs to a stranger, a youngish man, not clean, wearing a fisherman's hat and an army coat. Seeing that you are awake, he withdraws his hand.

I was just wondering, do you have any money I could borrow, he says.

Normally you would just say no. You give your time and money to the clinic. But things are different tonight. Your sense of well-being. The beauty that surrounds you. You wonder what you would feel if you took his hand.

You look for your purse. But there is nothing. You check your pockets in case you brought only your wallet or stuck your driver's license and a credit card in a pocket. Nothing. The man watches as you go through your contortions.

Probably you shouldn't have been sleeping here, he says. Probably someone got here before me, someone not so nice.

He pulls a pack of cigarettes out of the breast pocket of his coat and offers you one. When you refuse, he lights one himself and settles back on the bench.

When I saw you there, I thought, Now what's a nice lady like that doing in Lincoln Park in the middle of the night? he says. It was a real strange sight. But where are your shoes?

You look down. Your feet are bare and dirty. There is some dried blood on the side of your ankle. You reach down and pluck out a piece of glass. The hem of your pants is muddied.

Someone's been paddling, says the man. I can't say I blame you. It's certainly the night for it.

You notice that it's no longer quite as quiet.

Although the crickets have subsided, and the hum of traffic from afar has dwindled, there are other noises. You notice that the two of you aren't alone. The field surrounding you is dotted with dark shapes, people rolling up carts, unfurling blankets. A man and woman struggle with a mass of material that turns into a small tent. An encampment is forming.

The man continues to talk as he smokes.

You're new. You must prefer the shelters. A lot of the women do. You can stay cleaner there. But I don't care too much for the rules. In bed by nine PM. No liquor. No smoking. No getting up before six AM.

You must be a night person, you say. I always was, too. I'm a wanderer.

Wanderer. Wandering. Wanderlust. You like the sound of the words as you speak them.

You said it. Give me the park at night anytime. Hey, where's your stuff? I can help you settle in.

I don't know, you say. Home, I guess.

You have a home?

Of course. On Sheffield.

That's a pretty nice street! Where on Sheffield?

Twenty-one Fifty-three Sheffield. Right down the block from St. Vincent's.

I know that area. So you have a house there. So why are you out here, middle of the night, no shoes?

I guess I wanted some fresh air, you say. But now that he asks, you're not sure. The man's face has filled your mind, driving all other things out. His nose, his mouth. The grime in the considerable laugh lines around his eyes. A slight bruise on his cheekbone. The tufts of hair that stick out from under his cap. Not an unlikable face. A capable face, but capable of what?

What about your family?

They're all dead, you say. My mother. My father. Everyone died.

Hey, that's rough. Real rough. Mine all died too. I have a sister somewhere, but she doesn't talk to me anymore.

He takes a deep drag on his cigarette,

finishes it off, throws the butt on the ground, and grinds it in with his boot.

Hey, do you think we could go to your house? I sure would love to sleep in a bed for once. A bed with no rules.

We have a guest room, you say.

Well, that's just perfect. I would love to be your guest. Just love it. He stands up, dusts off his trousers, and waits.

You get up too. Your feet are sore. A slight stinging on your ankle. Can you walk? You can. But you're suddenly very tired.

Do you know how to get there? you ask.

I sure do. My old stomping grounds. And Antoine's, too. Let me get Antoine. He'd sure appreciate a guest room himself.

I only have one guest room. But it's a double bed.

Well, I could do worse than share a bed with old Andy. Let me find him. You just stay here. He runs off, glancing back at you every other step as if to make sure you don't go away.

You do as he says. You are grateful that someone has taken charge. You never let James do that. You must be getting older. Old. The desire to abdicate responsibility. To let others act, decide, lead. Is this what aging is all about?

Suddenly the man is back. With him, another man, slightly built. Cleaner than the first, but a less open face.

You finally ask the taller one, Are you my husband?

Excuse me?

How long have we been married?

The small man laughs. If she really does have a house on Sheffield, you could have a real sweet deal.

Yeah, but what if she does have family after all?

You heard her. They're dead.

Yeah, but she's fucking nuts. We don't really know what's what.

James? you say.

The small man speaks up. Yes?

No, you say. Not you. James.

The other man hesitates. Yes?

James, I'm ready to go home.

Okay, my dear. The man looks at the small man and shrugs. What have I got to lose? he asks. Okay, he says to you, let's go. Sheffield and Fullerton, here we come.

Seemingly hours later, you finally reach your house, unlatch the gate. The men stand aside, waiting for you to take the lead. A sign has been planted in the front garden. SOLD. Everything is dark. No curtains in the windows.

You walk up to the front door and turn the knob. Locked. You ring the doorbell. You ring it again. You pound on the door. James! You call. An arm grabs you from behind. Quiet. Do you want to wake the neighbors? You have forgotten. Right. The neighbors. You reach above the door and feel around the edge of the door frame. Nothing.

Doesn't she have a key?

387

Apparently not. The taller man retreats down the stairs and tries one of the ground-floor windows. It doesn't give. He tries the other. In the meantime you yourself have retreated to the front garden. You are turning over rocks. You know the spare key is here. You put it there yourself. The ground is cold against your bare feet. You step on something that crunches. A snail. Then another. You always hated them. Marauders. Thieves. Robbers of beautiful things. Fiona loved them, however. She would paint them brilliant colors using Amanda's fingernail polish, and set them loose. Living jewels among your petunias and impatiens.

You step on a sharp stone and let out a cry.

Shhh! says one of the men.

What's that? the other one says. Short bursts of sound, a *woop woop woop* from down the street. Red and blue lights flash.

Fuck, says the short man, and he's off like a flash, the other man after him. You go in the opposite direction, into the alley. Down three houses, one, two, three. Through the back gate and into the back garden. To the large white rock under the drain pipeline.

The key is under it, just where it should be.

Peter would tease Amanda. Keys every-where! he'd say. Scatter keys through the neighborhood! To every woman and every child! Amanda would just shrug. Better than being locked out in subzero weather, she said. Better than breaking a leg or having a stroke and no one able to come over and check on you.

You let yourself in. The house is silent, wait-ing. It smells stale, of mildew, a slight memory of gas. You flip the light switch but nothing happens. Still, it is Amanda's kitchen. No flowers, no fruit, but her photo-graphs, her furniture. She is not here. You know that somehow.

You wander down the hall. You know this house like your very own. Since you were pregnant with Mark. Amanda was the first person in the neighborhood to come to your door. Carrying not cookies, not a casserole, but a potted cactus. Ugly, with a small yel-low star-shaped flower on the crest of one of its spiny arms.

I know you by reputation, although you don't know me, she said. You treated one of my students who had an unfortunate accident with a firecracker. You repaired three of his fingers, and he still has use of two of them. Everyone says you are a genius. I admire genius.

Not a genius, you said. Just good at what I do.

You accepted the cactus. And promptly threw it in the garbage when Amanda left. You hate plants, and cacti most of all. You would have preferred cookies. But a few days later when you saw Amanda in the street, you stopped to say hello.

You remember it as clearly as if you were there now.

When are you due? she asked.

May 15. Just nine more weeks, you said.

You must be ready by now. How do you feel? Excited, I'd imagine.

No. My husband is. He's the one that wants children.

You waited to see what effect your words would have on this woman. She was tall, with impressive posture. Her back was straight, her gold hair curved in a shiny helmet that just reached her shoulders — you knew it was her real color. There were faint streaks of white — not gray — at her temples. Her tailored clothes were crisply ironed. You were conscious of your baggy cotton pants, your extralarge T-shirt billowing over your round belly, your worn sneakers.

Amanda laughed. You're what, thirty-five?

Thirty-five. It was time.

She smiled a little wryly. We're still trying.

You didn't even try to hide your surprise.

I don't give up easily. She reached out and patted your stomach — a gesture that too many people felt free to make. You found that you didn't mind. It wasn't presumptuous, but something else: There was yearning in it and a bit of awe. This made you speak more gently than you otherwise would.

Sometimes it's time to move on, you told her.

Not yet, she said. We haven't given up yet.

What about adopting? you asked, then

wished you could take back your words. Of course she must have considered it. How facile. And you actually found yourself blushing. But she didn't seem to mind or notice.

No. I need more control than that, she said.

That's an odd way of thinking about it, you said. You were becoming interested in this woman.

Nevertheless, control is what I want, said Amanda.

But if you could get a newborn, wouldn't that be control enough? you asked. You were genuinely curious about what she would say. You shifted a little on your feet. The baby was moving, thrusting its limbs so that your stomach got distended into strange, angular shapes.

After all, you continued, you'd have the child right away. You can even be in the delivery room in some cases, so the first person the infant sees is you.

Still not enough, Amanda said.

Enough what? you asked.

Control. That would take care of the nurture part. But what about the nature? That would be an unknown.

But you're a teacher, you protested. Surely you see how different children from the same households, raised the same way with the same food and the same experiences, can turn out differently?

Yes, Amanda said. You need to know that you're the source of whatever comes out. Otherwise you leave open the door for other emotions, other attitudes toward your child to creep in.

Emotions like what?

Contempt. Disdain. Or just plain dislike.

Let me get this straight. You can love a child who displays, let's say, unattractive traits or behaviors if you know he or she came from your genetic makeup. But if you don't know . . .

. . . then who knows what you might feel toward them? Amanda finished your question.

Like a body rejecting a donated kidney, you

said slowly.

Exactly. And because you don't know until you transplant it, why take the risk?

Because people need kidneys. And you say you need a child.

I do, she said. And the way she said it convinced you of her resolve.

But it didn't add up. You protested, But you've left half the chromosomes out of the equation. What about the genetic makeup of the father? That's certainly out of your control.

I can deal with Peter's genes, with any peculiarities that arise from them, she said. You wondered about that. You didn't believe at that point that you would ever consider James as something you'd have to deal with. You changed your mind later, of course.

The woman stopped. My turn to ask some questions, she said. Why did you resist having children? Is it your career?

No. I suppose it comes down to control as well, you said. I like making my own choices. I always have. But with a child you have no choice. When it is hungry, you must feed it. When it has soiled itself, you must clean and change it.

But as a doctor, aren't you constantly responding to patients' needs? When something happens during a surgery, you have no choice. You have to fix it. When an emergency arises, you have to respond.

That's different, you said.

How?

You spoke slowly, trying to work it out.

It requires the best of you, you said. Something unique. Not just anyone can perform a transfer of an intercostal nerve into the musculocutaneous nerve to restore biceps function. Or an open carpal tunnel release, for that matter. Even other specialists mess those up. Yet a child can love anyone. Children *do* love the most horrible, depraved people. They attach to warm bodies. Familiar faces. Sources of food. To be valued for such base requirements doesn't interest me.

You'll change your mind when you have the baby. I've seen it happen time and time again.

So people say. My anticipation is that I will hand it over to James and let him deal with it.

You interest me. Not many people would think this way, much less say so.

I usually say what I think.

Yes. I see that. And I suspect you don't have much patience for people who don't.

You're right. Not much.

Then suddenly your memory skips ahead to the birth, which was three weeks early. There were some problems with Mark's lungs. He came out furry, covered with lanugo. A small, red wheezing creature. He was your patient before he was your child, which helped the transition.

Naturally you breast-fed him, because of the antibodies. Did your duty in that regard, despite the inconvenience and pain. You didn't like being sucked dry multiple times a day, and the thought of it distressed you more than you expected.

You weaned him at three months and resumed your professional life once you no longer leaked milk at the slightest provocation. You hired Ana at that point — Ana who did all the things a good mother would do. You were not a good mother. And yet Mark clung to you. And, six years later, Fiona did the same. By then Amanda had stopped trying to conceive, even she admitted it was pointless.

When was the last time you saw Amanda? You cannot recall. You accept that she is gone. They are all leaving, every one of them. James. Peter. Even the children. A diaspora. But you are somehow drawing strength from that. With each loss, you are stronger, you are more yourself. Like a rosebush being pruned of extraneous branches so the blossoms will be larger and healthier next season. Sheared of this excess, what will you not be capable of?

You have a vision: Amanda, here, on the floor, her heart violated, her eyes still open. You always thought the practice of closing the eyes of the deceased a silly one. It's for the living, of course, who would like the dead to behave, to have death approximate sleep. But there is no repose for Amanda. She's on her back, her hands clenched as if about to engage in battle. Her legs akimbo. Are you making this up? Because there are others in the room, shadows are flickering. Words are being spoken. Must you do this? Yes, I must. Quickly then.

Your mind is full of other fantastic images, some in lurid color, some in black-and-white. It is like watching a compilation of movie clips filmed by a lunatic. A heap of harvested hands on the white sands of a turquoise sea. Your parents' house in Philadelphia, engulfed in flames. I am very far gone indeed. Here. So it was here. You can see the remains of the yellow chalk mark mixed with dust. What Amanda could never have abided.

Your filthy bare feet leave footprints. Shoes. You need shoes. Amanda was taller and heavier than you, but you wore the same shoe size. Eleven. Wearing boxes without topses.

You take the stairs to her room and find a severe blue dress with a belt and a pair of black flats. You try to wash your face, but the water has been turned off, so you spit upon a towel and scrub at the worst of the dirt. Then you lie down on Amanda's bed.

But before you sleep, Peter visits. He stands by the window, blocking the moonlight.

What did you do? he asks. Why did you do it? He has been digging in the garden. His knees are black with wet earth. He is holding one of Fiona's most brightly colored snails in his palm. *In the sweat of thy face shalt thou eat bread, till thou return unto the ground; for out of it wast thou taken.* You are sweating. Enough, you say. But he is gone, replaced by Amanda. She sits on the edge of the bed. She takes your hand. Hers is whole, unblemished. You are relieved: It was all a dream, then. All a dream. And finally you are able to sleep.

You are awakened by a crack of thunder, the sound of drumming against the window, on the roof. Outside the window you see gray and wet, but it is still warm. You see that you are already dressed, shoes even. You must have been on call.

Those days as an intern, learning to jump up from the soundest slumber, ready to slice. No transition from oblivion to hyperawareness. You are aware of an empty stomach, but when you go downstairs the refrigerator is dark and empty, and a sour smell emanates from it. In the pantry some dry cereal, stale. Rat droppings on the shelves, holes chewed in the bags of pasta, the cracker box.

You catch sight of the clock still ticking above the sink. Eight forty-five. The clinic opened at 8 AM. You are late. You stuff some cereal in your mouth, run to the front door. You do not have your car keys, you must take a cab. You walk swiftly down the street toward Fullerton, where the cabs stream past day and night.

You are already soaked from the warm rain. The first two cabs are occupied, but then you are in luck: The third one stops. To the New Hope Clinic, you say. Address? he asks, but you can't remember. He punches the name into a small machine mounted on his dashboard. Chicago Avenue, he says. Okeydoke.

He is dark, handsome. A Palestinian flag is draped over the front seat. His cell phone rings and he spits out a string of guttural sounds, hangs up. You brush off the water as best you can and try to relax. Chicago the gray lady. You don't mind.

Sometimes you want the outside world to match your interior reality, you said to

James once, trying to explain why you loved thunderstorms. Another boom overhead and a streak of lightning on the right. Awesome, says the taxi driver, and catching your eye in the rearview mirror, he smiles.

The taxi pulls up in front of a low gray building. Seven seventy-five, the man says. You reach for your purse. You begin searching around the backseat, you pat your pockets, you are frantic. The man looks more concerned than alarmed. You work here? he asks. Or a patient? You are a doctor, you explain, and the man nods like he expected as much. Perhaps you can borrow it, he suggests. I will wait.

You run through the rain to the front door. The waiting room is full of people, many more people than there are chairs. Jean is at the front desk, checking in a woman with a crying infant. When she sees you she looks startled. Dr. White! she says. What a nice surprise! Aren't I on the schedule? you ask. Then, without waiting for an answer, you say, No matter. Clearly you need me. I'll be ready in ten minutes.

You walk into the back area and are surprised at all the strange faces. A medium-size dark-skinned man stops you. I'm sorry, he says, staff only here. His name tag says DR. AZIZ. It's okay, you tell him. I'm Dr. Jennifer White. Apparently there was a schedule mix-up, but it looks like you could use the help.

Dr. White? he asks, but you are already at the back sink, washing up. You go to the wardrobe, take a white coat, button it over your dress. What do you have for me? you ask. The other doctor hesitates, then shrugs. Room three, a rash, could be shingles, could be poison oak, he says. The chart is on the door.

You give a quick knock for courtesy, then enter the room. The woman is perhaps thirty, African American, a fine strong frame. But she is holding on to her left side and her face is in pain. Let me see, you say, and she reluctantly lets go. You pull back the blue hospital gown to see an angry rash with raised red bumps and blisters that have erupted on the skin in a band that reaches across her belly and around her back.

Does this hurt? you ask.

Yes. It started out as a kind of tingling. But now it hurts. Badly.

402

You look. Some of them have become pus-filled, others are still in the early stages of formation. You motion for her to turn over. Nothing on the other side, just this broad swath down the right side of her body, her hip, thigh, and buttocks.

What is it?

Herpes zoster. Known more commonly as shingles, you say. I'm going to prescribe one of the antivirals. Acyclovir. It should decrease the duration of skin rash and pain. I hope we've caught it early enough. Also apply cold compresses to the rash three times a day. Above all, do not scratch or you risk infection.

How did I get this? You called it herpes. Did I get it from my boyfriend?

No, not at all. Shingles is caused by the same virus that causes chickenpox. You know, what you had as a child.

You are looking for your prescription pad. It's not in your pocket. You excuse yourself and go out into the hallway.

Excuse me?

Yes, Doctor?

I have misplaced my prescription pad. Can you get me one? You turn and nearly bump into another woman wearing a white coat. She does not have a name tag on. She looks frazzled. She examines your face with curiosity. Are you Dr. White? she asks.

You nod, yes.

I recognize your photo. I didn't realize you were still involved in the clinic. I thought you'd retired. Dr. Tsien still talks about how much you are missed at the hospital. She frowns, opens her mouth, closes it again.

You don't follow all of this. I come here every Wednesday, you say.

But today's Thursday.

You pause, think. I must have had a conflict this week, you say.

Everyone has been very grateful for your help. That a doctor of your caliber would work here pro bono has always meant a lot to us. Not to mention the other contributions you've made, of course. She still has a bemused look on her face, as if trying to remember something.

You turn to go. You face a bewildering mass

of doors. Where were you? You pick a door at random and go in. An older man is sitting in his underwear. He looks surprised. Is something wrong, Doctor? You tell me, you say. What brought you here today?

The man looks uncomfortable. As I told the other doctor, I'm having trouble going to the bathroom.

Does it hurt? Or do you have urgency but no voiding?

The second one. I think. I try to piss and nothing comes out. It hurts.

Any erectile dysfunction?

Excuse me?

Do you have trouble maintaining an erection?

No, of course not. The man doesn't look at you when he says this.

Liar, you think.

How long have you had this dysuria? you ask.

This what?

This urgency but no voiding.

About a month. It comes and goes.

Any blood in the urine?

He hesitates, then says flatly, No.

Any pain or stiffness in the lower back, hips, or upper thighs?

Maybe.

My guess is prostatitis, you say. Then, after seeing his reaction, you add: Relax, it's not cancer and it will not lead to cancer.

Is it curable? he asks.

Sometimes. Sometimes not. But we can almost certainly relieve the symptoms, you tell him. We're going to start by taking a urine sample to rule out bacterial prostatitis.

There is a slight knock at the door. A woman is standing there. Dr. White? she says. There is a cab driver who says you owe him money. He's kept the meter running, so it's up to sixty-five dollars now. What should I do?

406

I didn't take a cab, you say.

He says he drove a doctor here, a woman, and he described you. Perfectly. What should I do? He won't go away.

I'm busy here, I have roomfuls of patients to see, can't you take care of this?

He's really quite insistent.

Very well. You turn to the man. I'll be right back.

You follow the woman out of the room and nearly bump into a dark-skinned man going in.

Doctor?

Yes?

Was there some reason you were in with my patient?

To examine him, of course. He needs to provide a urine sample, have some blood work done.

Yes, I know. I'm surprised you found it necessary to interfere. I didn't ask for a consult.

407

There is a dark young man wearing a T-shirt and blue jeans standing at the counter, surrounded by people.

There she is, he says. He addresses you directly. You said you would borrow the money. Now the fare has increased. It would be even more if I were keeping the meter running now. I turned it off. Can you please pay me? It is now sixty-five dollars.

I don't know what you're talking about, you say.

I picked you up at Fullerton and Sheffield. In the rain. You left your purse at home. You said you would borrow the money.

The dark-skinned doctor is now standing behind you. Is there a problem? he asks.

This lady owes me sixty-five dollars. I don't know why she is lying. If she really is a doctor, she can afford it. If I lose this fare my boss will take it out on me.

The dark-skinned doctor reaches into his pocket. I have fifty dollars. Will that be enough?

The cab driver considers. A phone rings, he

picks up his cell phone and flips it open, and speaks in an unintelligible tongue.

Okay. Fine. But I am very upset with this. You're lucky I don't call the police.

I'm glad that's settled, you say, and return to the clinical area.

You are examining a five-year-old complaining of a stomachache when someone knocks on your door. Come in, you call. In walks a heavyset woman, short dark hair. A blazer. She is holding something in her hand.

Dr. White.

Yes?

You are scribbling instructions to the lab, trying to concentrate. The child's mother is asking questions in a language you don't understand, the child is whining, and your stomach is complaining from hunger.

Please get the nurse. I need a translator.

Dr. White, you'll need to come with me, please.

I'm not done.

You consulted the clock.

I'm here until four PM. I can see you then.

Dr. White, I am Detective Luton of the Chicago police.

Yes? You don't look up.

You and I have met before.

Not that I can remember, you say. You finish writing, hand the slip to the mother, and open the door to usher her and her child out. Then you turn to face the woman directly. No, you say, we have never met.

I understand that you believe that. But we actually have what you could call a relationship. At least I consider it so. Her brown eyes are so dark that the pupils are almost indistinguishable from the irises. She seems to be on edge, yet is speaking in an even voice.

What is this about?

A number of things. The most immediate is that you're practicing medicine without a license, since yours expired. Then there's some other outstanding business.

Such as? You lean against the examining table, cross your arms and your ankles. A posture that inevitably intimidated your residents. This woman doesn't appear in the least disconcerted.

There's the fact that you went AWOL from your residence yesterday afternoon. Your children have been frantic. The police have been looking for you for more than thirty hours. Funny, we never thought of looking here.

Why the police? you ask. I am an adult. Where I go and what I do is my own business.

I'm afraid not, the woman said.

That's ridiculous. I just saw Amanda this morning, you say. We had breakfast together. At Ann Sather's, on Belmont. Every Friday, it's our time.

Amanda O'Toole has been dead for more than seven months now, Dr. White.

Impossible. She was sitting opposite me eating Swedish pancakes this morning, you say. She complained about the coffee to the waitress, as usual. Then left an overly generous tip. A very typical meal on a very typical day at the end of a very typical week.

You need to come with me, Dr. White.

Faces are crowding up behind the woman's from the hallway. Faces curious and not particularly friendly. You unfold your arms, stand up straight. All right. But you are interfering with some important work. A lot of the people you saw waiting in the front office won't get seen today because of you.

To this the woman says nothing, but gestures toward the door. You hesitate before exiting the room in front of her. You feel her hand on your shoulder, guiding you. The people part as you walk silently out of the clinic.

You're in the front seat on the passenger's side of a small brown car with faded upholstered green-and-cream plaid seats. The seat belt is jammed, so you just hold it across your lap. The woman looks over and smiles. Hope we don't get stopped, she says. That would be something. She puts the car into reverse, backs up, nudges the car behind, then puts the car into first and inches away from the curb.

Your daughter has been worried about you, she says as she pulls out into traffic. It's now getting into late afternoon, rush hour has started, and Chicago Avenue is clogged in both directions.

Fiona? you ask. Why? She knows where she can find me. I'm here every week.

Nevertheless, the woman says. She is drumming her fingers on the steering wheel. She is in the right lane, behind a red Honda minivan when she puts her blinker on, sharply turns the wheel, and pulls into the left lane. Horns blare.

Are we going to the hospital? you ask. Have I received a page?

The woman shakes her head. No, she says. She picks up a small phone lying next to the gear box. She pushes a button and brings the phone to her ear, waits and then speaks loudly into it. Hello? Fiona? This is Detective Luton. I found your mother. The New Hope Clinic — she was treating patients.

I need you to come to the precinct. Call me when you get this.

And she hangs up.

Fiona is in California, you say.

Not anymore, says the woman. Just Hyde Park.

This isn't the way home, you say.

The woman sighs. We're not going there. Just to the station. You've been there before.

The words make no sense. She is your sister, your long-lost sister. Or your mother. A shape-shifter. Anything is possible.

The woman is still talking. There's no going back to your former facility. She gives you a quick sideways glance. You've deteriorated quite a bit since the last time I saw you.

There is such pity in her voice that you are jolted back into a more solid world. You look around. You're on the Kennedy now, heading south. This woman drives too fast, but expertly, taking a long off-ramp that swings around to the left and straightens out before passing directly underneath a long stone

414

building spanning the highway. Left, then right, then a glimpse of the lake before a sharp right turn, and down into an underground garage and into a parking stall with a screech. A sudden and absolute silence. A damp smell.

You both sit in the dim light for a moment without speaking. You like it here. It feels safe. You like this woman. Who does she remind you of? Someone you can depend on. Finally she speaks. This is highly irregular, she says. But I've never been one for following the rules. Neither have you, by the sound of things.

She leads the way to the elevator, pushes the up button. Something just wasn't right about this from the beginning, she says. Nothing fit.

When the elevator comes, she shepherds you inside and punches the number 2. The doors are dented and pocked, and inside it smells of stale smoke. The whole compartment trembles and shakes before slowly beginning its ascent.

When it opens, you blink at the sudden bright light. You are in a long, cream-colored hallway humming with activity.

Pipes run across the ceiling and down to the floor. Posters and flyers are tacked to the walls, ignored by the people streaming in both directions down the hall. The woman you're with starts walking, jingling a ring of keys, and you go on for some time, getting jostled by men and women, some in uniform, some dressed as if for the office, many casually, even sloppily attired. You wonder what you look like in your white doctor's coat, but no one gives you a glance. The woman finally stops at a door marked 218, inserts a key into the lock, opens the door, and gestures you inside.

Cool gray walls. No window. A gray steel desk, nothing on it except a cylinder holding a number of sharpened pencils and some photographs. The subjects range from faded black-and-white daguerreotypes of grim-looking men and women in clothes from a century ago to contemporary men and women, many of them holding children and many in uniform. No pictures of the woman herself, except one in the exact middle of the collection, of her and another woman, slim, with long ash-blond hair, standing next to each other, their shoulders slightly touching.

Sit down, the woman says. She pulls out a hard wooden chair. She then opens a corner cupboard, pulls out two bottles of water. She hands one to you. Here, drink this.

You gulp it down. You hadn't realized how thirsty you were. The woman notices the bottle is now empty, takes it from your hand, and offers you the other one. You are grateful. Your legs and feet ache, so you slip off your shoes, wiggle your toes. A long day of surgery, of holding steady, of not allowing your attention to flag.

The woman settles herself on the opposite side of the desk. Do you remember anything at all of the last thirty-six hours?

I've been at work. First surgery, then on call. A busy week. I've been on my feet for fourteen hours a day.

You bend your knees and lift up your feet as though presenting evidence. She doesn't look at them. She is intent on what she is saying.

I think you've been at the New Hope Clinic since this morning. But before that you were having quite an adventure.

You're not making much sense, you say. But

417

then you realize that nothing much does. Why are you sitting here with a stranger, wearing clothes not your own?

You look down at your feet and realize even the shoes are not yours: They are too wide and the wrong color: red. You never wore anything but sneakers and plain black pumps. Still, you slip them back on, struggle to stand up, fight the comfort of having firm wood support your thighs and buttocks.

It is time to go. Home again, home again, jiggity jig. You have a vision of a train speeding past a small plot of parched earth, of a clothesline strung between wooden poles from which hang a man's trousers, a woman's housedress, and some frilly dresses that belong to a young girl.

A tall dark man, a sweet melancholy face, kneeling by your side as you dig a hole in the dirt. He puts his hand in his pocket, brings out a fistful of coins, opens his hand, and lets them fall into the hole. Then he helps you push dirt over them, pat it down so there's no trace.

Buried treasure! he says, and laugh lines appear around his eyes. But you know what you need? he asks. A map. To remind you, so you can retrieve the treasure when you need it. I won't forget, you say, I never forget anything, and this time he laughs out loud. We'll come back in a year and see if you can find it, he says. But you never did.

It's time, you say, and begin to push yourself up.

The woman leans over, puts a hand on your arm, and gently but firmly pulls you back to a sitting position. You went away for a minute, she says.
  I was remembering my father, you say.

Good memories?

Always.

That's something to be grateful for. She sits for a moment, motionless, then shakes her head.

There was a disturbance at your old residence last night. A neighbor reported an attempted break-in. Was that you?

You lift up your hands, shrug.

If it was you, you weren't alone; the neighbor saw two and perhaps other people at your

419

former house. By the time we got a car there, everyone was gone.

There is a burst of music. A sort of cha-cha. The woman gets up and retrieves a small metal object from a table, holds it to her ear, listens, says some words. She looks at you, and says something else. Then puts down the device.

That was Fiona, she says. She's on her way.

Who's Fiona? you ask. The visions come and go. You would prefer them to come and stay, to linger. You enjoy these visitations. The world would be a barren place indeed without them. But the woman isn't listening. Suddenly she leans forward. She is focusing everything on you. She vanquishes the last remnants of your vision with her gaze.

It's time for the truth, she said. Why did you do it?

Why did I do what? you ask.

Cut off her fingers. If I understand that, I can put the rest together. If you killed Amanda, I believe it was for a reason. But I don't believe you would kill and then maim gratuitously.

Maim. An ugly word, you say.

An ugly business all around.

Some things are necessary.

Tell me why. Why was it necessary? Tell me. This is for me. Once I take you in, once you are committed to the state facility, that's the end of it. Case closed. But not really. It will never be, in my mind, unless I know.

She didn't mean for it to go that far.

What? What didn't she mean?

It was coming a long time.

Sometimes things build up. I understand. I do.

There's a knock on the door. The woman gets up, lets in a young woman with short hair.

Mom! She rushes over and hugs you, won't let go. Thank God you're all right. You had us all so worried. Detective Luton has been a godsend.

We've been going over things, says the older woman.

The young woman's face tightens. Yes? Does she remember? What has she told you?

Nothing yet. But I feel we're close. Very close.

That's great, the young woman says mournfully. She has not let go of your hand. If anything, she is clasping it even tighter. Mom, shhh. You don't have to say anything. It doesn't matter anymore. There's nothing worse they can do to you. You will not be judged fit to stand trial. Do you understand me?

A messy job.

The older woman speaks up. Yes, it was a messy job. How did you get rid of the bloody clothes?

Mom, you don't have to say anything.

They were taken away.

Who took them away?

You shrug. You point.

Mom . . . The young woman puts her hands to her face, sits down heavily in a chair.

Jennifer, what are you saying?

Her. There. She took the bloody cloth, the gloves. Cleaned everything up.

Detective Luton — Megan — I don't know why she's saying this.

But it's too late. The middle-aged woman has raised her head, the intelligence in her face aroused.

Three women in a room. One, the young one, deeply distressed. She has taken her hands away from her face and is clasping them tightly in her lap. Wringing them. Wringing her hands. A rough motion, this grasping and twisting of the metacarpal phalangeal joints, as if trying to extract the ligaments and tendons from under the skin.

Another woman, older, is thinking hard. She is looking at the young woman, but she is not seeing her. She is seeing images play out in her mind, images that are telling her some sort of story.

And the third woman, oldest of all, is dreaming. Not really present. Although she knows she is wearing clothes, sitting on a hard chair, that material is pressed against her skin, she cannot feel any of it. Her body is weightless. The atmosphere has thickened. It is difficult to breathe. And time has slowed. An entire life could be lived between heartbeats. She is drowning in air. Soon, scenes will begin appearing before her eyes.

The woman, the one that is neither old nor young, is opening her mouth. The words drop out, hang motionless in the congealing atmosphere.

At last, something is making sense, she says. A beat of silence. Then another. Perfect sense, she says. She stands up. She is working something out. Even if your mother were capable of killing, it's unlikely that she would have been able to cover her tracks so thoroughly. Not without help.

The younger woman's hands are now still, but they are gripping each other so tightly that all blood has drained from the knuckles. She closes her eyes. She doesn't speak.

The middle-aged woman's voice is getting louder. She is coming alive as the young and old women shut down. That's one of the things that saved your mother from being charged for so long. Her capacity for that kind of act was so obviously not there. But if she had assistance . . . Yours . . .

When the young woman finally speaks, her voice is so low you can scarcely hear it. What are you going to do? she asks.

I don't know, says the middle-aged woman. First I have to understand.

Understand? What is there to understand? The young woman is speaking faster now, agitatedly. Her voice is higher, pleading. She tugs at the edges of her shorn hair. Almost whining. You do not find it attractive. What does it remind you of? Stop that. Stop it now. She did it, the young woman says, loudly. I found out. I helped her cover it up.

Not so fast, the middle-aged woman says. I need to understand. She picks up something from the table, runs her fingers across it, puts it down before continuing. Did she give you any indication that she was angry at Amanda? That she was thinking about doing something like this?

Absolutely not. The young woman almost interrupts, she is so eager to answer. She places her hands in her lap, one on top of the other, like stacking bundles of kindling. Willing them not to move.

Then how did you know to go over there? The older woman's voice is rising. She is losing control even as the younger woman is regaining it. They are focused entirely on each other. One tamping down emotions, the other escalating them.

I went home to check up on her. I'd been worrying. And I couldn't sleep that night. I thought I'd spend the night there, give Magdalena a break.

Why didn't you tell us this?

Because one thing would lead to another and you would ask too many questions.

And so . . . ?

I pulled up into the parking space next to the garage. Behind the house. And saw my mother coming down the alley. She was spattered with blood. All I could get out of her was one word: Amanda. So I took her there. And found her.

Did your mother say why?

She said it was blackmail.

Blackmail?

Yes.

About what?

About me. The circumstances of my birth. That my mother didn't know who my father was. Not for sure. Amanda was going to tell.

Tell who? Your father was dead. Who else would care?

Me. How ironic. My mother killed to protect me. Or some idea she had about how I wouldn't be able to handle the truth. Or perhaps it was Amanda pushing things one inch too far.

And so you cleaned it up, the older woman says.

And so I cleaned it all up, says the younger woman. She is even calmer now. Almost relieved.

What did you do with the fingers?

I wrapped them up and tossed them into the Chicago River, off the Kinzie Street Bridge.

You did a good job of it. What about the scalpel?

You mean the scalpel blades? I threw them out with the fingers. I tried to take the scalpel handle, too. But my mother wouldn't let me. She took it home, along with the unused blades. You know the rest about those.

The older woman has been pacing. Back and forth, between the wall and the desk. Yes, she says. We know the rest. She is now looking at you again. They are both looking at you. You are now visible again. You are not sure that you like that. You felt safer floating in the ether.

But the fingers, says the older woman, suddenly. What about the fingers?

The younger woman shudders. She turns away from you, as if she can't bear what she sees. She answers the older woman without looking at her, either.

I don't know, she says. I haven't a clue about

428

that. It was just the way Amanda was when I found her.

The older woman is quiet for a moment. Then she comes over, sits down next to you, and takes your hand.

Were you able to follow this, Dr. White?

There are pictures in my head, you say. Not gentle visitations. The other kind.

Is that the way it happened?

A horrifying tableau.

Yes. Indeed it was. Can you tell us now why you dismembered her hand?

She had something I needed. She wouldn't give it up.

The woman is suddenly alert, her hand reaching out and taking hold of your arm. What did you say? she asks in a soft voice that belies the strength of her grip. What did she have?

The medal.

The medal? The older woman is not expecting this. The Saint Christopher medal?

The young woman sits up. She has a look on her face.

Mom.

You wave her away.

Amanda had the medal. She wouldn't give it up, you say.

But I don't understand. Why would she have your medal?

Mom . . .

There are voices outside the door, a shadow in the smoked glass at the top half of it. Then a loud knock — rat-tat-tat-tat. The woman gets out of the chair and reaches the door just as it is opening. She stops it with her foot, not letting whoever it is step inside. She speaks a few quiet words, then shuts and locks the door before sitting down again.

You were saying, she says. About the medal.

You do not know what she is talking about. The medal, you repeat.

Yes, the medal. She sounds frustrated. You were about to tell me about the medal. About Amanda and the medal. What did that have to do with the fingers? She gets up again, comes around the desk, reaches out as if to grab your shoulders. To shake it out of you. But what? You are no use to her. You shake your head.

The young woman opens her mouth to talk, hesitates, then speaks up.

Amanda had the medal clutched in her hand. She must have grabbed it from my mother's neck during the struggle. Then rigor mortis set in.

The older woman backs away from you, faces the younger woman. Her face is a study.

And so she cut open her hand to get it back.

Fiona, you say.

Yes, Mom, I'm here.

Fiona, my girl.

The older woman's voice is cold. A fine little actress. She pauses, addresses the young

431

woman. You know, we could charge you as an accessory.

The younger woman is now trembling. It is her turn to get up, begin pacing the small room.

Continue telling me about the fingers, please. Please, Jennifer. Try to remember.

But you are quiet. You have said your piece, nothing remains. You are sitting in a strange room, with two strange women. Your feet hurt. Your stomach is empty. You want to go home.

It's time, you say. My father, he gets so worried.

The young woman begins speaking again. I couldn't pull the medal out of Amanda's hand. She held it so tightly. Rigor mortis had set in. I panicked. I was certain someone was going to walk in. Then my mother just got to work.

Cutting off the fingers.

Yes.

She went back to the house, got her scalpel and blades. Washed her hands just as if she

432

were performing a procedure in the OR. She found a plastic tablecloth and a pair of rubber gloves from the kitchen. The tablecloth she positioned under Amanda's hand. Then she inserted the first blade in the scalpel and cut off the fingers, one at a time, changing the blade after each amputation was complete. She had to sever all four fingers before she was able to free the medal.

And then what did you do?

Took her home, washed her, put her to bed. Came back and cleaned up. It was easy — I just rolled up everything in the tablecloth and drove to the Kinzie Street Bridge. Then went home to Hyde Park and waited for the police to show up. I thought there was no way they couldn't know.

The middle-aged woman doesn't move for a moment.

Jennifer?

You wait for her to ask something else. But she seems to have run out of words.

Some things stick, you say.

Yes. Some things do. She looks miserable.

Defeated.

For myself, I don't care, you say. But Fiona.

The woman takes her hand away from you to watch Fiona, still pacing. Ten, twenty, then thirty seconds. A painful half minute. Then she makes her decision.

No. It's not necessary to mention any of this. Not to anyone. The worst has happened. Nothing will make a difference for Amanda. Nothing will change what will happen to your mother.

Mom. The young woman is openly weeping. She comes over and kneels by your chair, puts her head in your lap.

Thank you, she says to the middle-aged woman.

It's not for you. I have no loyalty to you.

No one is looking at anyone else. You reach out and touch the brightly colored head. You plunge your fingers into the hair. To your surprise, you feel something. Softness. Such silken luxury. You revel in it. To have regained your sense of touch. You stroke the head, feel its warmth. It is good. Sometimes the small things are enough.

■ ■ ■ ■

FOUR

■ ■ ■ ■

She is not hungry. So why do they keep placing food in front of her? Tough meat, applesauce. A cup of apple juice, as though she is a baby. She hates the sticky sweet smell, but she is thirsty, so she drinks. She wants to brush her teeth afterward, but they say, Not now, we'll do that later. Then, much later, the sloppy hard scrubbing, the rasp of the bristles against her tongue, the cup of water brought to her lips and then taken away too soon. Rinse. Spit.

The bulky diaper, the shame. Take me to the bathroom.

No, I can't, we don't have the staff today, everyone's on sixteen-hour shifts. Someone will change you later. Janice. I'll send her in when she's off break.

Jennifer, you are not eating. Jennifer, you must eat.

She shares her room with five other people. Four women and one man. The man sucks his toes like an infant. The nurses refer to them collectively as the Lady Killers.

There are no niceties. There are no soft edges. There is no salvation.

Once a day, they are let out of their room, allowed to walk around a cement courtyard. It is chilly, the season must be turning. Better than the suffocating heat. She takes care to stay away from the others, especially the contortionist, who is prone to bumping hard into people then daring them to complain.

She walks back and forth across the courtyard, head down, not seeing, not talking. It is safer that way. Sometimes her mother walks with her, sometimes Imogene, her best friend from first grade, chattering about monkey bars and ice cream. Mostly she walks it alone. She is having visions. Angels with flame-colored hair singing in that unending hymn of praise.

She's doing it again. A voice nearby.

Stop it! Stop her! Another voice, a smoker's voice accompanied by a cough.

The angels continue singing. *Gloria in excelsis Deo.* They are sending a savior. A very young man, but able. He will bring three gifts: The first gift she must not accept. The second gift she should give away to the first person who speaks to her kindly. The third gift is for her alone. *This is the word of the Lord.*

Her mother, her beauty known through five kingdoms, had three royal suitors. On Good Friday one brought her a rabbit, the symbol of fertility and renewal. Not to be outdone, on All Souls' Eve the second suitor gave her a black cat, emblematic of the witches' Sabbath. On the night before Christmas a donkey was found tied to a tree in the front yard. A donkey in Germantown! Let that be a lesson to you, her parents said. But she accepted none of these suitors because she was waiting. And then He came.

The laying of hands upon her, roughly. Now Jennifer, you have to stop that noise or we'll have to put you in solitary again. Yes. What are you wailing about this time? Can you use your words? Not today, huh? Okay, then you can just stay quiet. That's right. Shhh.

But when all is done, when the end is near, what is left? What is one left with? Physical

441

sensation. The pleasure that comes from relieving one's bowels under hygienic conditions. From laying one's head on a soft pillow. The release of the straps after a long hard night of pulling and pushing. To awaken from nightmares and find that they were, comparatively, the sweetest of dreams. Now that it is over, now that it's near the end, she can think. She can allow herself to drift to places that before she would not go.

It's the visions that make the waiting possible. And what visions! In glorious color, all senses activated. Fields of blooming, perfumed flowers, gleaming sterile operating rooms ready for cutting, beloved faces that she can reach out and caress, and soft hands that caress back. Heavenly music.

Jennifer, your visitor is here. Time to get up. Let's clean you up. You know the rules. Stay quiet, no yelling, keep your clothes on, do not grab or hit. That's right. Here we are. Now I'll just park you here. And look here is your visitor. You have an hour. I'll be back.

She does not know this person. Is it male or female? She cannot tell anymore. Whoever it is, they are speaking.

Mom?

442

She doesn't answer. She thinks something has happened, something important, but she can't remember what.

Mom? Do you know who I am?

No, not really, she says. But your voice is comforting. I believe that you are dear to me in some way.

Thank you for that. The person takes her hand, tightly. It is reassuring. It is something tangible in a world of shadows.

She's still not sure who this young person is, but she cannot stay here too long. There are a rabbit and a cat to feed and a donkey to ride.

How are things today? I'm sorry I'm late. Work's been insane.

Yes, she knows how insane work can be. One patient after another, bones bursting out of skin, how fragile the human body is, how easily penetrated and broken, how difficult to put together again. But the work doesn't need to be so sloppy. Who made this mess? She cannot believe it. She cannot believe her eyes. Who would do such a careless job.

You didn't clean up the OR, she says.

It's Fiona, Mom, your daughter. Here to say hello. Mark wants to come, but his work has been busy, too. He has a big case now, isn't that exciting? They finally trusted him with an important one. He promises to come soon.

Mark is dead.

No, Mom, Mark, your son. He's very much alive. He's doing well. Much better. You'd be proud of him.

She can't forget the OR. It is on her mind. Her vision of the day. A burning image.

You didn't adequately prep for your procedure, she says. It was a mess from start to finish! Wherever did you do your training?

My undergraduate and master's degrees at Stanford, Mom. You know that. And then back here for my doctorate at Chicago.

Sloppy. Sloppy and inexact. Have I taught you nothing? Skull base surgeries are delicate. Under the best of conditions you must be careful. But this is unsanitary, even brutal.

Mom.

That accounts for all the blood, of course.

Mom, please keep your voice down.

Then, louder, the man-woman person addresses the blue-suited woman sitting in the corner of the room. May we have a little privacy? We have some matters to discuss and it is difficult with a third party in the room.

It's against rules.

I know, but just this once? Here. Here's fifty dollars. Go have a smoke or a cup of coffee. No one will know. Nothing will happen. You can lock us in, that's no problem. Just give us a little privacy.

Okay, but I'll be waiting right outside.

The woman leaves the room. There is a rattling, then a click as the door is locked from the outside.

Mom, we're alone, we can talk now.

She's not sure what this person wants. She? He? has got both hands on her arms at this point, is squeezing too hard. It hurts.

Mom, are you remembering? Do you remember? What do you remember?

A botched job. Cruelty. You must never be cruel, however the temptation. And for many, it is a temptation.

What do you remember?

There is much pathology among surgeons. If patients knew, they'd be even more frightened of going under the knife than they already are.

Are you recalling that night?

I know some things.

What do you know?

I have these visions.

Yes? The person is growing agitated. Their green eyes are fixed on hers.

It can be difficult, she says. She is exerting herself, trying to break through the noise, trying to see past the blood. The clumsy job. The unmoving patient.

But you are having a vision now? Mom? Are you?

446

Quia peccavimus tibi.

What is that? Italian? Spanish?

Miserere nostri.

Mom.

My darling girl. Of course I had to help her.

The person is crying. Mom, please. The woman will be back soon. You must be careful what you say.

My darling girl. And yet I didn't want her. I took one look and said, No, take her away. Get me back to work, fast. Give me my body back, free of this parasite. And she turned out to be the most important thing. The thing I'd do anything for.

Stop, Mom, you're breaking my heart. The creature is now pacing up and down the room, beating its arms against its side, seemingly intent upon doing itself an injury. I would have told them everything if you had remembered. I would never have done this to you. Every day I think of turning myself in. No. Every hour. I'll never have peace again.

It stops for a moment, takes a breath, and

447

then continues.

Do you remember why? I want you to know why. I told you that night, but we never spoke of it again. I didn't want to ask. I didn't want to bring up something you may have put out of your mind. Do you want me to tell you again? It was for us, for the family. Amanda knew. She confronted me. She would have told.

Yes, I knew that she knew. That she would have figured it out. Too smart, my girl.

Mom, at first it was that I just couldn't make the numbers make sense. But I didn't know for a while exactly what Dad had done. Then it all became clear. The extent of it. It was a shock, I tell you. Dad!

The money was ours. James earned it.

You mean he stole it, Mom.

Yes.

And kept stealing. Until Amanda stopped him.

Yes.

And you told her that you had returned it. All of it. And were repaying your debt to society

by working at the clinic. But you hadn't. You managed to keep her from knowing.

It was our secret, yes, James's and mine.

Then Dad died. And you were deteriorating. I found it all out when going through your papers. At first I thought you didn't know about it, that it was all Dad. But then of course I realized you must have known. And ever since I assumed financial power of attorney, Amanda had been asking me questions. Probing. Somehow she found out there was money. Too much money. That she had been your dupe. That I'd been corrupted, as you had been. She couldn't stand that.

James had been right to worry about Fiona. It was too much for her.

And then she kept harassing you. Wouldn't give up. Despite your condition. That afternoon, you'd had a fight. Magdalena told me. You were terribly upset. She had to take you to the ER. They had to inject you to calm you down. Magdalena called me. She was furious. That woman has gone too far, she said. I wasn't able to get there until late — I had a faculty event I couldn't get out of. So I drove up around ten PM. I parked in front of your house, walked to Amanda's. I can still see the expression on her face when she opened the

door. Triumphant. No regrets. She had wormed what she needed out of you. And set to work on me. The things she said, horrible things. About you, Dad, and especially me.

Amanda told me, I put a stop to it back then, and I will not have you perpetuate it now. With your father dead and your mother the way she is, you can discover the past crimes of your parents and make restitution. Recreate yourself as an ethical citizen.

The person is deep into the story and startles when spoken to.

Keep an eye on Fiona, James told me when she was still very young. Not even ten years old. You know what worried him the most?

What, Mom?

All the caretaking. Of her brother. Giving it all away and leaving herself defenseless. She's at risk, he told me. Watch her carefully.

Amanda was going to report me, Mom. It would have been the end of us, our family, what little was left. And she told me such things. About Dad, about you. Nasty things. Amanda at her worst, her supercilious morality on full display. She would recreate me in

her image, she said. A righteous image. I was so distraught, so angry. I pushed my way past her into the house. I had no plans. But somehow I found myself shaking her by the shoulders — I had to reach up, she is so tall. She laughed at me — at my ineffectiveness, at my — my weakness. So I gave her a hard shove. And she fell backward, hitting her head on the corner of that oak table in her hallway. So much blood! And the world just stopped turning. I knelt down, tried to feel for a heartbeat: nothing. I was desperate. Bloodied and shaking with the chills and the horror of it all. I couldn't think clearly. I just ran — got in my car and began driving home, driving too quickly. It's amazing I didn't get stopped. I was past Armitage when I realized I didn't have my Saint Christopher medal. Your medal. It was there in Amanda's hand when I got back, but rigor mortis had already set in. I must have been sitting there for some time when you found us. I was just out of my mind.

All my beloved, gone. Except the one, the girl.

I didn't know you were there until you came up behind me, knelt down. You held me for a moment. Then you took me by the arm, pulled me up, and moved me away from the body.

A botched job. A cruel job.

451

I was out of my mind.

But that terrible tableau. There on the floor. All the blood. But worst of all, the look on her face. Horror, yes, but something else. Satisfaction.

You know the rest, and after, how I scrambled to remove any evidence.

An unwelcome vision. It keeps visiting me. But is it true?

The person covered its face.

The two people you love most in the world. And it's not the death that matters, but the look on your darling's face. The dark joy. Unbearable.

You never hesitated. You just set to work. No recriminations, no questions. You protected me. You saved me. The person is quiet for a moment. I guess you could say we managed to have a moment of grace in the midst of the horror. The person reaches out a hand.

Mom? What's wrong?

No. I will not go that far. I am not that far gone.

452

The person is starting to cry again. Mom? What are you saying?

She thinks then. She can still think sometimes. She knows this person. She knows what this person is capable of. She now knows. So this is how it ends. So this is what it feels like to get beyond pain. You can get beyond it.

Mom, please.

So this is how it ends.

Mom. This is not how I imagined things would be.

Each day slower than the one before it. Each day more words disappear. The visions alone endure. The playground. The white Communion dress. Playing kickball in the streets. James burning toast. The babies. The one she had to learn to love. The one she thought she couldn't love under any circumstances.

And that second one is all that matters now.

The large woman in blue is back, rattling her keys. Visiting hours are over.

Yes, I have to go anyway. The person is wiping its eyes. It is getting up. Mom, I'm going to have to skip tomorrow. You know it's a teaching day. But certainly on Thursday. I'll see you then.

What matters at the end are the visions. There is no one to hold up the books anymore, to ask if she remembers. But it doesn't matter. She doesn't need the photos now. Now they come directly to her. Her mother, her father. They have news for her, jokes. James, holding back at first, then allowing himself to be drawn in. And Amanda. Amanda is there, too, whole and strong. She is angry; who wouldn't be? But after her anger burns itself out, there will be something left.

Nurse, she's doing it again.

There is a good place here. It is possible to find it. With such dear friends. Even with the silent ones. Then there are the ones that have risen again. Sent by God.

Nurse, can you shut her up?

Accepting what you have done. Accepting the visions. Waiting it out in their company. In the end, that is enough.

ACKNOWLEDGMENTS

My heartfelt thanks to friends who commented on early drafts of this work, especially Marilyn Lewis, Jill Simonsen, Mary Petrosky, Carol Czyzewski, Christie Cochrell, Diane Cassidy, Marilyn Waite, Judy Weiler, Connie Guidotti, and Florence Schorow. I was thrilled to get the chance to work with Grove/Atlantic's legendary editor, Elisabeth Schmitz, whose insight and generosity of spirit made this a much better book than it otherwise would have been. My thanks also to Morgan Entrekin for his encouragement and support, and to Jessica Monahan, who held things together through the editorial process. My special gratitude goes to dear old friend Dr. Mitch Rotman for his invaluable advice on medical matters; however, any errors there are mine, not his. I can't thank enough my agent, Victoria Skurnick, of the Levine-Greenberg Literary Agency, whose utter professionalism was matched only by her extraordinary personal warmth: I know now why she is beloved throughout the industry. And of course I couldn't have done it without my family, who, after much debate, let me have the comfy chair to write in: David and Sarah, much love to you.

ABOUT THE AUTHOR

Alice LaPlante is an award-winning writer who teaches at San Francisco State University and Stanford University, where she was awarded a Wallace Stegner Fellowship and held a Jones Lectureship. Raised in Chicago, she now lives with her family in Northern California.